TORMINA

THE BOOK OF MALADIES VOLUME 4

D.K. HOLMBERG

ASH PUBLISHING

BACK IN CASTER

The Caster section was unique compared to the other sections in the city. It was old and run down, in a constant state of disrepair. Most of the stone buildings had crumbled, and there had been little effort made to restore them. Those that remained were elaborate and ornate, a reminder of better times years ago. Tall wooden buildings had replaced those that had crumbled, now towering above the rest. They were often times painted in garish colors, compared to other areas within the city and created in a mishmash of styles.

Caster was home to many thieves. Poverty was rampant here; Children begged in the streets and people sneaked through darkened alleys, doing whatever they felt necessary to survive. There were good people here, too, those who tried to come by their earnings honestly. Most of them worked in the fishing trade, signing on with the massive fishing barges, disappearing for a few days at a time before returning with a bit of coin in their pockets. It was dangerous work, especially as those barges went out to sea, ill-equipped for heavy storms.

Sam paused when she crossed the canal back into this section. She breathed in, taking in the faint scent of rot that mixed with other odors, those of wet earth and the sweaty funk of hundreds of bodies. It wasn't a pleasant aroma, but it was familiar to her.

Taverns lined one of the streets, and Sam made her way past most of them until she reached the one tavern she knew the best. She stepped inside and looked around. It was dark in here, the way Bastan preferred it. It was better for him to do his kind of business.

Sam glanced at the people inside, quickly taking stock of tonight's patrons. There was a certain type of person that frequented Bastan's tavern. Most of them wanted nothing more than the affordable ale or the decent food found here. Bastan was well-known for hiring people who could actually cook, and the food was often good. A few kept themselves hidden in the shadows, and it was clear that they wished to go unnoticed. Most likely, they were here to meet with Bastan about one of his jobs.

And then there were the people who worked here.

Sam smiled at Kevin has he stepped out of the kitchen carrying someone's dinner order. He gave her a quick smile and nodded to an empty table nearby. Taking his hint, she made her way to the table and threw herself into one of the chairs, happily anticipating the food that Kevin would surely bring. He always made sure she was well fed. She sat quietly for a while until Kevin returned and set a plate in front of her.

"Thanks," she said.

"I haven't seen you here in a while. There have been

rumors that something happened between you and Bastan."

"You know what they say about rumors," Sam said.

"That they have some basis in truth?"

Sam stuck her tongue out at him before taking a spoonful of food. It was smoked fish and delicious. There was something about the way that Kevin managed to smoke fish that she had missed. She would've expected the palace to have had better food, but that wasn't the case. Or maybe it was simply that the food served at the palace wasn't as familiar to her. They seemed to try too hard to make it fancier than was needed.

"Nothing happened between Bastan and me, I just…"

"I'm just glad to see you, Sam," Kevin said.

She smiled at him. "I'm glad to be here."

"He's here, if that's why you came."

"It is, but I figured I would talk with you first. Maybe get something to eat, maybe…" She shrugged. She wasn't sure why she didn't go directly back to Bastan. She wasn't afraid of Bastan. She had worked with him far too long to fear him, not the way that so many others did. Maybe that was a mistake. The only thing that had bothered her about Bastan in the past was that she was indebted to him. He gave her jobs and paid her well for doing them. But she'd had no choice. He'd manipulated her in a way that she was forced to serve him. Now that she had a sense of independence, she no longer felt quite the same way.

She no longer needed Bastan as she once had. But she couldn't deny that it was because of Bastan that she had been able to keep herself—and Tray—safe. Without him, she didn't know what would've become of them. Maybe she would have been lost on the streets. Maybe she would have been pulled in by the palace guards and placed in the prison. If that had happened, maybe she would have gained her mother's attention sooner.

"What have you been up to?"

"Not too much," she said.

Kevin shot her a look of disbelief, which she ignored. "Not too much? You haven't even been in Caster. Where have you gone? Have you figured out a way to get yourself in with the highborns?"

Sam paused in between bites. "I found my mother," she said.

Kevin studied her for a moment before taking a seat across from her. He had always been kind to her, and as much of a friend as she had in this world. "I thought your mother was dead."

"I thought the same thing, but it seems that she's not."

"Why do I get the sense that you aren't as excited about this as I would've thought you'd be?"

"You ever search for something for a long time, and when you finally get it, you realize you might have been better off not finding it?"

"Sam—"

Sam shook her head. "It's not quite like that," she started. "It's just that... I thought it would be different. Losing my mother when I was young—thinking her dead —I've always had a need to know more about who I am. With no one to ask, and no memories of my own, I have always felt... adrift. When I found my mother was alive, when I actually met her, I thought that I would finally begin to understand myself. Maybe find out more about where I came from and what I was supposed to do. Instead, it's left me with more questions than ever."

"About your mother?"

"About everything. My mother is not at all what I thought."

"Which means that you're not what you thought?"

She looked down at her plate and took another bite of food. "I don't know what I am, not anymore."

"So, not a thief?"

"I can still complete a job, if that's what you're asking."

Kevin grinned. "I wasn't challenging your capability. You've proven yourself too often for me to do that. But I'm guessing from the way you're talking and the fact that you haven't been seen recently that your mother is highborn."

Sam flushed. That was something of an insult in this section. And as much as Sam had wanted to be out of this section for as long as she could remember, now that she had connections to the palace, she wasn't sure what to make of them or even what to do with those connections. It was people like Kevin that she missed. They were people who had always looked out for her. Even Bastan had looked out for her, though he had done it in his own way. Caster could be hard; the life of a lowborn was never easy, but it was the people who had made it livable.

She looked around the tavern, seeing other familiar faces, and realized maybe that was what had troubled her the most. There wasn't the same sense of family near the palace as there was in Caster.

What did that say about her that the family she identified with was a bunch of thieves and lowborns?

"I don't know if she's highborn, but she has connections with them," Sam said.

Kevin chuckled. "And that's a bad thing? I seem to

remember that your friend was highborn, or close enough not to matter."

"Alec doesn't count."

"Is that right? Things have soured between you?"

Sam flushed. "That's not what I meant. All I'm saying is that he doesn't view the world in terms of highborns and lowborns." That was what surprised her the most. Alec wasn't from a true highborn section, but close enough that he was protected from the poverty found in the outer sections. Yet, Alec never made that an issue. Not that Sam would expect him to. It just wasn't in him. That wasn't the way Alec thought.

"No. He certainly wasn't as snooty as most of the high-borns who end up coming through here."

"There aren't any highborns that come through here."

"A few. And more than you would expect, especially how far out we are, but I think Bastan draws them."

"Don't tell him that," Sam said.

"Oh, Bastan doesn't care if we talk about it, but he's not interested in the highborns, other than what art they might have for him."

There was a time when Sam would have laughed about that, but that was a time before she knew Bastan wanted only to defend Caster. And that was before she had been outside the section to realize there was a certain appeal about being home and staying with what was familiar.

"Thank you," Sam said.

"What are you thanking me for now? I don't think that what I've given you here is that exciting. Food is fine tonight, but the fish... Well, that isn't quite as good as it usually is."

"No. Thank you for your friendship."

"You don't have to thank me for that. Besides, having you around has sort of kept Bastan calm."

"Calm?"

"Well, it's not something we talk about much, but before you came around, and he began to train you, Bastan was a lot different. He was harder. When he started working with you, he softened. Not a lot, but…" Kevin shrugged and stood. "Anyway. Good to see you, Sam."

He nodded behind her, and Sam turned to see Bastan watching. How long had he been standing there?

She got up and followed him into his office. He said nothing until they'd gone inside and he'd closed and locked the door. Sam looked around his office, taking in the painting of the canals. Given what she knew of Bastan, she wondered if he had painted that himself. She was glad to see it back up on the wall, along with his other paintings. She'd not been back since the night Tray had brought her here after Marin had poisoned her with her staff and thought back to what had happened here. Tray being attacked and left for dead. Bastan's art treasures tossed about, but not taken. It seemed like forever ago now.

"To what do I owe this pleasure?" he asked, taking a seat in his chair. Bastan had a massive desk, and stacks of paper sat on top of it, a few jars of ink on either side with a pen resting in the middle. He crossed his arms and leaned forward, looking at her.

"I can't come visit?"

"Since you *disappeared*, you haven't come to visit that often."

"I came when you needed my help."

"And I'm thankful for that," he said. He studied her. "You look well. They've been treating you the way that you deserve?"

"And what way is that?"

"Like someone deserving respect," Bastan said.

She shifted under the weight of his gaze, twisting the ring she now wore that signified her place at the palace and granted access that papers couldn't, signifying she had a place with the royals. After everything she had been through, Bastan was as much family as anyone, a fact that felt strange to realize. "They have been treating me well enough."

"What does that mean?"

"It means that they have been treating me well enough. It's sort of the way that you treated me when I first started training with you."

Bastan smiled. "A little tough love? Well, I can't say that I disapprove. Sometimes, you have to learn the hard way."

"I think my mother would agree with you."

His face clouded for a moment. "Why are you here?"

"Are you so eager to get rid of me that you keep pressing that?"

"You know that's not the case. Just as I know that you wouldn't have come here if you didn't need something."

"I shouldn't only come when I need something," she said.

"No. You really shouldn't. You should come as often as you want. Gods, if you want a job, I've got plenty of them."

Sam smiled to herself, thinking about what Elaine might say were Sam to resume thieving again. What would she do with that knowledge?

Then again, there was so much that Sam wanted to do, so much that she felt she needed to learn, that taking a job didn't feel quite right. Not only didn't it feel right, but with what she had been learning, she didn't think it was much of a challenge, either.

"I wanted to see if you might've heard anything about Marin."

"I thought you said Marin was taken care of."

"I said that Tray took Marin away. I don't know that that means she's taken care of."

"What do you think Tray might try to do?" Bastan asked. "Do you think he would do anything that might harm you?"

Sam paused before answering. There was a time when she would've said no immediately. There was a time when she would've done anything for Tray—and probably still would. Learning that they didn't have the same connection they believed had changed that, if only a little. Now, she no longer knew quite what to think. Even with what Tray had learned, when it came down to it, he helped Marin escape after the fight with Sam. And she had no idea where he was now, and if he was still with Marin. If she could only have some time with him, she might be able to ask him what he was thinking.

"What do you know?"

Bastan studied her for a moment. "I've heard rumors," Bastan said. "Nothing more than that, but…"

Sam frowned. It wasn't like Bastan to be so hesitant to answer. "You know something. Why aren't you sharing it?"

"I would say the same to you, Samara."

She glared at him. "I'm not keeping anything from you."

"No? I would argue that you're keeping a great deal from me. Maybe it's for the best. Getting involved with dangerous highborns isn't really what I want to take on, certainly not in a way that might draw attention to my business dealings."

"Business dealings?" Sam asked with a laugh. "I don't think anybody believes you have real business dealings."

"You may call it what you wish. It doesn't change the fact that I don't want to draw any attention to myself."

"And what do you know about Tray?"

"I know that someone who fits his description is working near the southern shores. It's not necessarily a safe place." Sam arched a brow at him. "Well, perhaps it's not any more unsafe than Caster, but that doesn't change that it's not the kind of place that someone wants to spend much time."

"Most of the highborns would say the same about Caster," Sam said.

"They might, but they'd be wrong," Bastan said, a smile trailing on his face.

"Which section?" Sam asked.

Bastan studied her for a moment before standing and making his way over to the map of the city. It was reasonably detailed, but mostly because of its drawings of the canals. Sam's only experience with the canals was jumping them, not traveling along them. She suspected that most of the barge workers would have a much better understanding of how to draw the canals and the way they circled the city.

The city itself was spread out in something like a

circle. To the far west, it was bounded by the steam fields leading to the mountains. To the north, there was the massive swamp that even the barge captains were said not to attempt to cross. To the south and east, they had nothing but the sea. In the confines of the city, there were dozens upon dozens of sections, each bound by canals that were both natural and artificially made.

Sam stared at the map. Caster was off to the far west side of the map, and practically at the edge of the city. From here, Sam could see the mountains rising in the distance, though she had never attempted to leave the city to see them up close. What point would there be? Even if she knew what might be beyond the mountains—and the more she learned about the Thelns, the more she suspected that was all that would be found beyond the mountains—there was no reason for her to leave the city.

Now that she knew of her ability as a Kaver, there was even less reason for her, at least until she better understood what that meant, and how she could use those abilities.

"We're here," Bastan said, pointing to Caster.

"I can see that," Sam said.

"Yes. I taught you well."

Sam ignored the self-praise. "I know where we are in the city, Bastan, and I can see where the edge of the city is, and where the mountains rise up, so—"

"Fine, Sam. I'm just trying to orient you."

Sam took a deep breath and shook her head. She wasn't angry with Bastan. In fact, it felt… nice to be back with him. Maybe she *should* take a job, if only to get back to some normalcy.

"I'm sorry, Bastan. Please go on."

"You don't have to be a smartass."

Sam grinned at him. "I didn't think that I was."

"You didn't think it all." He motioned to the map. "And here's the palace, with the university section nearby," he said, pointing toward two other sections that were now incredibly familiar to Sam. There was a time when she would not have known them, at least not well. They had been essentially forbidden, places she'd never imagined herself spending any amount of time, but now, she spent the majority of her time there. His finger trailed down the map, reaching the southern border where he pointed. "And here is the Thaylor section."

Sam's breath caught. She didn't know all of the individual sections in the city as well as Bastan—his *business* interests required that he know the city better than most —but she had heard enough about Thaylor that she knew it by reputation. Saying it was as bad—or nearly as bad— as Caster was no understatement on Bastan's part.

"And this is where you heard a rumor of Tray?"

"There aren't too many who fit his description, unless you want me to think that more of these... What did you call them? Thelns? Are in the city."

Sam stared at the map. There shouldn't be any reason for Thelns to be in the city, not now that the canal protections had been restored. Marin had attempted to poison them to allow Thelns access to the city, but Sam had thwarted her. "No. I don't think there are others in the city."

Bastan watched her for a long moment. "Then the description is of Tray. Perhaps someday, you'll tell me why he resembles these Thelns—or brutes, as I believe you once called them."

"Someday, I will."

"Is that a promise?"

Sam glanced over to him. Bastan traded in information as much as in actual goods, so she suspected that he truly wanted to know more about the Thelns—as well as about Tray. But while she might have need of him, she also didn't want to betray her brother to Bastan.

"There will come a time when I will tell you what I know," Sam said.

Bastan nodded. He returned to his desk, sat down, and took a scrap of paper on which he proceeded to quickly scratch out a note. When he was done, he handed it to Sam. "This is where you will find the person who matches Tray's description. I don't know if it's him, so don't be too angry if you get there and find that it's not, but…"

Sam glanced at the scrap of paper. There was a name and a diagram, drawn in Bastan's familiar style. Bastan had given her many of them over the years.

"A job?"

He clasped his hands together and grinned. "If you want to find your brother, you will do this for me."

She bit back the urge to swear at him, but that would only amuse him. Besides, she might enjoy taking a job. What would it matter, so long as she didn't let her mother know what she was doing?

2

SEARCH FOR A CONTACT

The sea crashed against the shore near Thaylor. It was an unfamiliar sound, one that Sam never heard in the Caster section. The smell of this section was different, though maybe no worse than it was anywhere else. She didn't feel as if she fit in, and moved cautiously along the street, subtly watching everyone she passed. She feared drawing unwanted attention, but with her cloak wrapped around her, that shouldn't be a problem. The cloak deflected light, making it harder for people to even see her, thus allowing her to move about stealthily. But why was it that she didn't feel it was as effective here?

Sam followed the map Bastan had given her. It wasn't difficult to follow now that she was here, and she hurried along the street, navigating by the diagram. She was tempted to place an augmentation. She and Alec had both agreed that she needed to have that capability, so he had helped her practice it a few times on her own, and she now traveled with a small vial of blood ink, ready for her to make a few notes on the scrap of easar paper that she carried. It was meant only for emergencies, and Sam didn't have the same creativity that Alec did, nor did she have the same knowledge that he did, so her attempt would be less likely to be as effective as anything Alec might do to help her.

A figure down the street was headed toward her, and Sam scooted across to the other side. The figure stopped and turned, coming toward her.

Kyza!

Sam reached into her cloak, where she kept the two segments of her canal staff. She curled her fingers around one of them and slowly pulled it from beneath her cloak. It would have been better for her to have the entire staff together, but in this part of the city—as in all sections except Caster—she feared it would draw attention.

The man—and it was most certainly a man—grabbed for her.

"What are you—"

The man tried to pull on her arm, and she jerked away. She wasn't quite as strong as he was, but she'd grown stronger during her training. She swung her staff as she pulled away, catching him on the arm.

The man jerked his arm back, and in a quick flourish of movement, he withdrew a knife.

Sam laughed darkly. "You're going to have to do better than that."

"A pretty girl like you coming out at night?" the man said.

"Aw, you think I'm pretty?"

He frowned, and in that moment, she darted forward, withdrawing the other end of her staff and swinging both of them at him. He ducked under the first one, but he missed the second swing, and she cracked it against his shoulder. She spun around, quickly twisting the ends of her staff together, giving her greater reach.

The man grabbed for her again, and Sam swore under her breath. She swung her staff, and it cracked against the side of his head, and he crumpled.

Was this what Thaylor was like? Why would Tray have come here? This wasn't like her brother.

Then again, she didn't know anything about what Tray would be like, especially now as he began to wonder about his connection to Marin. Now that he knew, what would he do with that knowledge?

Sam glanced down at the man, deciding to leave him where he lay. She didn't feel bad, especially not since he had attacked her simply for walking through the streets. Maybe Bastan was right. Maybe this section *was* worse than Caster. That was hard to believe, especially considering what she knew of Caster, but she'd never been attacked simply for walking along the street there.

But then, in Caster she had something of a reputation. Maybe that had something to do with it.

She looked around, but there was no one else out. Either their scuffle had sent other people into hiding, or there simply wasn't anyone else out at this time of night. Hurrying along the street, she made her way to the corner and quickly turned.

Knowing this wasn't her intended direction, she referenced the map again. She kept a more mindful eye as she wandered, not certain whether some other fool might attempt to come at her. Rather than keeping the staff separated, she decided to leave it together. It was easier to use in a fight, and the street was certainly wide enough for her to use it in that way, and it would make escape easier for her if needed. With the staff, she could launch to the rooftops, though many of the buildings in this section were so tall that it would make it challenging. She still hadn't learned to balance on the staff the same way that some of the other Kavers had shown, but Sam suspected she would be able to in time.

Noise in the distance drew her attention. It was coming from the way she had to go.

She moved forward cautiously. The half-moon over-head cast a shimmering light, too weak to push back the darkness along the street, but enough to make out shadowy figures in the distance.

Kyza!

Would she be forced to fight her way through?

There was only one way around it. Up. Sam planted her staff and shimmied up, pushing off to grab onto one of the windows on the second level of the nearest build-ing. She pulled her staff up with her, and scrambled up to the roof. From here, she could follow the street and go roof to roof to get where she was going. She was careful not to get too close to the edge, not wanting to fall here. A fall could be deadly. She could place an augmentation, but if she did that, would it be wasteful? She still didn't know what Bastan's job would require, and until she did—until she knew what he needed her to do—she had to conserve the vials of blood ink and the easar paper.

Sam scrambled across several roofs until she spotted the building Bastan had designated on his map. It was across the street.

There was a crowd of people below. They were loud—likely drunk. A few of them appeared to carry weapons, so she was thankful that she was above the fray, rather than down on the street. Eventually they passed, turning a corner and leaving the street empty once more.

Bastan had been right. This place *was* dangerous.

Why would Tray be here?

Maybe because it was dangerous. He could conceal Marin here and could hide her from Sam and others who might be searching for her. This close to the sea, it was possible that he could arrange transport away from the city, though she had a hard time believing Tray would do that.

Sam studied the building for a long time before jumping down. When she was back on the street, she looked around, making sure that no one else was there, and then headed toward the building. It was a simple matter to break the lock and get inside. Once inside, she paused, surveying what else was there. She saw an unlit lantern, and there was a single table, but nothing else. Sam started in, moving quietly—carefully—worried that perhaps she should have asked Bastan more about the job.

She found stairs leading to the second floor and started up. At the top of the stairs, she hesitated, wrinkling her nose.

There was a foul odor here.

Was that just specific to this section, or was there something else?

Sam didn't like the fact that something didn't feel right.

In here, her staff would be too long to fight easily. She broke it down and took one half in each hand, ready to use them if needed.

At a door along the hallway, she paused. The foul odor

she'd detected seemed stronger here. She pushed the door open with her staff and the odor poured out from inside.

Sam covered her face with her cloak. Even that wasn't enough to completely eliminate the stench. It reminded her of the odor she'd smelled when she had first found the princess, but this was worse.

Death. It was the smell of death.

A body lay in the corner. Sam looked around, making certain that there was no one else in the room, and crouched in front of the body. A woman. Blood pooled around a hole in her chest, but it was the crossbow bolt jutting out of her stomach that really drew her attention.

She'd seen crossbow bolts used before. She'd even survived an attack when she'd been shot with one.

The blood was still wet.

Why was the smell already so awful?

Sam slipped her hand into her pocket and pulled out the vial of blood and the scrap of easar paper. It was better to be prepared. If this attack had just happened—and this was where she was supposed to meet Bastan's contact, it worried her that she was already too late.

Sam scrawled a few words on the easar paper using her little finger. It wasn't nearly as neat as what Alec would do, and it didn't have the same level of creativity that he used to ensure that the augmentations were effective, but all she cared about was ensuring that it worked. They had practiced countless times, going over and over the different augmentations so that she could have strength and speed, enough to counteract most attacks that she might face.

A wash of warmth flowed through her as the augmentation took hold.

Using augmentations required drawing on the blood of both a Kaver and a Scribe. The combined effect was what was important. That, combined with what she documented on the easar paper, helped ensure that the augmentations held.

She heard movement, and she spun.

Augmented as she was, she spun around too quickly and nearly toppled over.

Sam jumped, bring her staff around, but there was nothing. The room was empty.

She hadn't imagined the sound. Someone else was with her.

She should have augmented her sight. Was there anything she could do that would help with that?

She tried to think of what Alec might do, but decided against adding an augmentation without having practiced it. Alec would have made it effective, but Sam didn't think she had the same skill, and feared that she might mess something up if she tried it. With her luck, she would end up blind, tormented because she had been too foolish with her augmentation. No, it was better to act cautiously. She had strength and speed, and she had her canal staff, which should be enough.

There was a sound below her.

Sam raced out of the room and back toward the stairs, reaching the main level just as the door into the building opened. A flash of moonlight revealed a shadowed figure leaving.

Sam raced out, chasing after the person. She nearly stumbled again. Maybe she hadn't performed the augmentation *quite* right. Could she have made a mistake with it? She didn't think so, especially since Alec had been the one to teach her the right words to write, and he'd made sure that she knew exactly how to put them on the paper. But maybe she'd forgotten something. Maybe in her eagerness to place the augmentation and face whatever danger she sensed, she had forgotten something. It would be something she would have to ask later.

She looked around the street, but it was empty.

With her enhanced strength, she jumped and reached the nearby rooftop. From there, she raced along searching for signs of movement. She saw the enormous group that she had seen before, and they continued to make their way southerly, where they would eventually reach the sea.

That didn't seem like the right direction.

She hesitated. If only she had thought to augment her hearing, too. She would have to ask Alec the next time they were together how to enhance her eyesight and her hearing, especially if she was to be active at night.

A figure moved in the darkness below.

There was something about it that caught her eye.

Whoever was down there cast an imposing shadow. Could it be Tray?

She hadn't come here thinking to see Tray. Bastan's contact was supposed to be the one to know where to find Tray, not the other way around.

She raced along the roof, trying to get a better look at the person below. There was another possibility as to who it might be, but it was one that she didn't want to believe. The protections on the canal were supposed to be enough to prevent the Thelns from reaching the city, but if they weren't, then maybe there was more to worry about than she realized.

Sam jumped and landed softly on a rooftop near where the figure had been on the street below.

Where had the person gone?

She felt movement behind her.

Sam swung her staff around, but there was no one there.

She hadn't imagined it.

She swung around again, and this time, she cracked her staff into the roof itself. Her arms jarred, and she nearly dropped her staff, but she managed to spin around.

Maybe she had given herself *too* much speed.

There was still that sense of movement near her.

Sam jumped and soared above the rooftop. Below, she saw a figure streaking along the street, now racing toward the canal.

She spun off the roof and used her staff to cushion her landing on the street. When she reached the edge of the canal, she hesitated.

The figure on the other side was familiar. There was no mistaking the sheer size. A Theln, but it was *her* Theln.

"Tray!" she called out.

He glanced back and shook his head as he disappeared in the night, joined by another figure.

Sam paused only a moment. She had been searching for Tray ever since that night when she had fought Marin at the canal bridge. Bastan had led Sam here to find her brother. How he knew, she didn't care. What job she had to complete, she didn't care. She just knew this might be her only opportunity to reach him. If she lost him now, she didn't know how long it would take to find him again, if she ever did.

Sam gathered herself, debating whether she should

place another augmentation, but decided the ones she had would hold long enough. All she needed was to reach Tray.

She jumped, clearing the canal in a single leap, and went racing into the night after her brother.

3

FINDING TRAY

Moonlight shimmered across the water in the canal far below Sam, in a way that made the canals seem almost peaceful rather than the dangerous—possibly deadly—thing that they were. Every so often, there was a splash, a reminder of the eels that swam through the water, and she shivered. She'd had enough encounters with the eels to know she never wanted to get close to them again. Then again, she now knew that those eels served as a line of defense. It was because of the canal eels that the Thelns were unable to enter the city in any significant numbers.

She forced her thoughts back to the task at hand. What would her brother be doing here?

He wasn't her brother—not by blood, at least—but it was difficult for her to think of him in any other terms. In her mind, he still was her brother.

With a quick leap, she jumped onto a nearby roof. She landed softly, silently, the enhancement that made her even lighter than usual helping grant her soft footing. She darted onward, streaking in the direction Tray had gone, keeping her cloak pulled around her so as to conceal herself better.

At the end of the street, she paused, searching for signs of movement.

It was late, and as was true in Caster, this time of night brought out only thieves—or worse. Sam wasn't sure what she qualified as. She wasn't a thief, not any longer, and she was certain she was anything worse. Now, she was only Sam, both more and less than what she had once believed herself to be.

Where was Tray?

Then she saw him.

He crossed the canal again, and she gave chase, keeping behind him. They raced through several sections, and as they did, she realized they headed toward the inner part of the city—merchant sections. It wouldn't be too far for her to head to Arrend and Alec's apothecary from here.

Maybe it *wasn't* Tray. She hadn't seen him clearly. But if it wasn't, it meant Thelns had reached the city again. She *thought* she, with Alec's help, had stopped Marin's planned attack in time, but what if they hadn't? What if the Thelns *had* reached the city?

She paused near a tall building. It was difficult to tell what sort of building it was from this angle, but there were dozens of merchants on the street. Most of the buildings were far nicer than anything that she had known growing up, far nicer than any that would've been found in the Caster section of the city.

The figure paused, glancing back. If Sam stepped forward, she would reveal her presence. Facing a Theln without solid augmentations would be a mistake, and she wouldn't make it unless she had no other alternative.

If only she knew that it was Tray. If it was, she had more questions for him.

But if it wasn't, she'd followed *someone* out of the building Bastan had guided her to, and that person was likely responsible for the death of the woman she'd found.

As he disappeared from view, Sam cursed to herself. As a Kaver, and someone who now worked on behalf of the throne to offer whatever protection she could to the royal family, didn't she have an obligation to discover whether it was one of the Thelns? And if it was, didn't she have an obligation to ensure that he didn't cause trouble in the city?

Sam crept forward, readying her staff. Even as she did, she knew the smart thing to do would be to wait, or follow closely and gather information, but when had Sam ever done only the smart thing?

She jumped. It carried her up and over the canal in a single leap. There had been a time when such jumps would've seemed impossible, and she would have needed to use her canal staff to clear the canal, worrying about whether the distance would be too much, but with her weight mitigated through the augmentation, that was no longer a concern.

She leaned up against one of the nearby buildings, wrapping her cloak around her. She held herself completely still, searching for signs of movement, but there was nothing.

Had the man known he was being followed?

When nothing moved in the night, Sam stepped forward.

Something whistled toward her.

Instincts honed over years spent roaming the streets late at night told her to drop. She went to her knees, and then she rolled, moving off to the side and out of the way of whatever it was that came toward her.

Sam jumped to her feet, spinning her staff around. When she had placed the augmentation on herself, she had added an enhancement to her strength. It was nothing like what Alec would have been able to give her—her skills with documenting and adding the augmentations were nothing compared to his—but more than she would have had naturally. That combined with the reduction in her weight made her movements considerably faster.

She still missed.

She rolled back, slapping her staff against the stone and pushing off, soaring into the air in a rapid flip. She surveyed the street in midair, looking for signs of the attacker, but saw nothing.

She landed with her staff held vertically in front of her and swung around it as she slid down, spiraling to the ground. Something else flickered toward her, tearing through her cloak.

A knife.

Her enhancements helped, but she could still be injured—or killed—like anyone else. Without Alec here to heal her if something happened, she didn't think that remaining exposed like this was a great idea.

Had she become so reliant on augmentations that she couldn't function without them? There had been a time—before she even knew about such augmentations—when she relied on her gut and her street smarts. Back then, having augmentations might have been helpful, but they certainly weren't necessary to remain safe on the streets. It almost embarrassed her.

When she landed, she spun around again, swinging her feet in the direction of the source of the knives.

Another attack didn't come.

Sam jumped, getting to her feet before anything could happen to her.

Was that movement? She wasn't certain. Rather than waiting to find out, she jumped.

But the augmentation failed. Her jump carried her five feet into the air, not enough to reach the rooftop as she had intended. She grabbed for the staff, sliding back down it.

She had easar paper and another vial of blood ink, but she would need time to apply it, and a sudden flicker of movement out of the corner of her eye told her she would not have that time.

Sam danced back, moving away from whoever this unseen attacker was. There came another flicker, and another knife whistled toward her.

She ducked, and the knife buried itself in the wall behind where she'd been standing. Thankfully, it didn't even tear through her cloak. She wouldn't want the questions Elaine would have if that happened.

She took another step back and bumped into something hard.

Sam spun around, and realized that she hadn't bumped into something, but someone.

"Tray?"

He grabbed her arm, but it wasn't that movement that drew her attention. It was the menacing look on his face, an expression that she had never seen from him before. Rage twisted his brow, anger that didn't fit with the boy she still knew him as.

Sam jerked her arm free. Or, at least she tried to.

Tray was strong, much stronger than she was, and he held her in an iron grip. "Get out of here, Sam."

She watched him, sadness welling up within her. This was her brother. This was the boy she had helped raise, ensuring that he was safe and unharmed on the streets. It was because of Tray that she had even risked trying to help the princess, but because of him, she had learned more about herself and what she could do.

And he was a Theln, at least partly.

"What are you doing?" Sam hissed.

Tray pushed her back, and she went stumbling. He positioned himself in front of her, blocking her view so that she couldn't see what was coming down the street.

Who was he working with?

"Where is she?" Sam asked.

Tray shook his head. "It doesn't matter. None of it matters, not anymore."

"It does matter. You know what she did to me, and the way that she treated you is just as bad."

"Go," Tray whispered.

Sam considered arguing, but what good would that do? What good would it do for her to argue with him when he could overpower her, especially without any augmentations. Even with augmentations, it was more about her natural reluctance to do anything that might harm Tray than anything else. She refused to attack her brother. She only wished that he felt the same about her.

"I've been looking for you throughout the entire blasted city. Kyza knows—"

Tray took a step toward her, and the look on his face screamed violence. Without wanting to and without meaning to, Sam took a step away from him.

"If you know what's good for you, you will go," Tray said.

"What's good for me? Listen, I don't think you understand what's been going on. Marin has protected you, and—"

Tray took another step toward her, and she jumped back. She didn't think he would do anything, but what if the ties of their childhood together no longer meant what they once had?

Sam refused to believe that was the case. She refused to view him as anything other than her brother.

But, after learning of the way that Marin had deceived everyone, she wasn't about to assume that her brother wouldn't do anything to harm her. She didn't think Tray would, but she hadn't thought Marin would betray everyone in the city, either.

She brought her staff around, placing it between her and Tray. Even without her augmentations, she wasn't entirely helpless. She had learned to fight with the staff, to protect herself and attack if needed. She had just never thought that she would need to attack her brother.

"I'm not going anywhere until you tell me what you did with Marin."

Tray watched her, and his eyes widened slightly.

Too late, Sam realized why—and what he had done for her.

There was movement behind her, and as she tried to

turn, something grazed her temple. She swung her staff around, but it was caught and torn free from her grip. Her vision blurred, and all she could think about was that the Theln in front of her was familiar.

Sam tried backing up, and she bumped into Tray.

She looked up at him, but the hope burning in her eyes faded when she saw the expression on his face again. Her brother was in there—she was sure of it—but he wouldn't help her. Maybe he *couldn't* help. Maybe whatever had happened with the Thelns—and with Marin—prevented him from being able to help. She hated that it could be true.

As she turned back to her familiar attacker—Ralun, the stupid Theln who had chased her through the city before she first learned of her abilities—she felt something else strike her from behind, and she staggered forward, practically into his arms.

Ralun grinned widely. "Kaver. I have so been looking forward to this."

4

THE PATIENT

Sun shone through one of the stained-glass windows at the university, sending streaks of color stretching across the interior of the library. Alec found it beautiful, but the rainbow of colors did nothing to help his mood.

Where was Sam?

Ever since rescuing her from Marin—at least, he liked to think that he'd had a hand in her rescue—she had been more present, and he appreciated that. Since coming to the university, he had begun to miss her, but he was torn. He craved what the university offered him, but he knew it was consuming almost all of his time, and he hated that it took away time that he could be spending with Sam. If anything good had come out of the attack, it was that he believed Sam now saw him as an integral part of what they did as Kaver and Scribe. And that was something.

Alec made another note in his journal, documenting what they had seen while on rounds that morning. It was another illness that he had seen before, though his experience treating illnesses of this type was quite a bit different from how most at the university would treated them. With this illness, it was abdominal pain, but he suspected it came from some other source, something his father called referred pain. Alec had always thought his father was teasing him, making up terms to test him, but he had seen it himself, and had seen how a problem in another area of the body could manifest as pain in the abdomen.

"That's an interesting thought," Beckah said, taking a seat next to him.

Alec looked over. She smiled as she took her place and twisted a ring on the middle finger of her left hand. Her eyes remained fixed on his journal as they often had over the time since they had met. "That's not necessarily my thought but my father's."

"Still, I think you might be right."

"Master Charles wasn't sure that I was right," Alec said.

Beckah waved her hand. "Oh, I wouldn't worry too much about Master Charles. Most of the time, he doesn't even know what he's talking about. You know, he *is* getting old."

Alec grinned. "I'm not sure that we should refer to Master Charles as getting old when Master Eckerd is considerably older than he is."

Beckah shrugged. "Eckerd is different, isn't he?"

"How do we know that Master Charles isn't different also?" They didn't speak about Scribes openly, not in the library, but it was fair to assume that, since they knew several of the masters were Scribes, many of the masters were. It was just that Alec didn't know which ones they were. Eckerd hadn't shared that with him in the days since the last attack, preferring to usher him back into his studies. Alec wasn't ready to know that information, at least according to Master Eckerd.

"We would know, wouldn't we?"

Alec shrugged. "I don't know. Without them sharing with us, I don't know how much we'd be aware of. Sam doesn't tell me what she's learned in the palace, though I suspect that's as much because she's not sure what to make of it."

Beckah leaned back and pulled a book off the stack on the table next to him.

Alec glanced over at it and looked at the title, then shook his head. "That's not anything exciting. It's just—"

"It's exciting because you thought it was important. Why choose this title?"

Alec wasn't exactly sure how to answer. That title was important to him because it spoke of countering unseen injuries. After what had happened during the last attack, he thought he should be better prepared for the possibility that they might face more like it. Tray had nearly died, and were it not for Beckah's insatiable appetite for learning and experimenting, which led to discovering that she was a Scribe herself, he might have.

Alec knew how much Tray meant to Sam. He also knew how much Sam meant to him, so he was willing to do whatever it took to ensure that she didn't suffer. Wasn't that his responsibility as her Scribe?

"Ah, I see why you chose this one."

Beckah's voice trailed off, and he reached across the table for her hand. There wasn't much he could do to soothe her, and there was even less he could do to reassure her that she would ever have the same connection to her Kaver as he did to his. Neither of them knew exactly what it meant that she was connected to Tray. For that matter, they didn't even know where Tray had gone. He had disappeared, taking Marin with him, presumably to get answers about what had happened to him. Sam had gone off thinking to help, but when she found Tray, she would have a different purpose to her search.

"Do you know whether Scribes ever pair with more than one Kaver?"

Alec shook his head. "I don't know. All I know is that the union is felt to be important." He didn't know much more than that, and without one of the Scribes sharing with them, they might never know.

"I think all we can do is prepare, and be ready if he returns," Alec said.

"It's easy for you to say. You have your connection to your Kaver. You still see her."

Alec stared down at the page, nodding to himself. He still saw Sam, and... he should have seen her by now, at least he should have gotten word from her by now. Usually, she was better at getting back to him, making sure that he knew that nothing had happened to her, so if she didn't, it left him worrying and uncertain. Knowing Sam, she was likely to get into trouble at some point. That was the entire purpose of their agreement. She would always send word, and if he didn't hear from her, he would have to assume that something had happened.

"You look troubled."

"It's nothing," he said. He didn't want to bother Beckah with his own concerns, certainly not when it involved his connection to his Kaver. It felt like rubbing salt in a wound.

"If you haven't heard from her..."

Alec sighed. "I should have heard something by now. It's just that I know Sam. I know what she thinks herself capable of doing, and I worry about her."

"You don't think she's capable of doing what she thinks she can?"

"It's not that, not at all. She *is* capable, even more capable than those who are training her would like to believe. It's just that because she's so capable and because she is as fearless as she is, I worry about her."

"Then place an augmentation," she said.

"If nothing is wrong? If she's fine, and I place an augmentation, then I run the risk of not only wasting easar paper, but once her strength fades, I weaken her."

"Only her?" When he frowned, she shrugged. "Are *you* weakened by the augmentation?"

"Well, most of the augmentations actually grant her some additional strength in some way. I'm weakened with it also, but the ratio of blood used in it determines how much—"

"I understand how the augmentations work," Beckah said, grinning at him in a mocking way. "It's more about what does the augmentations do to you?"

Alec had thought about it, and he had studied the possibility of what might happen to him, but so far, he hadn't detected anything that indicated he was lessened during an augmentation. The only thing that happened was a cold tingling that worked through him when he placed the augmentation.

He pulled out a small scrap of easar paper and grabbed a vial of blood ink made with Sam's and his blood, and dipped a pen into it, quickly scratching down an augmentation. As he often did, he focused on her size and speed, thinking that if nothing else, adding to her strength would benefit her most.

"You should hurry," Beckah said.

Alec glanced up and saw that they weren't alone in the library anymore. Master Carl had entered. He was a massive man, incredibly fat, and his large jowls drooped on either side of his face jiggled as he walked. He had a strange posture, keeping his back almost arched, forcing his enormous belly outward, almost as if he intended to use his enormous girth to intimidate people. And it worked. Alec knew he had a brilliant mind, but that wasn't what intimidated him. It was his sheer size—and his position of power within the university. The only people who weren't intimidated by him were the other masters.

Worse was the fact that Master Carl did not care for Alec. He had made that clear over and over.

Alec continued to scrawl his augmentation, hurrying now. He put less thought into it than he usually did, and felt cold wash over him.

For a brief moment, he feared he had made a mistake. If Sam was safe, all he would have done was add strength to her until it faded, leaving her weakened. Considering how he had placed the augmentation, he might have given her more strength than he had intended.

"Mr. Stross. I'm not surprised to see you sitting here with Miss Reynolds, though what do we have here?" He eyed the scrap of paper, and thankfully, Beckah had had the foresight to grab the vial of ink off the table and pocket it.

"Nothing but a few notes, Master Carl." Alec folded the paper and squeezed it in his palm. He hoped he didn't smear the writing. Ink on easar paper usually needed a few moments to settle. He hadn't bothered to check whether it set enough, or whether it had faded. That was the other risk. If their ink was stale—if the blood was too old—then it wouldn't even hold on the easar paper.

"Notes?"

Alec pulled out one of his journals, figuring that it would be better to offer that to Master Carl than to show him the easar paper. "I take notes on everything I see. This one was from this morning."

Master Carl glanced at Alec's hand before looking down to the journal. He scanned the writing quickly, and then he grunted. "A referral of pain is unlikely, with those presenting symptoms. You should rethink your treatment plan."

"My father saw—"

Master Carl glared at him. "You mean your apothecary father?"

Alec nodded. "My father saw symptoms like this before. Anytime the attempt was made to treat an abdominal source it was ineffective. There was always something else. Maybe heart, maybe—"

"Again. I think that you should take the word of a master physicker over that of a common apothecary, Mr. Stross. But if you feel that your father"—he spat out the word— "knows more than university masters, perhaps you'd be better served returning to his apothecary to resume your studies."

"I'll continue looking for alternative diagnoses," Alec said, lowering his head. It was better not to argue with Master Carl, especially about something like that. Alec thought that he was right, but knew all too well that

Master Carl had a sharp mind, and he had learned not to overlook that, knowing that if he did, he did so at not only his peril, but that of the person he was treating.

Master Carl glared at Alec before turning and moving past, heading toward the section of the library reserved for the masters. Alec watched him go, feeling helpless.

"You shouldn't allow him that power over you," Beckah said.

"What choice do I have? He's one of the masters and..."

"And you've shown that you know as much as most of them," Beckah said. "They know it. You have a quick mind. Master Eckerd said it himself."

Alec smiled. He had heard Master Eckerd use that compliment on him. He hoped that he was deserving of it.

"Did you finish?" Beckah asked.

Alec glanced down to his hand and unfolded the scrap of paper. The ink had dried in time, though it had smeared a little. Would it matter if the ink smeared? He hadn't tested whether the nature of his handwriting made a difference. There were times when he'd used his finger to write with, and he didn't know whether that made a difference or not. Maybe it didn't. Maybe all that mattered was the words on the page, and the combination of his and Sam's blood.

"I think so. I... I hope so."

He turned his attention back to the book, unable to take his mind off of Sam, though he knew that he should maintain his focus. She needed him to continue learning, because what he learned helped both of them. If he managed to learn enough to help them, then they wouldn't have to fear another attack. They wouldn't have to fear the Thelns. They might finally find a way to help Tray.

As he studied the page, he couldn't help but notice that Master Carl glanced over at him from time to time. He wanted nothing more than to avoid Master Carl's attention. Out of all of the masters, he was the one Alec wanted to notice him the least.

5

WAITING FOR SAMARA

Water from the canal sloshed gently against the edge of the canal, though Alec didn't know whether that came from the movement of barges through the canals or the gentle breeze that occasionally gusted around him. Maybe it was both. He stared out at the water, imagining what it must feel like for Sam to soar across the canal, using her staff as she jumped, leaping the distance. How freeing must that be for her?

"You still haven't heard anything from her?" Beckah said.

Alec glanced over. Beckah sat with her legs crossed alongside the canal, leaning over a journal that lay open before her. Since observing the way Alec studied, she had taken to copying him. She wasn't the only one who had. There were quite a few people at the university who now kept notes in a journal the same way as Alec. He didn't know whether to be flattered or worried. There was some advantage to him being the only one to study in that way. It allowed him to set himself apart, and to gain the notice of the masters. With what he wanted to do, he needed to gain their attention and their favor.

"I haven't heard anything other than a note that said she was fine." He fingered the scrap of paper in his pocket. It had been far too brief for Sam, which told him that something had happened, though she either hadn't felt comfortable detailing it in the note or she wasn't going to tell him. He wasn't certain which.

"At least you know that she's unharmed."

Alec nodded. "At least there's that."

"Did she say anything about her brother?"

Alec shook his head. "She wouldn't, not in a note like that."

"Who are you talking about?"

Alec spun to see Stefan approaching. He was tall and gangly, and he wore thick glasses. Alec wasn't sure whether Stefan's grandmother would share with her grandson the nature of what they did, but it would seem Master Helen had kept it to herself. Alec supposed he shouldn't have been surprised. If she was a Scribe—and the role she played during the attack on the canals had proven that she was—then she would be like all of the other masters who protected the secrets of the canals as well as the secrets of the university.

"A girl," Beckah said.

"You let him talk about another girl?" Stefan asked.

"Not by choice," Beckah said.

Alec frowned at her. "Would that be an issue for you?"

"Would it?" she asked with a hint of a smile.

Alec's frown deepened. "Beckah?"

She closed her journal and set it on her lap, grinning at

him. "You're so easy to harass. I suppose you know that, though. That makes it even more entertaining."

"I don't want to be more entertaining," Alec said.

"No? Even for that friend of yours?"

He appreciated that Beckah didn't use Sam's name, especially not until he knew exactly what to make of Stefan. He doubted that Stefan would do or say anything that would cause them trouble, but he didn't know him, not well enough.

"Is it somebody from the university?" Stefan asked.

Beckah stood and walked over to Stefan, elbowing him as she approached. "I thought we weren't going to talk about her around me," she said, glancing over at Alec.

"I thought you said you didn't care."

"Just because a girl doesn't care doesn't mean that you should go around flaunting other women in front of her. Especially that woman."

"What does that mean?" Stefan asked.

"Ask our friend here."

Stefan turned to Alec, looking at him with a curious expression.

Alec only shook his head. "I'm not going to justify that with a response."

"Does she have anything to do with that business on the grounds recently?"

Alec and Beckah shared a look before they both shook their heads at the same time. Alec hadn't realized anyone had witnessed or heard the encounter in the courtyard with Marin. He knew they'd been less than discreet in their escape from the building and their efforts to help Sam, but they'd obviously earned the attention of onlookers. They needed to be more cautious.

"What business is that?"

"Whatever it was that got the masters all up in arms," Stefan said. "Grandma Helen doesn't really talk about it, but then again, she doesn't really talk about much when it comes to what the masters are doing."

"She must say something," Beckah prodded.

"Only that she's annoyed with Master Carl and Master Eckerd and Master Charles and Master…"

Alec waved his hands in front of him. "You made your point. It seems as if Grandma Helen is annoyed with everyone."

"Pretty much. That's what I got to enjoy growing up. She is very particular about the people she associates with."

"Well then, perhaps we should see what she thinks of our friend Alec here. Most of the masters seem to have taken a shine to him."

"Not Master Carl," Alec said.

Stefan chuckled. "I don't think Master Carl likes anyone. So, don't think that makes you special."

"That's not what makes Alec think he's special," she said with a smile.

"What's that supposed to mean?" Alec asked.

Beckah only shrugged. She glanced at the canal, staring out at the water. "I think I'm going to take a stroll. I need to clear my head before our next talk."

When she disappeared, Alec stared after her. Beckah had been off since the attack, and he thought that it mostly had to do with what she'd discovered about herself —and about him—but maybe there was more to it. Could she be angry? Maybe not angry with him, but he wondered if she was angry that they hadn't discovered anything about Tray's whereabouts. For her not to have the chance to work with her Kaver, to never learn and understand exactly what she could do with these abilities. She had to be frustrated. Beckah was as motivated as he was, if not more so. Plus, she was smart. So for this potential ability to go untapped, unused, would be a significant loss.

"She's been bothered by something," Stefan said.

"I can see that," Alec said.

"I don't know that you do. I think... I think that she has feelings for you."

Alec turned to Stefan. His friend was staring after Beckah, watching her as she disappeared around the curve and followed the course of the canal. The university was situated on a massive section of land, close enough to the palace that he could see it from here, but far enough away that it created a separation from the rest of the city.

The university grounds were meticulously maintained. A thick carpet of grass created a lush blanket beneath their feet. Gardeners kept wondrous-smelling flowers lining the paths, and bushes had been sculpted into various forms, creating an artistic walkway for them to follow out to the canals. The buildings themselves were not nearly as ornate as the palace, but there was still a majesty to them, from the white stone that gleamed in the sunlight to the spires that rose toward the heavens, as if the knowledge within the university could challenge that of the gods.

"I don't think her feelings for me are what's bothering her now," Alec said. He hadn't thought about the extent of Beckah's feelings for him, though he knew she felt something.

"Do you have any sisters?"

Alec grinned when he looked over to Stefan. "You know I don't. My mother died before they had a chance to have another."

Stefan nodded sadly. "And I'm sorry to bring that up. It's only that… if you had sisters, you would understand that there's more to her actions than what she is saying. There always has been."

"Are you trying to tell me that Beckah has romantic feelings for me?"

"You can't tell?"

"Other than the fact that she harasses me every chance she gets and taunts me whenever she can, and the fact that I know she has feelings for someone else." He looked up at Stefan innocently.

Stefan blushed. "I don't have an interest in Beckah."

"Why not? She's lovely enough."

"She is. She has wonderful hair. The way it falls to her shoulders in waves…" Stefan blushed again. "But I don't have an interest in her."

"Why tell me this, Stefan?"

"I just want to make sure that you don't hurt her feelings. We still have years ahead of us at the university, and it's important to have good friends with whom you can study. Friends who understand what we're going through, because we are doing it together. I know I don't want to go through those years alone, and neither should you. My grandmother made it clear that was how she got through her time at the university. She had her own group of friends that ensured that she was supported."

Alec tried to think of what friends Master Helen

would have chosen back then, but fell short. "Do you know who they were?"

"Other than Master Eckerd, Master Carl, Master Charles..."

Alec grinned. "I can't imagine Master Helen being in the same group with them."

"Oh, she was. They were quite something, from what I hear. To hear her tell the story, they once were inseparable."

"Even Master Carl?"

"Master Carl wasn't always the way he is now."

"No. I suppose Master Carl once wanted more power," Alec said, thinking back to what Master Eckerd had told him. Carl had political aspirations, which wasn't unusual. Many who went through the university did. What was unusual was for someone who failed in their political ambitions to return to the university and rise to the level of master. That spoke of Carl's natural ability—at least when it came to medical knowledge. When it came to his political ability... That was a different matter. Likely as not, Alec conjectured, Master Carl had angered as many people in the political realm as he often did in the university.

Stefan smiled. "You know, I didn't come here to chat about Master Carl. He is fascinating, but..."

Alec looked over at his friend. "What is it?"

"I thought that we could study."

"Study?"

They shared many of the same classes, but when it came to their clinical exposure, Alec had been advanced to a level beyond Stefan. He had advanced beyond Beckah, as well, though neither of his friends seemed to mind. They both enjoyed the fact that Alec excelled, basking in his exposure, likely thinking they could borrow some of that shine.

"Yes, well, we were on rounds this morning, and we came across someone suffering with a strange ailment."

"I'm sure the masters knew what the ailment was. Just use what they gave you." Most of the time, they offered hints at the diagnosis. Sometimes, those hints involved treatment, and when they made their rounds, the students were expected to come up with their diagnosis and then a treatment plan. Few students at their level were ever correct. That was why Alec had the advantage. He had spent many years serving as his father's apprentice, years during which he had been given an opportunity to study and learn and test his own diagnoses, something that none within the university could claim.

"It's a difficult diagnosis," Stefan said. "At least, Master Jessup tells us that it is."

Alec didn't have much experience with Master Jessup; only that he was well-regarded. He hadn't discovered whether Jessup was one of the Scribes or not, though doubted that he was. If he had been, he suspected Master Eckerd would have shared that with him. Wouldn't he have?

"What do you know?"

"Well…"

"Do you want me to come with you?" Alec asked.

Stefan let out a relieved sigh. "Would you?"

Alec glanced along the canal where Beckah had disappeared. He had done most of his studying for the day, and he hadn't followed any complicated patients on the ward, so didn't expect to be needed. As he often did when looking out at the palace, he held out hope that he might encounter Sam or get word about where she had been and what she'd been up to. If he went with Stefan, any chance of discovering that would be gone.

But Stefan was his friend and needed his help. Alec knew she had different responsibilities at the palace, and that her connection there drew her in ways that he didn't fully understand, so he had to support her as much as he could. And he had to support his new friends here.

"Show me what you know," Alec said.

They wound their way back and reached the hospital ward. It was primarily a line of cots, and junior-level physickers wandered around through them, checking on the patients. Most were wealthy, a point of contention for Alec, though there were some—and often, the sickest—who were accepted, regardless of ability to pay. That was something that he had not discovered until they had gained entry to the university. Before then, when Alec had first been trying to understand what role he would have with the university, he had thought they only helped those with money. That went counter to everything his father had taught him about healing, so it troubled him the most.

"Which person here?" Alec asked. The students were all assigned someone to spend time with and to study, so he wasn't certain which was the illness that Stefan had been given.

"She's over here," he said.

Stefan led him between two rows of cots and stopped in front of a youngish-looking woman. She had dark brown hair, and it had gentle waves to it that reminded him of Beckah. Her face was pale, though many suffering from illnesses had pale skin. Her eyes were closed and sunken. A faint sheen of sweat covered her face.

As it often did, his training from his father kicked in. He immediately began trying to assess her symptoms, but other than the slight sweating and the pale skin, there was little that was outwardly wrong with her. Perhaps dehydration, but that was easy enough to resolve, especially for the masters as skilled as those here.

"She came here a week ago. She was complaining of cramping in her legs and difficulty breathing. After that, she went unresponsive and has been like that for several days. I'm not exactly sure what changed."

"What of the records?"

One of the things that Alec appreciated about the university was that they kept records much like his father did. His father archived everything, keeping notes about all of the illnesses that he encountered, including his treatment approach. His records were voluminous, reflecting the hundreds, if not thousands, of people he'd helped over the years. The plethora of records gave his father—and Alec—more data to help diagnose and treat those who sought help from the apothecary. It helped that the people of the Arrend section had little trouble with the apothecary prices. If they charged prices like were found at the university, his father would have had fewer people coming to him for help. Since his father was willing to treat anyone willing to come to him, regardless of ability to pay, they had more chances to gain insight.

It was an added benefit that Alec had not considered before coming to the university. He had always thought that his father choosing not to charge for his services was him simply doing the right thing, but Alec suspected he had known exactly what he was doing. His father was calculating in everything he did.

And might be something more than Alec had known.

He tried not to think about that, about the fact that his father might have used his knowledge in unsavory ways. He was equally complicit, wasn't he? Hadn't he been willing to use his knowledge to help Sam, and hadn't she used that skill set to attack and defeat the Thelns?

Stefan slipped a record into his hands. It was documentation of illness, one that was made for each person admitted to the hospital. In it, the presenting symptoms followed by all of the treatment attempts were noted.

Alec scanned the symptoms, searching for anything that might be different from what Stefan had summarized. As he'd reported, the woman had come about a week ago, complaining of cramping in her legs that she'd had for some time. She was the daughter of a canal captain and spent much of her time on board the barge. A day or so after reaching the university, she'd begun having shortness of breath and pain in her chest… and her stomach.

"She complained of stomach pain?" Alec asked.

"Is that important?"

"Probably not for what she has, but it helps me." Having more examples of what he suspected was a referred type of pain would only help him. Maybe not with Master Carl, but it helped him gain a greater insight as to the nature of some of the illnesses they might encounter.

"Is that what it says? She was having some abdominal pain?"

"It says that she had chest pain first, and then she complained of her stomach hurting."

"If that's what the record says..." His mind went to work on possible diagnoses.

"Interesting," he said, nodding his head.

"Do you know what's wrong with her?" Stefan asked.

"Perhaps. I suspect her blood was too thick, and she formed a clot that spread to her lungs."

Stefan's eyes widened slightly. "That happens?" He hesitated a moment. "And you can tell that from simply reading her records?"

"I've seen it before. Usually, it happens with people who are sedentary or who have been sick with something else or who have undergone various surgeries, but each time it is similar."

"The chest pain?"

"The chest pain is a sign that the clot went to her lungs." Alec motioned to Stefan and pointed at his friend's arm. "Think about when you cut yourself. Your bleeding eventually stops and forms a clot. It's that clot that prevents you from bleeding out."

"I've read through the hematology volumes," Stefan said.

"Then you know that the same thing can happen internally. It's not common, but when it does happen, it's painful and difficult for someone to withstand. If the clot is large enough, it may restrict their ability to take in enough air."

"And if she couldn't take in enough air..."

"She might become unresponsive," Alec said.

"Wouldn't she breathe more rapidly?"

"She would, but look at this." He pointed to a page on the record where different treatments had been tried.

Stefan studied it for a moment, and then his eyes went wide. "That would slow her breathing, wouldn't it?"

"It would. And if she can't take in enough air, and the medications you're giving her for pain are slowing her breathing, she would fall into a stupor."

"What happens if we withdraw the pain medication?"

"It's unlikely that anything would happen. She needs to be given something to help thin out her blood. Otherwise, that clot will stay there."

"And there's nothing that can be done to remove the clot?"

"Not easily," Alec said carefully. If he had easar paper, and if he were tempted, he could use that to affect a healing, but that wasn't what he generally thought about doing with the easar paper. He suspected that some of the master healers did. Why else would they have the paper? How else would they use it? But he hadn't seen evidence of them doing so.

Then again, even if they were, would he see that evidence? When he healed Sam, there wasn't any evidence left, mostly because he kept no records—other than his own, and the words he wrote on the easar paper.

"There are various blood thinners that you can suggest to Master Jessup. See what he thinks of that."

"He thinks that is a fine idea," a deep voice said.

Alec turned around and saw Master Jessup standing behind him. He was an older man with thick bushy eyebrows and deep black hair that was just starting to gray. He had a long face, and wrinkles at the corner of his eyes gave him an almost playful sort of smile. He regarded

Alec for a long moment before reaching for the record, which Alec handed over.

"Mr. Stross?"

Alec nodded.

"I see Mr. Jaffar brought help."

Alec glanced over to Stefan and saw that he was flushing. "Isn't that what physickers do when they struggle?" Alec asked hurriedly. "We share knowledge, doing whatever we can to help those that entrust us with their health. Mr. Jaffar was only trying to ensure that—"

Master Jessup shook his head. "I'm not criticizing that he brought you in, Mr. Stross. I'm only acknowledging that he sought help. That is a sign of someone who understands his limitations. Often times when we gain knowledge, we forget that we have limitations." Master Jessup cast a glance around him, and his gaze drifted over the junior physickers in the room. Each of them now practiced independently, though they still served under the direction of one of the master physickers. "Many of these in this room failed to believe they need help. Just think of this poor woman. Had we not chosen her as a teaching opportunity, would she have managed to get the help that she needs? Would we have been here, having this conversation, discussing the need for covain root to thin out her blood?"

Master Jessup pulled a jar out from his pocket and set it on the bedside table. He twisted off the top and carefully reached in, pulling out a slender length of the slimy root. Alec had some experience with covain, but not much. It was difficult to find and harvest, and his father rarely stocked it, not finding it beneficial in many of his treatments. Most of the time when he thought it would be beneficial, he sent the patient to the university. It was enough that Alec recognized it.

"It's best when you dice it and then provide a little pressure to release the moisture inside."

"Moisture?" Stefan asked.

Master Jessup glanced up, his eyes intent beneath his thick eyebrows. "Some would call it the juice of the root, but I prefer to use a more eloquent term. Moisture isn't quite fitting, but juice feels far too base for my tastes."

Alec smiled. He hadn't had much interaction with Master Jessup, but he found the way the man spoke amusing. It was almost as if he knew that he was amusing, and he chose his words to exaggerate the effect.

"Now, if you mix this… moisture… with a hint of terland leaves and perhaps even a pinch of albon ash to thicken it, it should create a paste that can be administered into her mouth even when she's in a stupor such as this."

"Why were you waiting on treatment?" Alec asked.

Master Jessup arched a brow, and Alec feared for a moment that he should have been more circumspect, but when it came to healing, what was the point of delay?

"Covain root is difficult to acquire, Mr. Stross. I suppose your father would know something about that, and likely would have been able to acquire it much more quickly than we have, but our suppliers struggled to find it in enough quantity."

"Quantity?"

"The treatment requires administering this dosage every hour for the next two weeks. Quantity becomes important with such frequent dosing."

He pulled another two vials from his pocket and

plucked some leaves from one and a pinch of blackened albon ash from another and mixed them with the juice—moisture—of the covain root. It thickened and took on a grayish coloration. Master Jessup dipped his pinky into it and ran it along the gum line of the incapacitated woman. He dipped his pinky into it again and did the same on the top gum line. When he was finished, he wiped his hands on the bed sheets and straightened his spine as he pulled a pen from his pocket, dipping it in a jar of ink that was resting on the table, and began making his notes.

"Mr. Jaffar will get credit for this diagnosis," Master Jessup said without looking up. "Perhaps Mr. Stross should also get credit?"

Alec shook his head. "I don't need credit for it."

"We should all take credit for our accomplishments."

"I'm happy enough that she will be treated."

"Did you think that we would not treat her?" Master Jessup asked.

"That's not it. I've just seen how diagnostic delays can happen, and even when you have the diagnosis, sometimes, you don't have the necessary supplies."

"Indeed. As I said, covain root can be difficult to acquire." Master Jessup smiled, the corners of his eyes wrinkling as he did, and he turned away, leaving Alec and Stefan standing side by side.

"That was strange," Alec said.

"Master Jessup? He's quirky, I guess, but he's a skilled physicker. I'm lucky that he has agreed to take on students this term."

"Not that. The fact that he seems to actually care."

"You don't think the master physickers care?"

"I believe they care, but I've seen too often here how

they are focused on other things. I've seen too often how they are more concerned about the money that can be made off of the people they are treating rather than making sure that everyone has the necessary treatment. Master Jessup seems to care."

"And that's a bad thing?"

"No. Just surprising."

The door into the hospital opened, and Master Carl entered with a bluster, leading a small cadre of students. Alec dipped his head down and grabbed Stefan's sleeve, pulling him out before they drew Master Carl's attention.

6

THE CAPTOR

When she awoke, ropes cut into Sam's arms, pulling far more tightly than was necessary. She jerked on them immediately, but without augmentation, there was nothing she could do to get free. She thought of the easar paper but suspected they had pulled it from her pocket while she was out. At least she had the sense to crush the vial of her blood before they were able to use that against her. She didn't want to think about what might've happened had they managed to capture a vial of hers and Alec's blood ink.

A cold hearth stared at her. Black coals lay within it, practically taunting her with the promise of warmth. The room itself was almost frigid, and Sam wondered what this place was. And where were Ralun and the others who'd brought her here? And why had Tray been there? After her capture, they had covered her eyes and carried her for a long time. She had fought for a while, but her strength was limited, and she didn't want to exhaust it completely attempting to escape her captors. Without augmentation, she knew she didn't stand a chance against Ralun and his Thelns. Her head was pounding, and she recalled being knocked out and was unaware of how long she'd been here. And where was here?

A part of her continued to hold on to the hope that Tray would release her, but he never came.

Was he so far gone now? Had Marin gotten to him? Sam wouldn't put it past the woman. She had betrayed them for so long, and had been so convincing, that it wouldn't be entirely shocking to believe that Marin was responsible for turning Tray. Then there was the hope, however distant and unlikely, that Sam might be able to get to him. If Marin could reach Tray, why couldn't Sam? She had a connection to him, too, and it was one that had been strengthened by their time together over the years.

A door opened, a small gust of wind the only sign that it had. Sam twisted, trying to crane her neck so that she could see, but it was too dark and whoever had entered stood at the edge of her vision.

The air had a slight stink to it. It was a mixture of sweat and dirt and other unpleasantness. She recognized it. The stench of a Theln. Ralun?

"Are you going to stand behind me, taunting me, or do you intend to come around and reveal yourself?"

A deep chuckling sounded from behind her. "You remain spirited."

Not Ralun. Not any Theln. Theln voices were different. While deep, they had a strange accent, and their tongues often seemed as if they were too thick with their words.

This voice reminded her of one she might hear in the city. A highborn voice.

"You're working with them, then," Sam said. I know they were here. I can still smell their stink.

"Ah, little Kaver, how little you know."

Sam bit back the first response that came to mind. She thought about swearing at whoever her captor was, berating him for calling her little—as if her height wasn't an insult enough—but she didn't. There were other ways to get to men like this, men who thought to use insults to reach her.

"By that, I presume you mean to imply that they're working with you?" Sam twisted and managed to push off with her chair slightly, enough that she could turn it and see this man out of the corner of her eye. He had a round head, but shadows covered his face, making him difficult to identify. He wore a long gray jacket, and that was what caught her attention.

It was a university jacket. A physicker jacket.

Could she still be in the city?

Sam thought that unlikely, especially considering the fact that they had carried her as long as they had. It was far more likely that they had taken her outside the city, either through the swamp or onto a ship and beyond the borders, attempting to wrest from her knowledge of what the Kavers might do to protect the city from the Thelns.

"I imply nothing, little Kaver."

Sam squeezed her hands, pushing back her irritation. It was what he wanted.

"Another traitor, it seems. The city seems overrun with traitors and Thelns these days."

"And what a wonderful collaboration, indeed, yes?"

What? Was there a conspiracy against the city that was born of collaboration? Who was involved? It seemed that

Marin had worked for someone, using her abilities to poison the eels in the canal. Sam had thought it was for the Thelns, but how was this physicker involved?

"What do you want with me?" Sam asked.

The physicker stepped forward. He moved slowly, carefully, and some of the training Alec had tried to impart drifted to the forefront of her mind. Was it joints that ached that caused him to move as slowly as he did? Or was it something else, weakness that came from age and time?

"You will find out soon enough what we want with you. Now that we have you, and soon we will have the other, there will be little that any of the remaining Kavers can do to oppose us."

The other? Alec? She didn't like the sound of that. She was bound to Alec through their magic. He was her Scribe, and she was his Kaver, which granted them both particular abilities. If someone like this physicker—or Marin—intended to take advantage of that, they could potentially use her and Alec's blood, forcing them to serve, and possibly using their power to augment others. It was something that the other Kavers—her mother—had warned her about.

But he said "soon." So, they didn't already have Alec. She needed to help him. To get word to him. But from here, there wasn't anything she could do, not without some way to reach her augmentations. And that meant having access to easar paper. Somehow, she would need to find a way to get ahold of paper, see if she could use any of the dried blood that now stained the inside of her pocket, and add another augmentation.

It was too much to achieve. It was unlikely to succeed.

"And who is this 'us'?" she asked. Maybe if she could keep him talking, he would reveal something about why he had captured her and what he wanted from her. Maybe it was about more than using her and her blood.

The physicker approached and wiggled a finger at her. "This isn't a discussion. Well, it's not a discussion that I will engage in."

"Fine, then at least tell me where my brother is."

"Your brother? Do you still believe him to be your brother? I would have thought that she'd have told you the truth before now."

There was a familiarity to the way he said *she*. It seemed almost intimate, and Sam suddenly understood. At least, she understood more than she had before. "You're her Scribe." The man's eyes twitched, the slightest movement providing acknowledgment of that fact. "I wondered what had happened to her Scribe. She never talked about you, so we all assumed you were dead." It was difficult enough to pair with a Scribe to begin with, and once that person was gone, it was nearly impossible to find another Scribe to form the connection with. Thinking that Marin's Scribe was dead was the most logical answer, at least to Sam.

"Yes, well, I am most decidedly not dead."

"Why are you helping her? And why are you working with the Thelns?" That had to be the reason Ralun had brought her to the physicker, but where was he? She thought she could smell him, but maybe that was only her imagination.

"For now, it's a mutually beneficial relationship."

"Poisoning the canals in the city was done on behalf of the Thelns. What was in it for her? Or you?"

"You know very little. Perhaps I will educate you. Or perhaps I will wait for Marin to do it. She would relish that opportunity."

Sam licked her lips, her mouth suddenly dry. The threat terrified her, especially as helpless as she was. Marin had betrayed her, deceived her, and had used the Book of Maladies to tear her memories from her, forcing her to forget her own mother and forcing her to believe that Tray was her brother. There was darkness within Marin, and Sam had very nearly died at her hands.

"Where is she?"

The physicker cocked his head, frowning at Sam.

"Marin. Where is she?"

"She is with you. And you will get her for me."

Sam was more confused than ever. When she had seen Tray, she had presumed he had begun working with the Thelns, especially since they had attacked her and he seemed to just stand there and watch. And the Thelns brought her here, to this physicker, so didn't that mean he'd know about Tray and possibly where he had taken Marin? But clearly this man didn't know where she was, and for whatever reason, thought Sam did.

That meant Tray was keeping what he'd done with Marin from this physicker—and maybe from the Thelns. He had to have a reason, and she'd find out once she tracked him down, but for now, she felt the best was to protect Tray was to assist him in his deception.

And here she had begun to worry that Tray might have become something other than her brother. It was almost enough to make her smile, though if she were to do that, she would have other questions to answer.

"What makes you think that I would be willing to get her for you?" Sam asked.

"You value your freedom, don't you?"

"I've lived most of my life in service to someone more powerful than me. Why should that change now?"

"Are you implying that you are offering your service to me?"

Sam laughed. "To do that, I would have to agree that you are more powerful than I am."

"We have you captured. Isn't that enough proof?"

"You have me captured because you used Tray against me."

"And I will continue to use him against you if you defy me."

"Oh, I will continue to defy you. Tray has betrayed me. I owe him no allegiance, not anymore. The only thing I owe him is a beating."

The physicker smiled slightly. "Most Kavers prefer to avoid conflict with the Thelns, and for good reason. You are too young to know better, but their poison would be fatal to you."

"Would it? If you know Marin, then you know that I survived their poisoning once already."

She watched his face, trying to gauge whether Marin had shared that piece of information with him yet or not. Was it possible that Marin had not shared it? If not, it was reason for Sam to question the interaction between this man and Marin.

Did he know about Tray?

He knew that Sam believed him to be her brother, but did he know that he was Marin's son? Did he know about how Marin betrayed the Kavers, and how she had used the Thelns?

"No one survives Theln poison. To do so would be—"

Sam shrugged. "Impossible, yes, that's what I was told. But I did." She glanced down at her shoulder. The scar was a reminder of her first exposure to the Thelns.

The physicker stalked over to her and jerked on her cloak, pulling it off her back. He tore back the fabric of her shirt, exposing her shoulder. His movements were rough, but he was very clinical in how he assessed the injury. His fingers traced over her shoulder, pressing into her skin and into the bones, before circling around where the crossbow bolt had gone in. The scar had faded considerably, now little more than a faint dimpling of the skin. But it was enough.

"If it hadn't carried poison, there would be no scar," Sam said. She looked up, meeting his eyes. "My Scribe healed me. But the poison made it impossible to remove all signs of the injury." She didn't know if that was entirely true, but suspected that it was, especially when the physicker shifted her cloak, covering up her shoulder again. He seemed almost... annoyed by the fact that she had recovered. Sam figured that was about as much reaction as she might get from him.

"Your Scribe should not have had the necessary training to do this."

"Maybe he should not have, but he did. His father taught him—"

"To be an apothecary, I am aware."

"If you're aware, then maybe you know how skilled his father is. From what I understand, he studied at the university."

"And washed out. He was deemed not fit to remain. Is that the sort of healer on whom you would hang your hopes of recovery?"

Sam glared at him. "Rather him than someone like yourself who has betrayed everything that you claim to hold sacred."

"And you know exactly what I claim to hold sacred? You know me so well as to know those intimate details?"

"I know that you're working with Marin, and I know what she has done in the way that she has betrayed her vows." That was vague enough—and especially true—that she could use it to anger him.

The physicker turned away and retreated to the wall. Turning back around, his arms crossed over his chest, he stared at her. He watched her almost as if she were a puzzle. And maybe to him, she was. "You will help me get her. Whatever you have done to her will be undone."

"What makes you think that I'm willing to help?"

"If you don't, I have told you what will happen."

"You've threatened." Sam leaned forward, testing the bindings around her arms. A chill began to wash over her, and she thought of Alec. She'd hoped that he would soon grow worried about how long she'd been gone. They had agreed that if that happened, he would grant her certain physical attributes, and she could use those in situations like this. "Nothing more than that."

The physicker continued to stare at her, and after a moment, his gaze dropped to where she pulled at the ropes. The smile on his face remained fixed in place, but then began to fade slowly before disappearing altogether. He took a step toward her, but he was too slow.

As the augmentation took hold, Sam jerked on the

ropes, rigidity to her skin protecting her from injury, and her strength allowing her to break free. She leapt from the chair and glared at the Scribe.

"And they were empty threats," she said.

Sam slammed her fist into his stomach, doubling him over, and caught him in the face with her knee, driving him back. He collapsed.

She raced toward the door and pulled it open. She used more strength than intended, and the door came flying free from the hinges, ripped out of its frame. At least her strength was significantly augmented.

She saw no one else in the small hallway. A door at the end beckoned, and she raced toward it, tearing it free as she escaped. Outside, she was greeted by the sounds and smells of the city. The stench of the canals loomed close—much closer than she expected. They *hadn't* taken her out of the city.

She glanced back to the building in which she'd been held. It appeared empty and unused. Did they own it, or did they just take advantage of an abandoned building and use it for their own purposes?

She couldn't race off—not yet. Augmented as she was, she wasn't in nearly the danger she had been. And there was something she still needed to do.

Sam hurried back into the building and ran down to the room she'd left, wanting to get there before the enhancements wore off. But the Scribe was gone.

Kyza!

She should have grabbed him as she escaped, but she hadn't wanted to be burdened with him. Now he was free, and likely as much of a threat as Marin.

7

RETURN TO THE PALACE

The augmentation began to fade as Sam reached the section that led to the palace, and though she knew she could cross the bridge by just flashing her ring, she was feeling the need to stay out of sight. She jumped, but the remaining strength augmentation was not enough to help her clear the canal, and she splashed down shy of the other side. She swore to herself as she landed, frantically swimming, not wanting to be in the canal any longer than necessary. Even though she knew the purpose of the canal eels, she still hated the damned things. Kyza knew that they had practically chewed through her cloak once. She didn't want to think what might happen if they managed to clamp onto her arm or leg. They had sharp teeth that could rip through anything.

She swam quickly, the water cold and making her teeth chatter. Maybe Alec would grant her another augmentation since she'd yet to return. One more might be enough help her reach the other side and climb out, but she wasn't quite lucky enough for that. Had he given up on her? Would he think to add an augmentation when he still didn't know what had happened to her? She had returned to the palace rather than going toward the university where she would find him. Maybe it upset him.

No. Alec wasn't like that. He wouldn't get upset by her not going to him. What would upset him would be learning that she had gone off and fought with a Theln without him. It wasn't that Alec wanted to fight the Thelns; it was that he understood the role he played, the way he could add to her augmentations, giving her enough strength to actually combat them.

When she reached the canal's edge and dragged herself out of the water, she was greeted by a pair of guards. She looked up at them, smiling. She didn't recognize either of the men, but that wasn't uncommon, at least not here in this part of the city.

"Can you let Elaine know that I need to speak with her."

One of the guards glared at her, but Sam put out her hand, flashing the ring that would tell them she was from the palace. They studied it for a moment before turning and stalking away.

When she stood, trying to squeeze the extra water out of her cloak, she watched them depart. They could have at least helped her rather than leaving her to drip across the stones on her way back to the palace. Typical. These pompous guards would rather leave a young girl cold and shivering, dripping from stinking canal water, rather than lift a hand to offer her help.

She glanced behind her. There was a part of her that

feared she might have been followed. If she had, she hoped it was Tray rather than Ralun. He might be working with them, but he still hadn't told them everything. If he had, they would have known where to find Marin. Which meant Tray wasn't lost—yet.

Sam shook her head. There wasn't anything she could do. If her brother was mixed up with Ralun, then she had to try to find a way to help him.

By the time she reached the palace, she had mostly dried. She'd received no more augmentations, though she hadn't entirely expected to. She started toward the side entrance when Elaine stepped out of the door, greeting her.

Her mother shared a similar size. Neither of them was very tall, and they both had dark hair, and easily tanned skin. Her mother had wrinkles at the corners of her eyes, and her jaw was sharp, lending to the severe expression she wore.

"Samara. I understand that you were found near the water."

"I jumped over the canal. And missed the landing. And the stupid guards who came upon me after I barely made it out of the water didn't feel the need to offer me any assistance."

"And why would you have needed to jump over the canal? You have the ring we provided."

Sam shrugged, looking behind her. There was that strange, unsettled feeling, again. Was she being watched? The itching between her shoulder blades told her she was, but that wouldn't be possible, not on the palace grounds.

"Well, I lost my canal staff." Even with it, Sam didn't think she would have been able to clear the canal. Using the canal staff to jump over the massive canal that separated the palace section of the city from the others would have been difficult if not impossible without any augmentations. With augmentations, she could clear the canal in a single jump even without her staff. At least she could with the right augmentations.

"And how did you lose your staff?"

The way she said it sounded so maternal, and it rubbed Sam the wrong way. Her mother had not been a part of her life for very long, so for her to act motherly felt... strange. And worse, it wasn't even her mother's fault that she had been gone. Not entirely.

"I was attacked. There are Thelns in the city."

"I know."

"Tray was with them, and they captured me and... Wait. You *knew*?"

"Do you believe that Thelns have never reached the city before?"

"No. I know they've reached the city. I seem to remember fighting with several of them before I knew anything about them."

"And you wouldn't have had to had you only left that to others who were more capable."

Sam glared at her. "More capable? You weren't there. While the princess was dying, you weren't there."

"I was searching for a way to help her," Elaine said. Her voice was pitched low and dangerous, and Sam knew better than to challenge. She didn't have many memories of her mother, but the tone that she took now was one that Sam wasn't willing to challenge. She knew better than that, even if she didn't know her mother that well.

"Fine. While you were searching for a way to help her,

I *did* help her. Just because I wasn't trained doesn't mean that I wasn't capable of helping," Sam said.

"I'm very aware of exactly what you did to help her."

Sam met her mother's eyes for a moment, before shaking her head. Was she trying to irritate her? No. Sam didn't think that was quite it. It wasn't that she wanted to irritate her, it was that she was...

"What are the Thelns doing in the city? You said you knew they were here, so what are they doing? Why are they here?"

"If you were captured by them, I imagine you know why they're in the city and what they're after."

"Marin?"

Elaine nodded. "Perhaps Marin, perhaps something else. Whatever it is that they're after, their presence here is dangerous to us."

"I met her Scribe."

Elaine frowned. "Marin's Scribe passed away many years ago."

"That might be, or it might be that he pretended to pass away. It wouldn't be the first time that Marin deceived someone."

"What did he look like?" She grabbed Sam by the arm and pulled her into the palace. Sam's cloak continued to drip, leaving pools of water across the pale white marble. There were tapestries hanging along the walls, pictures of royals that had once lived and served in the city, and Sam often wondered how many of them had been Scribes, much the way the princess was. There were few enough Scribes remaining, nearly as few Kavers.

"I didn't see him well, but I would recognize the voice. It was hard and angry."

Elaine glanced over, and her face was unreadable. "I was with Marin when her Scribe passed. There would be no faking that death."

"Are you certain?"

"When I told him I thought he was long dead, he replied, 'I am most certainly not dead.' That kind of confirmed it for me."

But then she wondered if she'd made a mistake. Had he only said that to confuse her? Maybe Marin had found another Scribe.

How often did that happen?

"It could be a different Scribe. It's possible that—"

"Possible, but extremely difficult, especially while in hiding," Elaine said, seemingly dismissing the idea that Marin had found another Scribe. "He simply let you get away?"

"I don't know that he let me get away. Alec gave me..."

Sam flushed. She wasn't sure she should admit that Alec had given her an augmentation, doing it remotely. Elaine wanted her to learn without augmentation, but she wouldn't have escaped otherwise.

"Alec gave you an augmentation. And how much paper do you have remaining?"

That was the real issue, at least to Elaine. Easar paper was valuable and limited in supply. Before long, someone would have to try and acquire more. Sam didn't know anything about the acquisition of easar paper, only that getting one's hands on it was difficult.

"Not much."

Elaine arched a brow. "That is vague."

Sam shrugged. "How specific do you want me to be? I don't have nearly as much as I once did and not nearly enough to practice using it." That wasn't entirely true. She still had a dozen sheets of paper, all concealed within the university, all held safe by Alec. That paper was the key to her rapid development. Most Kavers struggled with learning how to use their skills, partially because they were limited on how aggressive they could be practicing. Sam and Alec had never had such limitations—at least not quite the same limitations as others, because they had managed to keep a supply of paper.

"You understand the purpose of the paper is to protect the city. If you are hoarding it—"

Sam shook her head. "We're not hoarding it. And how can I know what I need to know to protect the city if it's limited?"

"There are other ways for you to train. There are other skills for you to learn."

"Such as what Marin knew?" Sam glanced over at her mother as they paused in front of a gilded door. On the other side was the princess's private quarters, a place that Sam once would have found overwhelmingly ornate. She still did, she supposed, but nothing about the palace overwhelmed her quite as it once had.

"Marin was always a skilled Kaver," Elaine said.

"She didn't need augmentations to challenge me," Sam said.

"No. She did not. Which is why you need to be cautious when you throw yourself against her."

"I didn't *throw* myself against anyone." Not that she would be opposed to doing so with Alec. She flushed again at the thought, and Elaine watched her, practically knowing what she was thinking. "Well, maybe I threw myself against a Theln. And Tray. Had my augmentations been enough, I wouldn't have been captured."

Elaine grunted. "You can't be so dependent on augmentations all the time, Samara. There will come a time when your augmentations will fail. They aren't indefinite. That's why we train so that we don't have to rely upon them."

"The Thelns don't rely on augmentations, and their powers don't fail.

"Their magic is different from what we possess."

If Sam had hoped that she might get a better understanding of the Theln magic, she was mistaken. It was something that she still didn't understand well. She had tried to ask questions, but those who knew didn't speak of it.

It was something that she would have to ask Tray. It was even more reason to chase her brother down and try to reach him.

On the other side of the door was a sitting room. Even that was enormous. It rivaled the size of Bastan's tavern, right down to the enormous hearth glowing with a crackling fire. There were none of the same pleasant smells that she always enjoyed in Bastan's tavern, but the princess had access to all the food she wanted, all with a simple summons. Several chairs were arranged in a half circle in front of the fire. Two massive wardrobes—likely filled with gowns and robes and other clothing that Sam could not imagine wearing—stood against the opposite wall. A folded screen created some privacy near a corner, and Sam wondered if someone hid behind it, listening. Knowing her mother, she likely wouldn't allow that, especially as the princess's Kaver.

"Why are we here?" Sam asked softly.

She didn't see any sign of the princess, but her mother seemed unperturbed by that. Sam could see her mother had a comfortable familiarity entering such ornate quarters. Sam wondered if she would ever reach a point of a similar comfort. It was unlikely that she would. As much as she had grown accustomed to her days in the palace, there was still something more comfortable when she was in the Caster section of the city. It was what she knew. She didn't have to thieve, not as she once did, though she couldn't deny that she missed it in some ways.

Coming to the palace had changed so much for her. Not only was she now training with a purpose, and she understood more about who she was and where she came from, but she no longer had to worry about capture by the city guards or drawing the attention of highborns. Kyza knew that *she* was practically a highborn now, even if she didn't feel that way.

"We're here because of your foolishness tonight."

A small figure stood from one of the chairs, and Sam realized that the princess was here. She had golden hair, and it had a luxurious sheen to it, braided and twisted up so that it formed buns on top of her head. Her pale blue eyes sparkled as she glanced from Sam to Elaine. She had a golden dress that matched her hair, something that Sam figured was intentional.

"Thelns have attacked in the city again," Elaine said, not even bothering to greet the princess.

Sam still wasn't sure what was expected of her. Was she to bow? She wouldn't curtsy. That didn't feel right. Bowing seemed somehow wrong also. This was a woman she had saved, and whether the princess acknowledged it or not—and often, she did not—she wasn't about to be deferential to her.

Yet she couldn't deny the young woman's regal air and the confident way she carried herself. Sam suspected she managed it without even knowing what she did. That was likely what happened when someone was born and raised in the palace, accustomed to all of the niceties that were found there. It was something that Sam would never feel. Regardless of what she was, she still felt like that lowborn girl from Caster.

"The Scribes have noticed a disturbance," the princess said.

"Sam claims to have been attacked by one or more of them."

"One," Sam said quickly. She wouldn't have the Scribes chasing after Tray. Not yet. There might come a time when they would have to, but she had no intention of putting them on her brother's trail too quickly. "And it was one of the Thelns I've faced before. His name is Ralun."

The princess flicked her gaze briefly to Elaine before looking back to Sam. "Are you certain?"

Sam nodded. "I've faced him before. He was the Theln who was in the city when you were poisoned."

"Not poisoned. Targeted," the princess said. "The Book targets an individual, and the disease takes hold. They used a wasting illness on me."

"I remember," Sam said. "I think I was the one who helped ensure that you were brought back from it." She didn't often throw that out at the princess, but now seemed the time.

Elaine was watching her. "Are you sure that it was Ralun?"

"I'm sure."

"Why haven't you told me about him before?" Elaine asked.

"What does it matter? I didn't realize that individual Thelns made a difference. When she was attacked"—Sam nodded to the princess—"there were three or four Thelns in the city." Sam lost track of how many there were, but knew that she had killed several of them, all with the aid of Alec's augmentations. Without them, she would have been strangled or poisoned or... possibly any number of horrible fates could have befallen her.

Elaine glanced over to the princess. "I've told you, she doesn't know enough. We need to share with her."

"It's because she doesn't know enough that we can't share with her," the princess said.

"Share what with me?" Sam asked.

The princess considered her for a long moment. "Are you certain it was he?"

"I'm certain. I told you, I've had enough experience with him that I would recognize him. He's the one who shot me with the poison crossbow bolt and later destroyed Alec's father's apothecary. Why is he important?"

"He is important because he is dangerous."

"All Thelns are dangerous," Sam said.

"And he sits high among them. If he is here, we need to know who he intends to target."

"Target?"

The princess nodded. "When you encountered him at the university while you and your Scribe were working to save me"—the princess looked right at Sam at that moment, and she felt a surge of satisfaction at the recognition—"it was not the first time Ralun had used the Book against us. If he is here again, it means that he intends to use it again, and whoever he is here for is in grave danger."

8

FATHERLY ADVICE

Alec crossed over the bridge leading to the palace section. He hated that it had come to this, but he should have heard from Sam by now, and the fact that he hadn't bothered him much more than it should. He tried to ignore Beckah watching him as he made his way across the bridge between the university section and the palace, but he felt her gaze practically burning on his back. Could Stefan be right? Could Beckah's feelings for him be more than just friendship? He didn't think so. He attributed her intensity to her struggle to learn what she needed to do with Tray. But if Stefan was right, he'd have to address it at another time.

On the other side of the bridge, he encountered a pair of guards. Thankfully, Sam had given him a ring like hers, signifying his right to at least enter the palace grounds, and he flashed it at the guards. They waved him past, and he felt the same flush of excitement he got each time he used it. It still amazed him that he was allowed to come onto the palace grounds, though he suspected that it amazed Sam even more. She didn't talk about her feelings about it, not like she once did, but he knew that she viewed herself as less than what she was.

Once on the other side, Alec looked around. He had rarely come here on his own, but he'd grown tired of waiting for Sam. He didn't like being separated from her, any more than he liked not knowing what had befallen her. He had the sense that something had happened to her, which was why she had not reported back to him after the augmentation he sent, but what? And why was she keeping it from him? What was she thinking she could do on her own?

More than he could do on his own. He knew that. Sam was skilled, whereas he was... he was a healer. Not a physicker, though he had to believe that he would eventually reach that point. And he wasn't an apothecary, not anymore. It left him questioning what he was and what he was meant to be.

What was he doing here? He didn't even know whether Sam was here, and if she was, would she be free to visit with him? Or would he only end up disturbing her? She had other responsibilities. He knew that. But then, he thought that she would want to see him.

When he reached the main entrance of the palace, he paused. Alec glanced around, looking to see whether there was anyone here who he might recognize. He'd only been here a few times, not often enough that he thought he should recognize someone, but if there was someone here he might know...

The door opened, and a familiar face appeared.

"Master Helen?"

She looked over at him, and a dark expression clouded

her brow. "Mr. Stross. I didn't realize that you were granted permission to leave the university and come to the palace."

Alec blinked. Was he supposed to get permission? He didn't think that was required, but then again, he hadn't been at the university long enough to know for sure. What if he was supposed to get permission? And what if his leaving got him into trouble?

Alec could only imagine just how excited Master Carl would be at learning that Alec had ventured beyond where he was supposed to go, and how excited the master might be to enact whatever discipline such an unsanctioned departure warranted.

"Relax, Mr. Stross. I have no intention of telling Master Carl that you left the grounds."

A flush washed over his face. "Thank you. I mean..." He shook his head. What did he mean? And how had Master Helen even known what he was thinking about? Was he that transparent that he was known by the other masters?

"I don't believe your—*friend*—is here."

Alec flicked his gaze to the palace. "Do you know where she might be?" Never mind the fact that he didn't know why Master Helen would care where Sam was, or why she would keep tabs on her comings and goings. What mattered more to him was that he didn't know what happened to her, and he was getting concerned—and maybe a bit afraid.

"She has an assignment."

"An assignment? I would think that if she had an assignment, I—"

"Would you? You are a student at the university,

studying to become a physicker. Don't presume that places you in any greater position than anyone else, Mr. Stross."

Alec's mouth went dry. "I wasn't trying to—"

"I know exactly what you were trying to do, Mr. Stross. There are a great many things you can still accomplish at the university, but you must be there in order to do so. There is a process, a stepwise manner to your training. Don't think that you can step beyond it, regardless of how accelerated of a student you might be."

She pushed past him, and he turned to grant her space and watched her go. He stood at the doorway, feeling foolish. At least she had complimented him in her chiding, but even that compliment was a challenge. He felt taken aback and didn't know how he should react, or what he should say.

His gaze drifted back up to the palace. If Sam wasn't here, there was nothing for him here. There was no reason for him to remain. It would be better for him to go back to the university... Only he didn't really want to go back, not without knowing more about what had happened to Sam, and he didn't like the idea of bumping into Master Helen again, either.

Alec sighed and turned away, crossing the grassy yard leading toward the bridge that would carry him away from the palace. There was another bridge that had been damaged, and it was undergoing repairs, but that wasn't the way he wanted to go, anyway. His steps took him from section to section, quickly passing from one part of the city to another, and he finally reached his father's rebuilt apothecary shop.

A few lanterns glowed inside, giving off light despite

the early hour. It was his father's way of alerting others that he was there. He often lit lanterns inside, and there was something comforting about that, a warmth to the apothecary shop that no other place really rivaled.

Alec pushed the door open, enjoying the familiar sound of the bell tinkling above as he entered. His father sat at the back of the shop and looked up when Alec entered.

His eyes widened, and he smiled at Alec. The same warmth that he'd always known evident on his face. "Alec. Has the university granted you a break?"

"I have completed my studies for the day, if that's what you're asking."

His father nodded. "Good. Good. I wasn't worried. I think you have an advantage that most who go to the university do not. How many have had the opportunity to practice before they even study?"

Alec snorted. "Not many. That advantage is nice, Father, but it often sets me apart."

His father glanced back down to where he was documenting. He wrote on a nice parchment, likely expensive, imported specifically for Aelus by Mrs. Rubbles. "As well you should be. You have a brighter mind than most in the university."

Alec took a seat across from his father and rested his arms on the table, simply enjoying the familiarity of the shop. It wasn't the same shop he had known growing up, but that didn't matter to him, not entirely. That shop had been destroyed, and his father had rebuilt this in much the same image.

His father set the pen down and looked up at Alec. "Out with it. What is it?"

"It's nothing, Father."

"Nothing? You come to see me when I would think you'd be studying, and sit here with your shoulders slumped and a deep frown on your face. I don't need to be a master physicker to know something's wrong. I suspect if I were to check your pulse, your heart would be palpating, and with your quickened breathing—"

Alec waved his hand, cutting his father off. "I'm not some patient who came for healing."

"You're my son. I am willing to do whatever it takes to ensure that you understand how much that matters to me."

"I know how much it matters, Father."

"What is it then?"

"It's Sam."

"It often seems that when you come here frustrated, there's some problem with that girl. It was often the same with your mother and me."

"This isn't like that."

"Isn't it? Perhaps it's not, but perhaps you would like it to be. Could it be that you're here because you aren't receiving the affection you would like?"

"Father—"

"Don't father me. I'm only asking because I care and because I want to know what I can do to help. I don't want to see you in pain."

"I'm not in pain. I'm just..."

His father smiled. "I understand. You're just like every other young man who finds himself in a position where you have someone you care about but you aren't sure what they feel about you."

"I know what Sam feels about me."

"You do? Is it a shared emotion?"

"Shared emotion? Father, you don't have to talk quite so clinical all the time."

His father breathed out a sigh. "I'm sorry. I find that talking clinically makes it an easier conversation. After your mother…"

"I understand."

"I'm not sure that you do. After your mother, I've not been able to connect to someone else, not nearly as easily as I would like. I've tried, and the gods know that there have been opportunities—"

"Father!"

"You're old enough to have heard this."

"Maybe you should check with Mrs. Rubbles."

He waved his hand. "Rubbles is not quite my type."

"Not your type? Father, this is Mrs. Rubbles we're talking about."

"And I told you that she isn't the kind of person who appeals to me."

"You mean someone caring? Someone who goes out of her way to make sure that you have all the paper that you need? Someone who ensures that all of your supplies are ready?"

"You would lecture me? You have this nice girl that you have been partnered with, and you've done nothing but create reasons why the two of you aren't a good fit. You're not convincing anyone."

Alec sighed. "Father, this isn't why I have come here."

"It may not be why you came, but now that you're here, I intend to give you every bit of advice that I can."

"I think we've already proven that you are not fit to give advice."

"Not fit? What kind of statement is that?"

"An appropriate one."

His father chuckled, and they sat in silence looking at each other for a long moment. "Are you going to tell me what happened?"

"I don't know quite how," Alec said. "Something happened with Sam, but... I'm not sure what it was. I don't know where she's gone, or if she's safe, which is all that really matters, but..."

"But you worry about her."

"I worry about her," Alec agreed.

"I imagine you also feel as if you have been left out."

"It's not quite like that," he said. "I don't mind the fact that she's off with the princess and whoever else training to be a Kaver, but I do mind that I don't know what she's involved in. I know how dangerous it is."

His father sat silently then leaned forward, resting his elbows on the table between them, steepling his fingers together. With one arm, he shifted the papers that rested on the table, nearly disrupting a vial of ink in the process. "And you would like to be a part of the danger?" his father asked.

"It's not the danger I want to be a part of. It's everything else. It's what she's going through."

"Have you told her?"

"I've tried, but she—and everyone else—thinks I need to keep my focus on what I'm learning at the university."

"I think I like this young lady more than I realized," his father said with a smile. When Alec started to object, his father waved his hand. "I know the role you have in her life puts you in danger, and I'm not trying to keep you from helping her. In fact, I'm very proud of your efforts not only for her, but for the others you've helped, including the princess. I'm just saying that I appreciate that she sees the value in you continuing your studies. It's more important than you know."

"I'm very aware of how important my studies are, Father. I understand the necessity of continuing to train at the university, and I understand why I need to be there, and what I can learn, it's just that…"

"It's just that you would like to do something else, is that it? You like the thrill that these dangerous situations present?"

Alec sighed and leaned back in his chair. He thought of all the times he'd been in danger since meeting Sam, and everything they had been through, and knew that wasn't what he wanted. He didn't want to be the one in danger, but at the same time, he didn't want Sam to be, either.

Before he had a chance to say something else, the door to the apothecary opened, and his father jumped to his feet, hurrying to the door. Alec stood, and clasped his hands behind his back as he often had when he was younger, prepared for whatever his father might ask for him to do.

It was a younger man who entered, escorting a woman about the same age. Dark curls framed her face, which was drawn and pale, reminding him of the woman Stefan had taken him to see at the university and the illness she had presented. Unlike that woman, if this young lady had stomach pain, it wasn't from illness. Her large belly told Alec she was pregnant, though he couldn't tell how far along she was. From the look on her face, she was near term, and likely had come to his father to help with the delivery. It wasn't uncommon for people to come to his father rather than a midwife. Especially when they had nothing to offer in payment.

"Alec?" his father said.

It was all that he needed to be spurred into action. He hurried off, disappearing to the back of the shop to gather rags and a few blankets. He had been part of many births while studying with his father. It was something that even few within the university could claim. Most pregnancies were managed by a midwife, and there was little that the physickers were needed for when it came to the delivery. By the time a physicker might be necessary, it was often too late.

When Alec had all of the supplies gathered, he returned to the front of the shop. His father had positioned the woman on a cot, and she writhed as a contraction overwhelmed her. His father patted the woman's hand, trying to soothe her while her husband looked on worriedly.

Alec hurried over and grabbed the man's hand, guiding him away. It wouldn't do for him to get in the way of his father as he worked. It would only delay the care she needed.

"Come on now," Alec said, ushering the man away. "Give them some space. Let the birth happen naturally."

"Natural?" the man said. His voice was hoarse, as if he'd been yelling. "The midwife said this was not natural."

Alec frowned and glanced over to his father. "Why not?"

"The baby is backward," the man explained. "The midwife said she couldn't deliver our child."

Alec let out a frustrated sigh. If the baby attempted to come out backward, it would be a difficult delivery. His father had been successful several times delivering a breech child, but there were just as many times when the child died.

He wasn't sure that he wanted to be present when a young couple lost their child. He checked his pockets, searching for easar paper, but there was none. He must've left his supplies back at the university. That was a mistake. He should have known better than to leave them behind, but then again, how was he to know that he was going to come to his father's apothecary and feel compelled to help a couple as they attempted to deliver their child?

He patted the man on the hand and nodded to his father. "I'm going to help. You need to stand off to the side —or sit, if that's easier—but don't get too close. You will hear some screaming. You will hear us reassuring her. And when you hear your child crying, then you can approach."

The man glanced over to Alec and bobbed his head in a nod.

Alec left him and approached the woman. She was panting now, and with every contraction, she cried out, her moans filling the shop.

"The man says they went to a midwife, but she told them the baby was breech," Alec said.

"I can feel that their child is breech. If you place your hands right here"—his father motioned for Alec to set his hands on the woman's belly—"you can feel the positioning. Continue to move your hands around, get a good feel for which way the child lies, and once you do, you might be able to shift it."

"You're intending to reposition the child within her womb?" Alec asked.

"It is possible."

"What if it's unsuccessful?"

"If it's unsuccessful, then there may be nothing we can do. The child will need to be delivered, but…"

"There's another option," he said.

"No."

"You don't even know what I was going to say."

"I know what you were going to say. I know that you've been in the surgical suite. And this is not the right place. The apothecary is not prepared to operate on this woman."

"If we don't do something, the baby will likely die."

"And I've told you that we won't be performing surgery in the apothecary."

Alec stood back and watched. His father went to the shelves and quickly began gathering supplies before returning and setting a series of jars next to the woman. He began mixing them, and it appeared that he was mostly focused on trying to make sure she was comfortable. There were a few—mostly bagil leaves—that would be necessary if she were to lose the child.

Could his father already be preparing for that possibility?

"Father—"

His father glanced over at him, and the heat in his eyes made Alec take a step back. "You are in my shop," he whispered.

Alec nodded. If nothing else, he would see the way that his father worked up close, having now spent time with the masters at the university. It wasn't that he didn't know how his father worked—they had spent so much time together over the years that Alec knew exactly how he

92 | D.K. HOLMBERG

worked and could anticipate his needs—but having been away for as long as he had and having spent time with the masters, it would be good for him to see the limitations of his father's abilities.

Aelus quickly mixed a soothing concoction and spooned some into her mouth. She took it and began to relax. As she did, he worked his hands around her belly, *pushing* with more force than Alec would have believed necessary.

"Many at the university would have you believe that surgery is the only way to save this child," Aelus said. The words were directed at the woman, but Alec knew who he really intended them for. "There are other ways to reposition the child within the womb, though it takes a delicate touch."

"There's nothing delicate about the way you're pushing on her belly," Alec said.

"Fine. Deft might be a better description, anyway."

Alec stood back while his father continued to work, pressing on the woman's belly. With each movement, he saw shifting beneath the surface of the skin, and he realized exactly what it was that his father attempted.

The woman continued to moan, but the medications that his father had administered had soothed her, easing some of the discomfort that would come from his attempt at forcing the child around. When he was done, she lay still for a moment, but only a moment.

Then another contraction came.

His father nodded to Alec. "It is time."

Alec positioned himself so that he could assist his father, maneuvering in such a way that he was behind him and ready to help grab the child. Had he been successful?

He couldn't imagine that his father's efforts shifting the positioning of the infant could have been completely successful. But...

She started to push.

Alec had been part of enough deliveries to know and recognize what a normal delivery was like. When she pushed, and he saw the head coming first, he knew that his father had been right. He stared for a long moment before the woman's scream drew his attention back to the task at hand. He shook his mind free, turning back to assist his father and readying the supplies he needed.

As they completed the delivery, Alec couldn't shake his amazement at his father. He had always known how skilled his father was, and seeing him in action again only reinforced that. Was that what he was bound to become? Was that the level of skill he was destined to attain if he remained at the university?

And what would happen if he went off with Sam on her missions and he didn't have that opportunity? Would he always feel unfulfilled?

Those thoughts lingered as he watched his father wrap a crying baby boy in a fresh blanket and hand him to the father. The man sobbed as he stepped next to the woman, holding the child together.

9

THE SCRIBES CONVERSE

Alec sat at his desk and finished making his notes, detailing what his father had done. He wasn't certain he could replicate the same maneuver, but having seen it once, he thought it was possible. It was unlikely that he would ever have the need. Why would he ever be asked to deliver a child? He wasn't an apothecary—not anymore—and the longer he stayed at the university, the less likely it would be that he would be asked to perform a task like that.

The door to his room opened, and Beckah poked her head in, grinning at him. "You're back."

"I wasn't gone that long."

"You were gone long enough. I wasn't sure when—or if—you were going to return."

"That sounds like you weren't sure if I was going to come back at all."

"It's true. I'm never sure, Alec," Beckah said. She stepped inside and closed the door. She was wearing a long flowing gown that accentuated her small frame. Her hair was pulled back and tied behind her head with a length of ribbon. She looked quite lovely.

Was that for his sake? He decided it was better to ignore that thought.

"What makes you question if I will return?"

"Because of who you are. Because of what you are."

"But you're the same thing."

"But I'm not. I might have that potential, but the person that I'm connected to has disappeared. Regardless of what I might want, the fact that he's missing and I can't find him…"

Alec looked up. "You've been looking for Tray?"

"Why wouldn't I? Don't you think I deserve to have the same opportunity as you?"

"Of course you do, it's just that…" Alec didn't know what to say. He agreed that she deserved the chance to understand what it meant that she had a connection to a Kaver, and that she could be a Scribe, but he wasn't sure whether that was even safe for her. Then again, it wasn't his place to protect her, was it? She was her own person. He had willingly exposed himself to dangers that put him at risk in his efforts to understand what it meant to be Sam's Scribe, so he couldn't fault her for wanting the same.

She took a seat next to him and looked over at his journal. She scanned the page—always impressing him with how fast she read and how quickly her mind worked —and looked over at him.

"You were present for a delivery?"

"I went to visit my father, and a pregnant woman and

her husband came for help. And it wasn't the first time I've seen a birth."

"This one sounds like it was complicated," she said.

"The baby was breech."

Her eyes widened. "Most don't survive without surgery, and most of the time, the university doesn't get an opportunity to help because the women don't make it to them in time."

"I know," he said with a smile.

"And your father managed a breech delivery without surgery?"

"I tried to convince him that we needed to perform surgery, but he was adamant that he would not."

"Why not? I thought you said he trained at the university, in which case, wouldn't he have some skill with surgery. Maybe not as much as you…" She added with a hint of a smile.

Alec shrugged. "I don't know. My father has always shown a resistance to surgery, ever since I first started studying with him. I don't understand where it came from, and whether it simply has to do with the fact that he doesn't want to draw attention from the university masters, preferring them to see him as nothing more threatening than an apothecary, or if there is more to it."

His father had been willing to do minor surgeries, such as cutting out infection and suturing injuries, but anything more than that, he avoided. The first time Alec had ever been allowed to participate in any sort of surgery was at the university. It appealed to him, mainly because it made him feel like he was actually doing something.

Healing by using the knowledge of medicinal herbs

was rewarding in a different way. It was a challenge, and it forced him to use his mind, to think through what diagnosis he might make, and find the best way to help, but there wasn't always the same immediacy to the reward. Maybe that was why he enjoyed using the easar paper. There was an immediate reward. He knew right away whether his treatment had been effective.

"The university already knew about him. He'd studied here. Why would he have cared about drawing their attention?"

Alec shrugged. "I don't know. When it comes to my father, there are many things I don't know."

And of all the things that he had recently learned, about himself, about Sam, the Thelns... His world had been turned upside down, and what was most surprising was learning that his father had hidden secrets from him. That wasn't the kind of thing he would have expected from his father. He thought him nothing more than a healer, and apothecary, a simple, compassionate man who served the community—the larger community than even their immediate section—never wanting anything more than what each person could pay. Discovering that there was more to his father... he still didn't know what that meant for him.

"Why do I get the sense that you're annoyed by that?"

He set his notebook down and regarded Beckah for a long moment. "Tell me what you remember of your family?"

"Remember? My family is not gone."

"Then tell me about your family," he said.

"My parents are of a middle class. We have lived in the

Parnum section of the city for my entire life. My father has served as a section chief, and my mother helped him. I've told you all of that."

"I know you have. What of your brothers?"

"I have an older brother. He has followed after my father. He has ambition, much like my father does. If it were up to him, he would end up leading in the section, and possibly moving on to take a greater role within the city."

"And your other brother?"

"He's not well," she said with a whisper.

Alec hadn't known that. "What happened to him?"

"He's never been well, Alec. He was born sickly. He's younger than I am, you see, and my mother spends all of her days caring for him. I think she once had a much more prominent role in the running of our section, but when my brother was born, she had to make a decision about whether she was going to continue with her civic responsibilities or commit to taking care of my brother full time. It was an easy decision for her. She dotes on him, constantly doing everything she can to ensure that his needs are met." She smiled almost wistfully. "He has a better connection to her than the rest of us because of his illness." She caught herself and covered her mouth. "It's not that I resent him. I love my brother. He's the reason that I'm here."

"I thought you were here for political ambition."

"That's what I let others think. My father having his role makes it an easier explanation. It doesn't draw attention to my brother, but both he and my mother know the real reason I'm here. If there's anything I can do that will help others like my brother, I want to do it. I feel that's my calling."

Alec studied her. They came from such different places within the city, and they had such different perspectives, but she was caring. She was the kind of person that he had hoped to find at the university but had begun to fear he wouldn't.

"Now imagine that your mother was hiding something from you. Imagine that you believed she'd spent all of her time doting on your brother, but you learned she had a secret that she'd hidden from you. Imagine that she didn't actually spend all that time with your brother, but rather disappeared for stretches of time, doing secretive things, and never explaining to you where she went."

"That wouldn't happen."

"But imagine that it did."

Beckah sat silent for a moment, and then she nodded slowly. "I see what you're saying. Then again, your father has always been strange, hasn't he?" When Alec arched a brow, she laughed. "You know I'm just kidding you. He did choose to abandon his training at the university and go off on his own. There aren't many who would do that, and certainly not many who have the raw talent that your father appeared to have. The gods know that if he didn't, you wouldn't have learned nearly as much as you did. I think he could have been a master physicker had he stayed here."

Alec still didn't know why his father had left the university. He had his suspicions, and it seemed as if perhaps part of it was tied to what had happened to his mother, but maybe there was more to it.

"He is strange," Alec said. "He's also caring. Intelligent. And serves the city in a way that I don't yet understand."

He frowned as he said it.

If his father served the city, and if he wasn't a Scribe, maybe he served the city in a different but related way. Maybe he worked on behalf of the Scribes.

If his father wouldn't tell him what he did, was there another way for him to find out?

And if he did, would it upset his father?

Alec didn't know whether that mattered quite as much as it once would have.

It was a strange realization for him. He had moved on, no longer needing his father the way he once had. He no longer needed his approval. Now that he had come to the university for his studies, he felt as if he could make his own way. It might be through becoming a physicker, or he might choose his father's path, deciding to take over the apothecary. But if he were to do that, it would be *his* choice and not his father's.

There was another option, and it was the one that Alec hoped would come to fruition, but it was the more dangerous one. That involved him learning and understanding what was needed for him to be a more effective Scribe.

And without Sam, he couldn't.

As much as Beckah was annoyed that she couldn't find Tray, Alec was equally annoyed. He was accustomed to having Sam with him, working with him, and her prolonged absence troubled him.

There was a knock at the door, and Alec looked up.

Could it be Sam?

When he opened the door, a messenger stood there,

holding a folded piece of parchment. It came from the palace, and he knew immediately that it was from Sam. He unfolded it, scanning the contents, once again reassured that she was fine, but elaborating no more than that.

He crumpled the page up and tossed it off into the corner.

"That good?" Beckah asked.

"She's fine. I guess I should be pleased that she let me know that she's unharmed, it's just that…"

"It's just that you're angry that you don't get a chance to work with her."

Alec nodded. "Angry might be a bit strong, but I am disappointed. She knows that I worry about her, and the fact that she's been gone for as long as she has bothers me."

"Why does it bother you? She's capable. I've seen it."

"She's capable." Alec smiled to himself. "She might be more capable than most who share her heritage, partly because her background was unknown to her growing up, and she had to find a different way. But because of that, she often finds herself in trouble." He looked over at Beckah. "I hate worrying about her. I hate not knowing what's happening and fearing that something unfortunate has occurred, and never knowing whether she will send word to me. Never knowing whether my augmentations have made a difference, or if I'm simply overreacting. All I want—"

"Is her."

He looked over and Beckah shrugged.

"You care for her. It's more than just a Kaver and

Scribe connection. I can see that. It's obvious in how you look at her."

"Beckah—"

Beckah grinned at him. "I'm not jealous. I'll admit that when I first met you, there was an interest on my part, perhaps an appeal, but I understand that you have someone who is important to you, and you need to work on that. Maybe you need to share with her how you feel."

"I don't know how I feel."

"I think you do. I think that you're afraid to share your feelings. Gods, Alec! You're one of the brightest people at the university, but you can't even diagnose yourself?"

Alec's gaze drifted to the stack of books near the corner of his room. "There aren't books on things like that," he said.

"No. I suppose there aren't. If there were, maybe I wouldn't be miserable."

"Why are you miserable?"

"Oh, there are many reasons for me to be miserable. I suppose mostly, it's a frustration that there's knowledge I'm not able to tap into."

She tipped her head toward one of his journals. It was one where he had a folded scrap of easar paper hidden. Did she know that was where he kept it? Back before they discovered she was a Scribe, she'd broken into his room and altered his journals, thinking it a great joke on him. But that was before she knew anything about him or about easar paper. Now she knew the value of it and what it could be used for. Her knowing where he kept his small supply felt like a violation, almost a betrayal.

Or was he overreacting?

Alec wasn't sure. He wouldn't put it past himself to

overreact. When it came to easar paper, and the scarcity of it, he had overreacted in the past. It wasn't something that he was proud of, but they had such a limited supply, and such a need for him and Sam to practice—and to do whatever it took to keep her safe—that he needed to maintain all of the supplies he could.

"I think the master physickers—at least those who are Scribes—will train us when the time is right. We already have Master Eckerd and Master Helen in our corner, I think. But this is all new, to us at least. Once we become more familiar and they become comfortable with us, I think they will take us under their wings and teach us," Alec said.

"Do you believe that? They already know what *you* are, but have they come to you offering to teach?"

Alec swallowed. "No."

"Have you thought about why that might be?"

"I haven't. I've been—"

"Focused on where Sam might be. And I get that. But I need your help on this."

"And what is this?"

"Don't you agree that the masters' secrecy seems to have increased, not decreased since we helped with the Theln attack? Why? Why haven't they reached out to us to teach us? We could be helpful, especially now that it's known that you're a Scribe and that I *could* be a Scribe." She gave a sigh of exasperation. "That's what makes me miserable. It's almost like they're trying to keep us from it."

"I don't know that they're trying to keep anything from us. There's a level of knowledge required—"

"And you have that knowledge. You've shown that you

can do things that they didn't think were possible, at least not for someone of your level. Don't get into the same mind trap that they would have you in. Don't believe that you're less than what you are."

"It's almost as if you want to force me to confront Master Eckerd."

"Not confront. I only want you to think about what we might be able to learn."

Alec had to admit that having a chance to work with a master physicker who was also a Scribe appealed to him. How could it not? He had so many questions and wanted to be ready for whatever Sam might need from him, if she ever returned to him. Without having an opportunity to work with her and practice, he needed to have a different way to gain that skill, and there was an opportunity for that here at the university. There were those with the necessary knowledge, if only they would agree to share it.

That seemed to be the common thread with everything at the university. There were those with knowledge and they needed to be willing to share.

He'd seen it from the beginning. Some had a willingness to use their knowledge on those with the ability to pay. Others had the willingness to share knowledge with students. And still others simply wanted to practice, using their knowledge to heal. They didn't teach, which meant their knowledge wasn't passed on to those who followed after them.

"I'll think about it," Alec said.

Beckah smiled. "By that, you mean that you will consider it if your friend doesn't come back to you."

Alec sighed. "Fine. I'll consider it if Sam doesn't return. Is that what you want me to say?"

"I want you to admit what you're doing. That's all. There's only so much you can learn by studying with your friend. At some point, you'll run out of the paper, and then what will you do?"

"We'll find more."

"What if there isn't more? What if the palace limits your supply to it? What if—"

"I will consider it," Alec said again.

But what she said had merit. If he didn't have access to enough paper, having someone like Master Eckerd who could instruct him would be valuable to him. If he had someone like that, he could learn tricks, techniques that he might not have considered on his own.

Beckah watched him, saying nothing. She seemed to be studying him, the same way he would study someone who came to him with an illness. It made him uncomfortable, and he turned away rather than answering any more of her questions.

Even if he went to Master Eckerd, would he be willing to share?

The master physicker had invited him into the surgical suite and had continued to advance him through his training, so maybe he already had recognized that Alec had potential, and was intending to take advantage of that. Was there any way he could accelerate it? If he couldn't, would that put him and Sam at a disadvantage somehow?

And what did it even matter? Sam was training much the same as he was. Why would they need it to be accelerated? There were others who had the ability to counter the threat of the Thelns, especially now that they knew such a threat existed, and that they had penetrated so deeply into the city.

Yet Alec couldn't shake the idea that he and Sam had a role to play, and he had to be ready for it. If Sam wouldn't return to him, it meant that he needed to do everything he could to be prepared.

And if he had to force his way onto Master Eckerd, then that was what he would do.

10

RETURN TO THE ATTACK

The splintered door to the building was a dead giveaway that something untoward had taken place in the building. Sam stood in front of it, averting her gaze from Elaine, avoiding meeting her mother's eye. Instead, she looked along the street, wondering if anyone had noticed that the door was missing.

"This was reinforced," Elaine said.

Sam turned her attention back to the door and realized that iron was worked into the frame, reinforcing it as Elaine had said. Tearing it free would have been difficult, even enhanced. How much of an augmentation had Alec given her?

She needed to get to him before he got too upset. She'd made sure to send word to him, but it was one thing to alert him that she was unharmed and another entirely to avoid a visit, though in truth, Sam wasn't avoiding him, really. She had been dragged back to the place of her captivity by her mother.

"I was thinking only of getting free, I wasn't thinking about the reinforcement."

"This would have taken considerable strength, Samara."

"Are you saying you don't think I would have such strength?" She glanced over at Elaine, frowning at her. "Are you thinking that even with augmentations, I shouldn't have been able to do it?"

"You still have so much to learn," Elaine said.

"What does that have to do with anything?"

"It has to do with the fact that there are limits to your abilities. If you waste them, if you risk them unnecessarily, you place not only yourself in danger, but you place your Scribe in danger."

Sam frowned as she studied the doorframe. Other than the iron that had been worked into it, there was nothing unique about it. Well, nothing other than the fact that it had been torn free, destroyed as Sam had exploded her way to freedom.

"Alec wasn't in any danger."

"Are you certain? You don't even understand your abilities, and yet now, you make claims that he wouldn't be placed in any danger by mixing his blood with yours to create a magical ink to use on the easar paper?"

She had lowered her voice at the end, but she had made her point.

When Sam used an augmentation, though it enhanced her abilities temporarily, there was a cost. Using augmentations took physical strength from her, and though she had grown more skilled with them, and had begun to handle the strength required in ways that she hadn't before, she still felt the drawing of power from her as she used the augmentation.

It was the same for Alec, though she didn't know the extent. She'd seen how weakened he got when placing augmentations, but had that improved since they had started practicing more regularly, or did he still suffer the same way?

Kyza. She hated working from a place of ignorance. More than that, she hated the way Elaine looked at her, treating her as ignorant, regardless of whether or not Sam *was* ignorant.

"He was down here," she said, pointing down the hall, deciding that it was better to redirect their attention.

"And you left him, rather than thinking to bring him with you when you escaped?"

"All I was thinking about was escape," Sam said. She shouldn't have to argue this, not with Elaine. Had she remained the man's captive, would it have mattered?

"Another sign of your lack of training. Had you more training, you would have thought about doing whatever it took to keep him in your custody."

Sam smirked at Elaine. "Custody? I'm not one of the city guards."

"No, you are not." Disappointment laced her words.

Elaine made her way along the hall, her canal staff gripped tightly in her hand. Every so often, she would tap it on the ground, reminding her of how Marin used to do the same thing. She didn't know the purpose, but maybe Elaine would tell her if she asked, since she couldn't ask Marin. The echo it made reverberated along the hall. Was there anything she learned by tapping her way along her path?

At the end of the hallway, she paused in front of the other door that Sam had torn free. This one had not been reinforced, not in the way that the other had, but Elaine still ran her hand along the outside of it. When she was done, she glanced back at Sam, the frown that had been evident on her face before even more pronounced. "We will have to have words with your Scribe."

"Why?"

"You need to understand the limits of your augmentations, Samara. These are dangerous."

Sam joined Elaine at the door and looked to see what had drawn her attention, but couldn't find anything that would seem to matter. It was a broken door. It was made of a heavy oak, but even that shouldn't have mattered. It wasn't the stoutness of the wood that mattered when using an augmentation, it was more about how much force she used. And Alec had discovered that augmentations sometimes benefited from the nature of the words used on the easar paper. It wasn't so much the ratio of blood used—though that was often part of the key to an augmentation—but how Alec documented what he was doing. In that, Sam thought Alec was better prepared than many at the university. That was a part of his training with his father, an advantage that few of the other Scribes had.

"Why are these dangerous? What is it here that you're concerned about?"

"The fact that you don't recognize it is what troubles me."

"Then help me. Show me what it is that I'm supposed to be recognizing here."

Elaine considered her for a moment before breathing

out heavily. She tapped on the doorframe. "Do you hear that?"

"I hear you knocking. Am I supposed to hear anything more than that?"

"Focus, Samara. What do you hear when I knock?"

She knocked again, and Sam listened. It sounded no different from what any knock on wood would sound like, though there was almost a slight rattle to it. "Is the wood loose? Is that why it's rattling?"

"So, you *do* hear it."

"I don't know. I'm not exactly sure what you're trying to get me to hear," she said. She knocked the same way that Elaine had, and focused again, listening to the wood, thinking that if there was a rattle, maybe it meant that something hid behind the doorframe. As before, it rattled, but it seemed to come from within the wood, vibrating against her hand.

"I feel it almost as much as I hear it. Something behind it?"

"There is intent behind it," Elaine said.

Sam smiled slightly. "Intent? What does that mean?"

"What does your Scribe do when he uses the easar paper?"

"He documents what he's trying to accomplish," Sam said. "He does it almost as if he's trying to document an attempt to heal."

"Yes. Your Scribe has a unique approach, and it's one that the other Scribes have attempted to replicate with some success."

"Other Scribes aren't able to do things the same way as Alec?" That was news to her. She had thought that the easar paper had been the key for Kavers and Scribes, and she still thought it was, but maybe Alec's training made him unique.

"Easar paper is unique. Everyone has their own experience with it, and even experienced Scribes don't always know how to best use it. Your Scribe found a way that was *different* from how most others use it."

"What do you mean by intent?"

"What I mean is that easar paper is not the only way Scribes work. The key isn't the paper. It's a specific focus and intent."

Sam ran her hand along the doorframe, frowning as she did. "Is this what you mean?"

"Whoever reinforced these doors used power, and that power had an intent behind it. When you knock, you can feel traces of that energy, and it grants you an ability to detect just what went into it. That is what I'm picking up on."

"What does it mean?"

"What it means is that whoever was here knew enough to use a Kaver and Scribe together, and mixed it with intent. Doing so isn't easy, even for someone with significant abilities." She glanced over at Sam, eyeing her for a moment. "For you to have escaped is perhaps lucky, but perhaps it was something else."

"I don't know what you mean."

"I don't know if the intent was sabotaged, or whether your Scribe simply managed to overpower what was placed here. If he *had* overpowered it, it would have taken more strength from you to overcome it than what it appears it did. You aren't weakened, not nearly as much as I would've expected."

Sabotaged. That could have been Tray, or maybe there

was another answer. "Could it be that they simply made a mistake placing the augmentation on the door?" It didn't seem like quite the right word, but Sam wasn't sure what fit. An augmentation seemed more appropriate when using easar paper and placing it on a Kaver, but perhaps it was the same thing—or near enough—that calling it an augmentation was fitting.

"Someone who knew enough to place that intent on the door would have known enough to do so correctly," Elaine answered.

She continued running her hand along the doorframe, and Sam frowned as she did, thinking that there had to have been something more to it. When Elaine was satisfied with what she found—or didn't find—she entered the room.

Sam followed her in and made a circle, coming to stand in front of the chair where she had been bound. Elaine glanced at the remnants of the rope. At least the Scribe had not taken those, giving proof to Sam's story.

"You tore free of those?"

Sam nodded.

"It seems as if you're Scribe is cleverer than I expected."

"Why would you say that?"

"Only because he thought enough to place a protection on your skin, which allowed you to break free. Without that..."

Sam smiled to herself. Without that, they had already discovered what would happen. If her muscles and bones were strong but her flesh was not, it was easy for her to get injured. She could bleed out, and without Alec there to provide healing, she wouldn't survive injuries like that.

Practice had taught them what was necessary to provide protection.

"Why would Ralun and the physicker have brought her here?" Sam asked. That had been troubling to her. They hadn't taken her out of the city, though doing so would have allowed them to control her more easily, and she would have had a harder time escaping.

But then, the physicker hadn't expected her to attack her, much less escape, had he?

No. Ralun probably assured him she was controlled, and without her Scribe, she couldn't have been augmented. Even once she'd received Alec's augmentation, the man still seemed to think he could control her.

She was missing something. It was about more than Tray and his apparent involvement with the Thelns, though she was convinced that mattered. Ralun was in the city again, and she knew that was important, if not why. If he had a piece of the Book—not even the entire Book but only a page—she knew how dangerous that would be. She had seen it firsthand with what he had done to the princess.

"Whatever the reason, it seems that Marin is important to the plan. The physicker wanted me to bring her to him. She's involved in it somehow," Sam said.

"This is more than simply being involved. This is bringing resources to the city. If Ralun is here, they have brought significant resources."

"Ralun was already here."

"As a way to bring down the Anders. That would be worthwhile to them. But now…"

Elaine turned and looked over at Sam, watching her

with a deep frown on her face. She studied her for a long moment before shaking her head.

"Ah, blessed Talissa," she said, invoking one of the lesser gods, "I fear that she's now got you mixed up in this."

Sam shook her head. "I've been mixed up in this from the beginning. Ever since I attempted to help the princess, I've been mixed up in it."

"This is different."

"How is this different?"

"This time, I worry that *you* might be the target."

11

PRACTICE

S am gripped the length of the new staff Elaine had given her, spinning it in the air. It was slightly lighter than her old one, and had a little more flex, but it felt comfortable in her hand. She darted forward, trying to maintain her balance as she did, and nearly stumbled over her own feet. This would go so much better if she had an augmentation.

"You need to focus on your technique," Elaine said, smacking her on the arm with her own canal staff.

"I could do this better with an augmentation."

"And so could I. That's my point. You're skilled. I know that. But you also become dependent on your augmentations. Why else do you think I wanted you to practice your attacks without it?"

"Because you want to annoy me?" Sam asked.

Elaine darted forward and caught Sam on the arm. None of her blows were terribly hard, but they stung just the same. Each attack was sharp, leaving a painful welt wherever it landed. So far, Elaine hadn't allowed her to go to Alec to be healed. Sam knew that with his help and the easar paper, she wouldn't have to suffer the pain, but without his help and without the easar paper, the pain of a dozen different bruises was her constant reminder that her training was not going well.

Sam and Elaine had been working for the last three days, and her mother was pushing her. She wanted her to develop her skill, wanting to challenge her so that she could fight without augmentations, but Sam doubted it would matter. She had been surprised by Ralun the last time, but now that she knew he was here, she would remain vigilant. And she had no intention of going against him without augmentations.

Elaine watched her, staying back a step, then quickly unscrewed her staff and darted toward Sam, flipping up while in the air and swinging around one end of the staff.

Sam blocked that one, but she missed the other.

It caught her on the side, and she grunted, falling to the ground. Experience had taught her that Elaine would not slow once she was on the ground. She would continue to attack, driving with the free end of her staff, unmindful of the pain that each smack would cause her daughter.

"Good. At least you avoided the first hit. It was a basic attack, but—"

Sam swung around with her staff, hoping to catch Elaine, but missed. Her staff caught nothing but empty air.

Elaine chuckled. "Another good try." She struck at Sam again, catching her with the end of her staff. This one caught her leg. That bruise would be painful. Likely, Sam would end up limping from it. "You're like most in your position who come to depend on their augmentations. I was the same way once. I quickly discovered that relying on my augmentations is a sure way of ending up dead." Elaine stalked over to her and leaned forward. One foot pressed down on Sam's staff, preventing her from moving it. Sam jerked on it, but Elaine held firm, despite the fact that she wasn't very heavy and shouldn't be able to hold her down. "It's my job to ensure that you don't end up dead."

"Just because I'm a Kaver?"

Elaine glared at her. "Is that what you think? You think that I'm only here trying to help you because you're a Kaver?"

"I think that's the primary reason," Sam said.

It was hurtful, and Sam knew that it was hurtful, but she hoped to disrupt her enough that she would be distracted, and that Sam could then take advantage.

Elaine eyed her for a moment, and then she laughed. "That's a good attempt. Distract your opponent, bring them outside of their comfort, and you have an advantage. Is that a skill you learned from Marin?"

"Why would Marin have to be the one to teach me that?"

"Because you worked with Marin. I thought that—"

"You thought that because you weren't there." Sam spun around, swinging her staff, forcing Elaine back a step. She jumped, bringing the staff around again, and Elaine took another step back. "You didn't come looking for me. You knew that I was missing, and you didn't know what had taken place, but you left me."

With each word, Sam spun with more force. Now she was fighting with anger, and she knew better than to do that. She knew better than to allow herself to get trapped in the emotion, but facing Elaine made that difficult. Any time she spent with her, she was left with a sense of emptiness. Elaine could have found her all those years ago. Sam was certain of that. Yet she had chosen not to go in search of her own daughter. She had been so focused on remaining a Kaver, that she never tried.

"Do you really believe I intended for you to stay with Marin?" Elaine blocked her attack, spinning her staff around so that she could keep Sam from connecting. "Do you think I wanted *her* to train you? She took you from me. It's her fault that you don't remember me or any of the lessons that I taught you."

"What lessons?" Sam asked. "What is there that you taught me? What should I remember?"

"I wish you remembered the way I would put you to bed. The way I smoothed your hair. The way I—"

Sam realized almost too late that Elaine was using the same technique on her, only she did it without anger.

She jumped back, swinging her staff around, blocking the blow that she almost missed.

Elaine smiled.

"Even in that you attempt to train me?" Sam slammed the end of her canal staff down. It was a nicer staff than any she'd had while growing up, and she appreciated that they had given her such a quality staff, but it didn't do anything to cool the anger that burned within her, nor did it reduce her frustration of being unable to remember any time before Marin, any time with her mother. Still, Marin had taught her how to use the canal staff, and Marin had trained her, showing her some of the ways to be a Kaver. Marin had prepared her for this life.

And why?

Sam still didn't know. And perhaps that was what bothered her the most.

"You need to be trained with everything. You're unfocused. That's what my purpose is. I need to help you find that focus, to hold it, to turn you into the Kaver that you need to be."

"Then let me go see Alec." She slammed the staff down onto the ground again and glared at Elaine.

"Will seeing this boy help you find focus?" Elaine asked.

"I don't know if I'll find focus. All I know is that together, we're better. I know that with him, I am better able to do what I need to do."

"And what happens when you don't have him?"

There was a distance between them. Even if Sam jumped forward, without any augmentations, she wouldn't reach Elaine before she managed to either move out of the way or block her attack.

"Why wouldn't I have him?"

"I'm not implying that we would do anything to him. Scribes are rare enough, and good Scribes are even more rare. It seems as if you found yourself a good Scribe, the kind who will help protect you and who knows enough to act creatively. Too often, they are so rigid, though I suspect that comes from their university training."

"You didn't answer the question."

"You won't always have your Scribe with you," Elaine said. "Without him, you need to be more than just a small girl with a staff. You need to be someone who others fear. You need to be someone who can take care of herself, who can defend herself if necessary. You need to be imposing and able to manage everything that comes your way."

"Do you believe that everything you've taught me will help me do those things?"

"If you continue to study and focus, I think you will be able to do those things."

"What about finding Marin?"

Elaine cocked her head to the side. "That's not what this is about for you, is it?"

"What's it about then?"

"It's about you finding Ralun. You think that, through him, you can find the Book."

"You don't want me to find the Book? You don't want me to learn what happened?"

"Do you believe that destroying that page will allow you to regain your memories?"

"It won't?"

"I don't know. It's difficult enough to deal with one of the pages from the Book. You were lucky when you managed to destroy the page that influenced the princess. With this one…"

"What?" Sam asked, glaring at her mother. The palace loomed in the distance, too close for Sam's comfort. All around them were others training, most of them soldiers, though there was another pair of Kavers—both of them older—working nearby. From what Sam had learned, there weren't many Kavers remaining. Those that did remain were valued and stayed outside the city, keeping the Thelns from the gaining access. Or so they thought.

"I don't know. It's been a long time. That page has been used on you for over a decade. Long enough that the effects may be permanent. Besides, at this point, what would having your memories back change?"

Sam stared at her. She couldn't believe that Elaine was

asking her that. What would it change? How about every-thing! She would be able to fill in the gaping hole of who she was, what her childhood was like, how her mother apparently put her to bed and smoothed her hair... Yes, it would change everything.

"I guess it would change nothing." Sam untwisted the ends of her canal staff. She was done sparring with Elaine, ready to return to her room—or anywhere— where she could sit in silence. Alone. Better yet, if she could go off with Alec, perhaps train with the augmentations, that might make her feel better.

"Exactly," Elaine said. "It would change nothing. I think it's important that you recognize that and recognize that you need to move forward. Understand what your role is now that you know who you are."

Sam bit back the response that came to mind. She *didn't* know who she was. That was the problem. How could she move forward until she did? She might know that she was a Kaver, but she knew nothing else about herself. Anything that Elaine could share she kept hidden from her. Why was that? Was it out of a lack of caring? That was the way it seemed to Sam. Or could it be because she did care, and it was too hard for her, much as Elaine had claimed?

"Am I allowed to go speak with Alec?" Sam asked.

"Do you feel as if you're restricted?"

"I tried crossing the bridge, but the guards turned me back."

"Is that your only way off the island here?"

Sam glared at her. "You intend for me to jump over the canal?"

"I seem to recall that you have done it before," Elaine said.

Sam shifted the direction of her gaze, looking over at the canal. It was wide, practically a river here. The grassy lawn ran all the way up to the edge of the canal, ending abruptly in a rocky wall that created the canal. No barges were permitted to traverse the canals between the university and the palace. Those here were isolated, trapped on the island, the bridges being the only way off, short of jumping. But, without an augmentation, there was no way she could jump that far.

And she wasn't about to swim.

Sam had too much experience with the damned canal eels, and regardless of what purpose they played for the city, she wasn't about to get in the water with them, not voluntarily. It was better to remain trapped here until Elaine chose to allow her off.

"Without my augmentations—"

Elaine tipped her head forward in a nod. "Without your augmentations, you think that you're trapped. I understand that. What I'm trying to tell you is that without your augmentations you are only limited. Don't think of it as a restriction, think of it as an opportunity to practice and develop your other talents."

"What other talents?"

"You faced Marin and you question what other talents you might have as a Kaver?"

"Marin wasn't exactly forthcoming about what abilities she has," Sam said.

"I didn't expect that Marin would be forthcoming. What I'm trying to tell you is that you didn't need Marin to *tell* you anything about her abilities for you to recognize that she did not require her augmentations."

"You keep saying that, but what if she's getting them the way Alec does? Those augmentations could be done from a distance." But they'd need some of Marin's blood, and if Tray still kept her secluded, maybe the Scribe didn't have any.

"As I've said, I don't know how this could be her Scribe. She *had* a Scribe, but he was lost during an attack. Few Kavers ever claim another Scribe when theirs is lost."

"How did you not find her?"

"We didn't expect her to settle in Caster. How could we?"

"Because it's a lowborn section?"

"Because it's an ancient section," Elaine said. "There's something off about it."

"Why would you think that?"

Sam didn't think there was anything off about the Caster section. It was familiar to her. It was her home, as much as anywhere could be. Certainly not the palace. Though she might be allowed access to it, and though she was training here, the palace wasn't her home. It was strange to think that she didn't really have any place other than Caster, and what she knew about that home was different now. It had changed when she had discovered what she was and Marin's role in it.

"The Caster section is one of the earliest sections. It came from a time before the Anders claimed the city as their own, leading the city out of a sort of darkness."

Sam frowned. She didn't realize that the Anders had taken over a city that already existed. It made sense, though. The Caster section *was* different from many of the others. It was full of lowborns—thieves and people like herself and Bastan—and more rundown than other places within the city. Still, there was the familiarity to it that she appreciated.

"Why would you claim that something was off about the Caster section?"

"Kaver magic—our magic—works a little differently there. We don't know if it's tied to something done by the original founders of the city or if there is something else to it, but whatever it is, we know that we need to be careful when we enter that section."

"That seems like a perfect place for a rogue Kaver to have set up," Sam said. "Why wouldn't you have looked there?"

"We looked everywhere. *I* looked everywhere."

She stared at Sam, daring her to challenge, but Sam didn't take the bait. "So, if I want to get off the island and away from the palace, I need to find a way across the canal without an augmentation and without my ring?"

"You can always swim," Elaine said.

Sam grunted. "Why don't you swim and I'll follow you?"

Elaine grinned. "I think that would not be my first choice. Now, if that's all, I think you and I will resume our session tomorrow."

"If I'm still here?"

Elaine nodded. "If you're still here."

She turned away and headed back into the palace. Sam watched until she disappeared and then turned her attention to the others still training in the yard. One of the other Kavers—a woman by the name of Raylene—worked on something like a dance with her staff, keeping her feet off the ground, twisting the top of the staff, tapping it as she bounced along the ground. It was a delicate and difficult maneuver. Sam had tried something similar, and had some success with it, but she wasn't nearly as skilled as that. Thoren had tried teaching her something like it, but she didn't have the necessary skill.

Maybe it was what she needed to try. Maybe in order for her to get off the island as she wanted, she needed to practice dancing across the ground the same way that Raylene did.

She was determined to get away from the palace section. Even if it was only so that she could find Ralun and discover what he might do with the Book, she was determined to do it. And there was another benefit of escaping the island. She would go looking for Marin's Scribe, and though she wasn't sure whether she could find him, she suspected that she knew where to look. If she could find Tray, she could find that Scribe. And with him, she had to believe that she would find the Theln she wanted, as well.

Almost as much, she wanted to get off the island so that she could go to Alec. She missed seeing him, studying with him, just *being* with him. Even if she didn't have any augmentations, she wanted time with him.

Sam planted her staff, and began her attempt at dancing across the ground. If nothing else, she would try to mimic Raylene. She might not be nearly as skilled as the other woman, but she could try, and if she were able to succeed, she would have a way off of the island.

12

WITH THE ROYALS

S am stalked through the halls of the palace. She glared at everything she saw around her, looking for something familiar, but there was nothing. Every day had been the same. She continued to practice with Elaine, working with her staff, growing in skill—that much was evident to her in that there were fewer and fewer bruises on her arms—but not managing any greater success with attempting to dance on the end of the staff. She had taken to watching Raylene, taking advantage of every time she was out in the yard to copy her, and the woman had begun giving her pointers, tips that would help her improve her ability to remain aloft on the end of the staff. Those pointers had helped, but Sam still wasn't able to manage much more than staying up for a few moments at a time. If she could have found Thoren, she would have asked for his help, but he had been gone.

When she turned a corner, she came face-to-face with someone she hadn't expected to see here, not so soon.

"Helen?"

The physicker had always been kind to Sam, but it had been a while since she'd seen her. What was she doing here now? When she had been here before, she had attempted to extract Sam's memories, thinking she might come up with a method to pull them back out, but she hadn't been successful. For the longest time, Sam had been disappointed, until she finally accepted that there was nothing Helen would be able to do. Not without the Book of Maladies. Not without help from the Thelns.

"Samara. I understand that you remain well."

"As well as I can be."

"Yes, I have heard the likely cause for your lack of memories. If that is true"—there was a hint to her tone that made it seem as if she wasn't completely convinced —"then there may not be much that we can do. It is possible that with time, and with enough coaxing, we may be able to ease some of those memories free."

Sam doubted that. Even if it were possible, Helen didn't seem convinced that anything could reverse what the Book put forth. And considering the way the Book had been used on the princess, and the fact that all the healing attempted had failed, why would her situation be any different?

"Are you here to see me?"

"Not you, Samara. Though, I would be happy to speak with you when I'm done with this task, if you would be so willing."

"Of course. Anything that you think might help."

Helen smiled. She had a gentle face. She had deep wrinkles at the corners of her eyes, and her graying hair was pulled up into a bun. Sam had taken an immediate liking to her—even if she hadn't originally been comfortable with the sessions they'd had talking about her memories and her mother—and suspected that everyone who encountered her felt the same way. She was the kind of person that Sam always imagined a physicker to be. She was skilled, caring, and warm. The next time she saw Alec, she would have to ask him about her.

"If you will excuse me," Helen said.

Sam stepped away, allowing Helen to move past her. She hurried off down the hall and disappeared through a door into a part of the palace that Sam never visited. It was an area that primarily housed the royals, and even though she'd spent some time with the princess, Sam had no interest in getting too caught up in what the royals were doing and what they were after.

She turned away, thinking to head back to her rooms when she saw Elaine marching down the hall and through the same door Helen had.

Her curiosity was piqued, and she changed direction.

Where would they have gone?

Sam suspected that Elaine was responsible for getting Helen to help her in the first place but didn't know for certain. If she was, Sam should be appreciative. Helen had helped her, though possibly not in the way that Elaine might have intended.

She paused at the door. It was open a crack, making it so that anyone could enter, but she only heard a few voices. She recognized Elaine's and Helen's, and there was a third, a deeper male voice. It wasn't one she'd ever heard, which given the fact that Helen was here, made her suspect it was another one of the physickers. Likely one of the Scribe physickers.

Sam pressed on the door, pushing it open just a little.

Hopefully, they wouldn't notice. Hopefully, no more people would be coming to this meeting, as she didn't want to be caught eavesdropping as they approached. At this point, what did it matter? If she irritated Elaine, would it even be a problem?

"You're certain that's what you heard?" Elaine asked.

"I have been looking around, but there's no sign of any Thelns in the city."

"She was certain that was who she saw. She said it was Ralun."

"Ralun would never come to the city." This came from the deeper voice. Sam couldn't identify it, but it sounded familiar. She didn't know why.

"She seems to think that this is the second time he's been in the city, Sire."

Sire?

Sam froze. Could it mean that she was eavesdropping on the king?

She'd never seen him, other than from afar, but there were rumors about him. Even in the palace, he was rarely seen. She knew better than to put much stock into rumors, but rumors about the royals had a strange way of being accurate.

"The second time? Ralun wouldn't risk coming to the city once, let alone a second time."

"He would if he thought that he was safeguarded somehow," Elaine said. "We've already seen that the protections placed were incomplete. If he believed that the secondary protections were absent, he would risk coming to the city, especially if the prize was valuable enough."

"And what prize do you think would draw Ralun to the city?"

"The first time it was your daughter, Sire. This time... this time I think it was mine."

The king grunted. "Why would he risk coming here for her?"

"I don't know. She's beaten him at least once, and I think that angered him."

"Ralun doesn't operate from a place of anger. He's too calculating for that."

"All I can tell you is what I've heard."

"Does she know?"

"She's the one who shared with me that he was here."

"Does she know the rest?"

There was a moment of silence, and Sam found herself leaning forward. What rest would they be referring to? What else were they keeping from her? She was growing weary of Elaine keeping things from her, all because she thought to protect her. Sam didn't need her to protect her. She had done well enough on her own, thank you very much. What she needed was to know what was taking place. She didn't want to be kept out of any of the planning for thwarting the Thelns, nor did she want to be left in the dark about anything the Thelns might have planned for her.

While leaning, she bumped into the door, and it swung open.

Sam stood there, framed in the doorway, frozen in place.

Elaine and Helen looked over to her. Sam started to back up when the deep voice rumbled, "Who is this?"

"This is Samara," a voice from behind her said.

Sam turned, swearing to herself. How could she have allowed herself to get caught like this? She knew better. She had too much training and experience to allow it to happen, and yet... Here she was.

"My apologies, Princess. I'll just be on my way," she said with as much deference as she could muster.

Lyasanna stared at her for a moment, and there was a hint of a smile that quirked her lips, enough that Sam wondered if perhaps her presence here amused the princess rather than annoyed her. If it did—and if the princess thought it was funny that she was here—maybe she wouldn't get into trouble for eavesdropping.

That still seemed too much to hope for.

Lyasanna pushed her into the room. She was strong—much stronger than Sam would have expected given her smaller size—and she ignored Sam's attempts to push her way back out.

Sam gave up and turned to face the King. No good would come from opposing what was happening now. She could run—but she doubted she could run fast enough to escape, and now that she'd been discovered, what point would there be in attempting to run?

"You are Samara?" the king asked.

Sam looked over at him. He was a solid man, tall—though most people were tall compared to her—and had deep black hair with a few streaks of gray peppered through it. He had a strong jaw and a serious set to his eyes. There was something about him that reminded her of Bastan.

"I'm Samara. Sam."

The king frowned. "Sam?"

Sam shrugged. "I don't really care to be called Samara. It's a little too formal for me."

The king glanced from Sam to the others in the room. She used that moment to see who else was there. In addition to the king and the princess, she saw her mother, but she had heard her, and there was Helen, who was studying Sam with a mixture of amusement and irritation on her face, and one other person, someone who'd yet to speak. He was younger, and reminded her of the king, only twenty years his junior.

Could it be Lyasanna's brother? She knew there was a brother, but didn't know enough about him. He was rarely seen outside of the palace, much as Lyasanna had rarely been seen in the city, until recently. He had the same serious expression as his father, and, for that matter, the same serious expression as his sister. Though, Sam had seen Lyasanna smile, it was rare.

"Why are you here? Why are you listening to our conversation?" asked the king.

"I didn't mean to," Sam began. She kept her gaze on the king only. If she looked over to Elaine, she expected to see her mother frowning at her, and she had no intention of getting distracted as she lied to the king. "I just heard voices I didn't recognize."

"You didn't recognize the voice of your mother?" he asked.

"Not at first. When I did…"

She hoped that trailing off would distract him, but the king only watched her, that frown pinned to his face making it difficult for her to know whether he was annoyed with her or amused.

"You were talking about Ralun. I've seen him. I can help."

"Ralun would not have come to the city."

"And I tell you that is who it was. When Lyasanna was poisoned—I mean, *Princess* Lyasanna—it was Ralun who was responsible. I thought that I'd stopped him, but he got away."

"How certain are you that it was Ralun?"

"Very certain. I saw him again outside my friend's apothecary, and a Theln with him referred to him as Ralun. And when he returned, when I saw him just a few days ago in the city, he was here for something else."

It wasn't Sam. Regardless of what Elaine said, it wasn't Sam that Ralun was after. It couldn't be. Why would he care about what she did? Why would he care about her presence at all?

"Yes. We have been discussing what Ralun might be interested in, if indeed it was Ralun." He glanced over to Elaine, almost as if seeking confirmation that Sam could be trusted to identify Ralun.

"They're interested in Marin. Tray took her from me after the attack on the canals. I tried—"

"Samara, we will not be discussing this here," Elaine said.

Sam looked over to her. Why was Elaine trying to silence her? Was it because she thought Sam couldn't be trusted to participate in this conversation? Was she ashamed of the fact that Sam was her daughter—and a Kaver who hadn't developed nearly as fast as she had hoped?

"If not now, when? Marin hasn't stopped her attack. If Tray took her away, it's possible that she's still on the loose. He will protect her, because he wants to know more about her."

"This is the half-Theln that we were talking about?" the king asked.

"Yes. Trayson. This is the one Marin used to bind Samara more tightly to her," Elaine said, pointedly looking at Samara.

"She used her own son. I find that horrifying, yet I still wonder whether there is something we're missing. Marin was always calculating, and she would be unlikely to have done something so cruel without a plan behind it."

"I'm sure there was a plan," Elaine said. "It's discovering that plan and finding what exactly she might have been after that is the challenge. Now that she has brought her son into it..."

"But Tray wasn't brought into it. He didn't know anything what she was doing. He's trying to figure that out. He's trying to find out who he is," Sam said.

"And yet he has helped a known threat to the kingdom," the king said.

"Helped? He isn't helping her. He simply took her away after I defeated her."

"And did that not help her? Did that not allow her to have a measure of freedom?"

"I don't know that it helps her at all. If he has her, and if he's questioning her, she's going to be forced to share things with him that she doesn't want to share."

"How certain are you that it wasn't all part of her plan," Elaine asked softly. "Marin is nothing if not clever, Samara. It's entirely possible that she is using Tray to keep herself safe. It's entirely possible that all of this was part of her plan."

Even though Sam knew that it was possible—she had become all too familiar with the lengths to which Marin might go to deceive—she didn't think that was the case with Tray. Marin cared about him, regardless of what else she said and claimed. She was trying to protect him, if nothing else. She had encouraged Sam to protect him. That had to mean something, didn't it?

"You may go, Samara," the king said.

Sam looked at the others, hoping that Elaine or Lyasanna or even Helen might say something that would allow her to remain, but none of them did. And why would they? To them, she was nothing more than a novice Kaver, still in need of training. To them, she was nothing more than an inconvenience.

Which meant that she would not be a part of whatever took place with Marin.

More than that, it meant that she wouldn't be a part of whatever happened with Ralun. And if she wasn't a part of that, how was she supposed to discover anything about the Book?

That was what she wanted more than anything. She needed to find the Book. And she wanted to know why Marin had used it on her. What was the purpose of taking away Sam's memories? Why would she torment her like that?

SEARCH FOR THE MASTER

The hallway was quiet and dark. A lantern flickered in the distance, giving a little light, but not enough for Alec to see clearly. He watched for shadows, any sign of movement. There were many masters who might come through these halls that he wanted to avoid, but one in particular worried him the most. If he encountered Master Carl, he would have to turn away. It would be difficult for him to justify his presence here. At least when he'd come to the masters' quarters before, he had a pressing need. Now, there wasn't quite the same urgency.

He glanced behind him. He saw no movement, nothing that would signify that anyone was aware he was here. It wasn't that he was trespassing by coming to the masters' quarters. It was more tradition that stated that the students should refrain from coming this deep into the masters' section of the university. Alec had already violated that tradition more than once.

He started forward. He had a vague idea of where to find Master Eckerd's rooms, and thought that if he could reach them, and he was there, maybe Alec could get answers. If he wasn't there, maybe he could find something in his room that would allow Alec to discover those answers on his own.

As he made his way along the hallway, the sound of voices came from the stairs behind him.

He had to hurry. He didn't recognize either of the voices, but neither was the booming voice of Master Carl. His was easy to hear. He never lowered his volume, even when it was unnecessary for him to yell.

Alec reached the end of the hall and found the door to Master Eckerd's quarters. He knocked, thinking that it would be better for him to have permission to enter rather than barging in, but there was no answer.

The voices continued along the hallway. They were louder now, and he thought that he recognized the sound of Master Helen's voice. He couldn't be certain. If she found him here, he didn't want to think of what might happen. She would be unlikely to react well to his presence.

Alec checked the door, and it was unlocked.

He flung the door open and stepped inside.

The room was empty, but a door separating it from another room was cracked, and light glowed from the other side.

"Master Eckerd?" Alec said, stepping forward.

No one answered, and Alec took another step forward. Was Master Eckerd even here?

There was movement in the room; he was certain of it. With the lantern there, he had to believe that Master Eckerd was here, but if he was, why wouldn't he answer Alec?

He stepped up to the door and pushed it open a little further.

When he did, in the faint orange glow of the lantern, he saw a face looking back at him.

"Master Jessup?"

Master Jessup took a step forward. His eyes seemed to catch the light from the lantern and almost twinkled. Then a hint of a smile spread across his face. "Mr. Stross."

"I... I was looking for Master Eckerd."

Master Jessup smiled, and he nodded. "As was I. I don't know where he is. I haven't seen him in days."

Days? How long had it been since Alec had seen him? Surely, it hadn't been days. Then again, Alec hadn't gone looking for him. Maybe it *had* been days.

"I didn't mean to interrupt..." Alec looked around. What was Master Jessup doing in these rooms? A simple knock on the door would have told him Master Eckerd wasn't here. And if he had any concern, and found the door unlocked as Alec had, a quick look around would have confirmed the man wasn't in, much less in his other room. There should be no reason for him to be here, not without having Master Eckerd present. It was unlikely that any other master would have gone into another's quarters without invitation. That seemed strange to Alec.

Master Jessup smiled broadly. "Ah, I was looking for something we shared. It was a joint project that we were working on."

Alec looked around the room. Master Eckerd had a unique set up. It was much like many of the other masters —at least as much as Alec had seen. Within the room, he had rows of shelves on which a variety of books were stacked. Most of them probably had been borrowed from the library, though a man like Master Eckerd would likely have his own collection, and it was that sort of collection which set him apart.

On a nearby table sat a row of glass jars. Alec conjectured that they contained various medicines and different concoctions that he would have mixed himself. Those alone would have been incredibly valuable, especially if someone knew they had come from a master physicker. Being treated by a physicker was incredibly expensive. Having treatment from one of the master physickers would be even more expensive. Only the richest of the highborns would have been able to afford it, other than those who came with great need to the university.

There were other assorted items, but none of them was easy to identify in the faint light. What would Master Jessup have been after? What project would he and Master Eckerd have been working on together?

Something that was none of his business. As a student, especially a low-ranking one, he had no reason to question what they might have been working on together. He could wonder, but neither man was obligated to share what they had been doing.

"I won't disturb you, then."

Master Jessup smiled again. "You're not disturbing me at all, Mr. Stross. I was just getting ready to leave."

He turned and grabbed something off of one of the nearby tables, slipping it into his pocket. Alec frowned, but when Master Jessup turned back to him, that disarming smile on his face, he bobbed his head. "Now. Would you escort me back down to the ward? I have something that I need to reevaluate, and I would welcome your company."

Alec nodded. Even if he had somewhere else to go, or a good reason for his presence here, he couldn't refuse a request from one of the university masters to accompany him to the ward. Even if he could, Alec wasn't sure he would want to. There was much for him to see and learn by shadowing him.

They made their way along the hall, and when voices drifted up to them, Master Jessup tapped him on the arm and guided him down a different hallway, leading him to a narrow stairway that wound around the inside of the university. It was a way that Alec had never gone, and he was surprised to find that it led directly into the student section. From there, it was an easy walk to the ward.

"Sometimes, I find taking the back way is beneficial."

"Beneficial?"

"There is something to be said about returning to where you first learn. In my case, that is here. Like nearly all students, my first experience with learning about the requirements to be a physicker came from here. It's something that I recall with fondness."

"Why do you say 'like nearly all students'?"

Master Jessup glanced over at him with that beaming smile. "Well, there is you. Unlike most of the students who come to the university, you had extensive experience at healing long before you came to learn in these hallowed halls. I even had a place in the lower sections I used to go to as a student." He smiled at Alec. "There aren't many places for students to sneak away alone, and a few of us from my time had such a place."

They continued past the student section and down the hall until they reached the ward. They passed no one else along the way, and for that, Alec didn't know whether to be grateful or surprised. At this time of day, it would be normal to find students out in the hall, but there was no one.

Even once they reached the ward, there was a single junior physicker working, but she only nodded to Master Jessup and otherwise ignored him.

"Who are you treating? Is it the woman with the thickened blood?"

"Ah, she is well enough, I suspect. After a single treatment of the covain root, she began to show signs of improvement." He glanced over at Alec. "And, of course, we had to reduce her sedation. We needed her more alert. The junior physickers always think to treat pain with sedation, but often times, they do so far too aggressively. Pain is beneficial, I think. It shows us signs of what is wrong. Without it, we might never know what more we might need to do."

"My father believes that pain is often beneficial. No one ever wants to have pain, but he believes in taking the edge off of it, not masking it completely, not unless there is a good reason."

"I think I would like to know more about your father," Master Jessup said.

"What's there to know? He studied here, long ago. I don't know who he might've studied with or who he might have known."

"He never talks about it?"

"I didn't even know that he had studied here until recently."

Master Jessup stopped at a cot in which an older man lay. Sleeping or unconscious, though maybe sedated. He looked to be in his forties or early fifties and had graying hair. His brow was lined, and he took slow breaths, but he appeared comfortable. Alec quickly scanned his body, searching for any sign of visible defects, but there were none.

"Why is this man here?" he asked, beginning to reach for the record.

Master Jessup grabbed it, pulling it away from him. "I thought that perhaps you might show me exactly how much you know. I haven't spent much time working with you, though I deserve most of the blame for that. I have been a bit preoccupied," he said with a smile. "But I hear nothing but good stories about your skill. You are quite well regarded among the masters. I thought that perhaps I should spend little time with you, get a sense of how much you know... Not that I think to test you, Mr. Stross. Consider this a chance for you to demonstrate your knowledge."

Alec studied the man. He was accustomed to being tested. It was something his father had taught him from the earliest days. He thought there was value in having him demonstrate what he knew. Somehow, his father always managed to give him things to read that happened to come in around the same time. By having him demonstrate, it helped reinforce what he was reading about and gave him a practical approach to learning that wasn't practiced even here in the university. Alec had a much different experience from anyone else here.

"Can you tell me what he presented with?"

"He presented like this," Master Jessup said.

Alec glanced up. "He came in unresponsive?"

"As I said, he was brought in like this."

He smiled to himself. Master Jessup might claim that

this wasn't a test, but that was exactly what it was, and he intended to challenge Alec to see exactly how well he could diagnose a condition without having much information at hand. It was a difficult challenge, and it was the kind of challenge that he would normally be offended by, but there was something about Master Jessup that he was drawn to. He felt compelled to try and please him.

Alec carefully rolled the sheet back, revealing the man's gowned form. There was nothing unusual about the skin color of his face or extremities, and by simply observing the rise and fall of his chest and the pulse in his neck, he didn't detect any visible breathing or circulation issues. He shifted the gown off to the side, giving him full access to evaluate the unconscious man.

"When you have someone unresponsive, if they are stable, you can take the time to evaluate them thoroughly," Alec said. Now that he understood that this was a test, he thought about what his father would have expected. His father would've expected him to talk his way through what he was doing, detailing each step along the way.

"And how certain are you that he's stable?"

"You told me that he's been here a few days. I can see that he's breathing regularly. His coloration is adequate. If he were unstable, more would have been done for him in the meantime."

"A reasonable conclusion."

"His age limits some of the possibilities, but not so much that it is beneficial."

Alec started with checking the man's pulse. It was strong and steady, supporting his observation of the great artery in his neck. He hadn't expected anything otherwise, but knowing that was the case, he was reassured by that.

He lifted the scope to listen to the man's heart, and leaned forward, pressing it against his chest and into his ear. As he listened, he heard nothing unusual. Occasionally, when listening to someone's heart, you can hear an extra beat, or sometimes, a strange rhythm, and less commonly, there might be a strange whooshing sort of sound that could indicate a problem with the function of the heart.

"And what do you hear?" Master Jessup asked.

"I don't hear anything, not clearly."

"Do you believe that his heart is responsible for the symptoms?"

Alec shook his head. "I doubt that this is from his heart. If it were his heart, he would not look quite as healthy as he does."

"Then why are you listening?"

"It's part of being thorough."

"You find that necessary, even when you know that you won't learn anything from it?"

"My father taught me that there are times when you think you might know what you'll discover but be completely wrong."

Alec remembered a time when his father had his mind made up about a diagnosis, but it wasn't until he started examining, listening to the way the body talked to him, that he came up with an alternative diagnosis. That had been the key to healing that person.

"Go on," Master Jessup said.

Alec moved on to listen to the man's breathing. His breaths were shallow, but they weren't raspy or wheezing. There was nothing unusual to the lung sounds. He set down the scope and placed his hands on the man's belly. As he did, the man began to writhe, though not awaken.

Alec paused, reducing the pressure on the man's belly, but not removing his hands altogether. It was the only reaction from the man so far, so he focused there for a time.

Alec moved more carefully, starting at the periphery of the abdomen and pushing slowly inward. After each pressure application of pressure, he lifted off, trying to figure out where inside this man's stomach that the pain was coming from. As he moved upward, he felt a pulsating beneath his hands.

He paused. That pulsating was unusual.

Normally, the stomach was soft. There were parts of it that were firmer than others, and for the most part there was minimal pain when pressing on the stomach. Why would this man have such pain and be unresponsive like this?

He started checking off ideas in his mind. The first thing that always came to mind when someone was unresponsive and otherwise looked well was the possibility of a poisoning. He had seen that firsthand with the foxglove, but he didn't think that was the case this time.

He moved his hands away from the man's belly. The pulsating was surprising, but he couldn't allow himself to be distracted. It could be that it was a distraction, a way of pulling his attention from something else that was the true culprit.

Yet he couldn't shake the fact that the man had reacted, clearly in pain, when he pressed.

There were other things that could cause abdominal pain, and he tried thinking of what they might be, keeping his mind off of the possibilities of referred pain, doubting that the severity of the man's discomfort could be explained in that way. He moved on, looking at his skin, examining his legs and arms, but finding nothing. He propped open his mouth and brought a candle over so that he could look inside. Other than some mild dryness, there was nothing in his mouth that would explain the symptoms. Some poisons could discolor the mouth, and some habitual use of herbs would cause other effects, such as staining on the palate or gums. He saw neither of those. He pinched the man's nose, and it was unremarkable. He rolled the man over to look at his back. The skin there was no different from anywhere else on his body.

It was troublesome. Without knowing anything more about this man, it was a mystery. And maybe that was why Master Jessup had challenged him with this case.

Could it be that the masters didn't know what was wrong with him?

Alec frowned. He didn't want to become so arrogant that he would believe he knew more than the masters, but he had seen things that they had not. It was possible that some of what he had seen allowed him to have a better feel for some of these diagnoses, though again, he did not want to presume that he knew better than the masters.

"What has been tried on him?"

Master Jessup shook his head. "What would you try?"

Alec frowned, biting his lip. He had abdominal pain, and there was the strange pulsation in his belly. It could come from a naturally occurring deformity. There were enough of those that Alec wasn't beyond believing that they could occur. And there was the pain. Could it be an infection? They could sometimes occur internally. Could it be something else?

"His reaction to the belly pressure told us he has pain

in his abdomen. I imagine he was given something to relieve the pain," Alec said. "Otherwise, he wouldn't be resting so comfortably. And there is what you told me about the junior physickers and their desire to treat pain aggressively."

Master Jessup smiled. "You are exactly what I was led to believe."

"What does that mean?"

"It means that you're right. The junior physickers have treated his pain. I wasn't totally forthcoming about how he presented. When he came in, he was moaning and in great discomfort, and they were unable to perform a full assessment. Without doing anything for his discomfort, they couldn't continue, and they have been unable to provide a diagnosis."

Jessup replaced the records at the end of the bed. "As is often the case, it seems they might've been a bit aggressive with the dosing to relieve his discomfort. But I feel they are overly aggressive with treatment quite often. Had you not examined his belly, you might not have known that he was having the abdominal discomfort."

"And the pulsation?"

"Pulsation?"

Alec placed his hands on either side of the central portion of the man's stomach. He pressed down, collecting the middle section of his stomach between them, and once more felt it. "It's there. I don't recognize it but suspect there might be some reference to it in one of the old patient records on file."

The librarians were incredibly skilled at searching the records for symptoms. It was part of what made the university so powerful. They had countless volumes of records, and each of them was cataloged, and those catalogs were tied together, so that the librarians could search them quickly, finding references to various illnesses. It was also a way of searching for symptoms that might be similar to those of another illness. It was time-consuming, but the librarians were skilled at it, and managed to do it much more quickly than Alec could ever imagine.

Master Jessup stepped next to him and pressed his hands on the man's stomach. He frowned as he did, holding them in place for a long moment before pulling them back. "Yes. Surprising. He does not appear to have any discomfort when you place your hands there, though."

"No, but if you press here"—Alec pressed on the upper right portion of the man's stomach—"this is where he begins to have pain."

It was subtle, but as he moved his hands around, he could focus on the pain. There were a few different organs in that area of the body, and it would take a surgeon to determine which of them was involved, though it was possible to use a combination of medicines to better elucidate it.

"Very good, Mr. Stross."

Master Jessup grabbed the record and made a few notes, and then he turned away from the cot.

Alec stared at the man a moment longer before covering him back up. He shifted the gown into place, and then covered him with the sheet, before racing off after Master Jessup.

"Is that it? That's all you wanted to do to test me?"

"You'd already proven to have an astute mind," Master Jessup said. "I was curious what your examination skills might reveal. It appears that your father has taught you well there, as well."

"What now?"

He half expected Master Jessup to share something with him, perhaps invite him to be a part of some study, but it was not to be.

"Now you return to your studies, Mr. Stross. And I will return to mine."

Alec paused at the student section, and Master Jessup took the stairs back up to the masters' section, not looking back at him. Alec wanted to follow him and talk to him. He wanted to find out more about what it would take for him to understand his role as Scribe... and as physicker. But the man was gone. An opportunity lost.

TO THE SWAMP

S am paced in her room, irritation filling her. It had been another three days, days full of nothing but training, working with her staff, attempting to improve her skill, but feeling as if nothing had changed for her. Elaine hadn't even bothered to work with her, and that bothered Sam more than anything else. If Elaine wouldn't train with her, it told her that she meant nothing to the woman.

Why was she so hard on Sam?

All she wanted was to find some way to get to Alec. She could continue sending him notes, but what more could she tell him? How many times could she simply say that she was well? She couldn't tell him that she felt like a prisoner here in the palace. What if the note was intercepted and someone told the princess, or her mother?

What would Alec do anyway? He hadn't tried to come for her, so it would seem he had no interest in seeing her, much less any concern for her safety . He was busy with the other students, probably that Beckah, the woman who had gotten so close to him. She was pretty; Sam couldn't deny that. But Alec needed someone who could challenge him, beyond how his studies challenged him. He needed to be brought out, away from the books and back into the real world, something that Sam could do. Could Beckah?

But maybe he no longer wanted what the two of them shared. Maybe he didn't want to be her Scribe, much less her friend.

Whenever they were together, she put him in danger. Maybe that was not the life that he wanted. He was a healer and was now on his way to becoming a physicker, and if Sam knew Alec—as well as she thought she knew him—it wouldn't surprise her if he quickly progressed to become a master physicker. He was incredibly smart, much smarter than she, and considering everything he had gone through, he was stronger than most would be, as well.

Her door opened, and Elaine poked her head in. Sam glared at her. "What do you want? You want to tell me that I can't even leave this room now?"

"Are you feeling as if you're trapped here?" Elaine asked.

"I've told you that I'm trapped."

"And I've told you that you are not. All it takes for you to get off the island is to find your own way."

"You've prevented me from crossing the bridges."

"Have I? Is it all my fault that you are unable to cross the bridge?"

"You don't want me to cross over."

Elaine shrugged. "As I said, I have done nothing to prevent you from accessing other parts of the city. All it takes is for you to use your abilities and you are free to leave."

Sam frowned again. "Is that why you're here? Did you think that you needed to taunt me more about my inability to get off this section? Because I *will* get off."

Elaine nodded. "I hope so. But no. That's not why I came."

"Why did you come?"

"It's time for an assignment."

Sam sat up, looking over at Elaine. "What kind of assignment? I've been practicing with all of the different Kavers that I can. What more do I need to do for my training?"

"It's not that kind of assignment."

Elaine motioned for her to follow, and Sam hesitated only a moment before jumping off her bed and grabbing her canal staff. She hesitated at the door and turned back to grab her cloak. It was a cloak that Marin had given her long ago, and because of that, Sam knew she should have destroyed it, especially knowing that Marin likely had some ulterior motive for giving it to Sam, but she just couldn't. The cloak had protected her over the years. It had allowed her to sneak along the streets, not drawing attention to herself, and to use the shadows to bend light around her. There was something strange about the fabric that shifted though shadows, making it difficult for her to be seen.

With her cloak now on, and staff in hand, she caught up to Elaine at the end of the hall. Elaine glanced over and saw Sam wearing her cloak, hood pulled up as she often did, and nodded to her. Sam felt foolish for a moment, wondering if perhaps this wasn't the kind of assignment that Elaine had in mind, but even if it wasn't, with her cloak and staff, she was ready for anything.

"Where are we going?"

"As I said, on an assignment."

They quickly crossed the grounds, and Sam saw where they were heading.

A narrow barge waited near the shore.

That alone was unusual. It was rare for boats to be this close to the palace, and when they were, there was usually a particular reason for it. They weren't even allowed nearby for trade. Merchants were required to bring things across the bridge from one of the outer sections.

"That?"

"Are you afraid of boats?" Elaine asked.

"I'm not afraid of boats, just asking whether that's where you intend for us to go."

"That will be our transportation."

Sam's gaze drifted from the boat to the other side of the canal where the university rose up. Its white walls caught the sunlight, and made it feel like it was close to her, yet at the same time, it was so far away. Alec was so far away. All she wanted was a moment. If she could reach the other side, and if she could get to Alec, she could tell him that she was well, that she was unharmed, and... They could work together, using augmentations to help find Marin. Sam had no idea where to begin, especially now that she couldn't get off the damned palace section. She felt they were stronger when they worked together, studying problems as a team rather than individually.

"Focus, Samara."

Sam shook her head and pulled her attention back to the barge. They paused at the shore, and someone pushed a plank across from the barge over to the shoreline. Sam and Elaine crossed over, stepping onto the barge. Sam had never spent any time on the boats that traveled the canals. This one was narrower than most. It had none of the scale or enormity, and it didn't have the massive crates stacked atop it as many of them did. This was not meant to transport items. Rather, it seemed designed to transport people. With the slim hull, it would likely be sleek, and she suspected it traveled through the waters rapidly.

Once they were on, Elaine nodded to a man standing near the tiller. He wore a leather jacket that hung to his mid-thigh, and he had long boots that pulled up to his knees. He was thin, and he swayed with the movements of the boat, clearly comfortable on the water.

There were two other men, but neither of them spoke. Both were younger, and one had a scruff of a beard, while the other looked as if he could barely grow anything on his face.

They pushed off, and the two young men used long poles to push through the canal. Sam watched with fascination. It was an unusual way of travel, and though she had seen the barges making their way along the canals for as long as she could remember, she never paid any attention to how they moved. They didn't have sails or any other way of propelling themselves, she hadn't realized that they used something similar to her canal staff to push along the waterways.

Once they got going, they moved with a reasonable speed. It wasn't any faster than what she thought she could walk, but traveling by canal, they were able to bypass the slowdown of traveling through the city. It was somewhat more efficient. She imagined what Bastan would think of traveling on the canals. He had long had a fascination with the canals, going so far as to place maps of them around his office. Sam suspected that was for another purpose, and that he used them to help with his smuggling operation, but it was equally possible that he simply found the canals interesting.

"We could move through the city just as fast augmented," Sam said softly.

"As I have told you, you rely too much on your augmentations. I'm not denying that we could, what I want you to realize is that there are other ways that you can travel. There are ways that do not require you to be augmented. What you need to learn is what you would do if your augmentations failed. I fear that you don't have anything in mind for such a scenario."

"I've lived without augmentations most of my life. I know what I would do if I didn't have them. I would walk."

"And what if you needed to move quickly through the city?"

"Then I would move quickly through the city by walking—or running."

"And what if you needed to get out of the city?"

"Then I would go to the edge of the city and leave."

Elaine smiled at her. "It's not quite as simple as that."

"Why not?"

"Have you ever tried to leave the city?"

Sam hadn't, but she didn't want Elaine to know that. All that would do would be to give her another reason to torment her about her inexperience. "What reason would I have had to leave the city before?"

"You want to call yourself a Kaver, and you haven't even left the city?"

"How often have you left the city?"

"My responsibilities carry me from the city frequently. Where do you think I was when Lyasanna was attacked?"

"I thought you were out searching for some way to heal her."

"Once I learned what happened, I certainly did. Before that, I didn't know that she was in any danger. Why should I? We've kept the Anders safe for many years. And Kavers have long protected the city, staying outside the borders to provide that protection."

"Only the Anders?"

"The Anders came to the city and settled here as a way to get away from the Thelns. They created the protections, and they were the first who helped give the people here the freedom to live without fear of what the Thelns might do to them. In that, I serve the Anders."

"But not all Scribes are from the Anders line," Sam said.

Elaine settled near the center of the barge, looking out at the water. "Not all Kavers are from the Anders line, either."

They were traveling along a canal that took them past several of the highborn sections of the city. Sam had never seen them from this vantage. Seeing it this way, with buildings rising up on either side, there was something *magical* about the city itself. Every so often, they would pass a street, and Sam would glance down it, looking to see movement from the people who lived in the section. They were still in the highborn section, but from out on the water, it was difficult to tell the difference between sections. There were certain parts of the city that had elements that reminded her of Caster.

"What do you know about the founding of the city?" Elaine asked softly.

"I'm not a scholar. I never went to school, so I never studied the history of the city or anything else."

Elaine glanced over to her. "And yet, I suspect that you should."

"Why should I? What benefit would there be for me to study such things?"

"The benefit is obvious. When you learn about where you live, and where you come from, you can understand things better."

"Which is why I'm trying to find Marin and the Book," Sam said. Was that so hard for them to understand?

"Finding the Book will do nothing other than create trouble for you," Elaine said. "And your interest in finding Marin is not entirely about the Book."

"No? Then what is it about?"

"You want to know why she used you. You want to know why she was willing to use Trayson."

Sam shook her head, trying to suppress the frustration that surged through her. There were times when Elaine tried to act as if she knew her so well, but how could she? She hadn't been a part of her life. They may share a blood-line, but that was about it.

"And you want me to know about the history of the city, but not care about the history of me?"

"I'm not saying that you should be uninterested in your past and where you came from. All I am trying to say is that you should be aware of the intent behind what you choose."

Sam snorted at her choice of words. "Intent? Like what you showed me on that doorway?"

Elaine tipped her head, and she nodded. "Intent is much the same," she said.

"Except I'm not trying to fortify some door so that I can prevent it from being kicked in."

"Or are you? The door may be symbolic, but it's still a door."

"Now you're talking in riddles."

"There's no riddle. All I'm saying is that you have fortified yourself. You're strong, Samara. I won't deny that. If you weren't strong, you wouldn't have survived nearly as long as you have. You wouldn't have been able to withstand the Thelns' attack the first time. You wouldn't have survived a poisoned bolt to the shoulder." Elaine glanced at Sam's shoulder.

Most of the Kavers she'd now met didn't believe that she had survived a Theln poisoning. It was rare. Anyone who had survived had done so with the help of a fully trained Scribe. For her to have done so with Alec, and with neither of them having had any training at that time, unsettled the other Kavers.

"Maybe I wouldn't have had to fortify myself in such a way if I had my mother there with me," Sam said.

Elaine considered her for a moment before shaking her head and looking away. "You blame me for something that was out of my control."

Sam had given it a lot of thought. There was a part of her that thought blaming Elaine for something that she really couldn't have controlled was irrational, but another part of her said it wasn't irrational at all. Had Elaine put *any* effort into finding her, she would have been able to. It wasn't as if Sam had been hiding. It would've been easy enough to find her. Marin hadn't even changed her name, though maybe she couldn't have. Maybe there was no way to do so and maintain her identity. When she found Marin, she intended to ask about that.

Rather than continuing the conversation, Sam fell silent. There was no point in arguing. Elaine would only justify that she had done what she could, and that she had been limited, that there was no way for her to have found Sam in a city that size.

They made their way along the canals, and Sam watched as they passed from section to section, eventually moving into a part of the city that was entirely unfamiliar to her. They traveled north, a direction that she rarely went, and she marveled at how different this part of the city was. Caster was on the western side of the city, near the edge, and beyond that was nothing but the steam fields that eventually led up into the mountains. To the north, there was swamp, making it difficult for anyone to enter the city that way. To the east and the south was the sea, leaving them essentially isolated. Now that Sam knew about it, she suspected that meant they were protected, though it didn't always feel that way. It felt isolated. Trade had always been difficult, requiring ships to bring their wares to ports along the coast, then offload them onto barges that came up the canals, and all trade was restricted by the royals—all highborns—who prevented anyone they didn't want to trade from entering the city. Could all of that been about trying to restrict access by the Thelns?

"Where are we going?" Sam asked.

"I thought you would recognize this. Didn't you tell me that you have wandered the city?"

"I have, but I haven't gone this far to the north."

"It's not much farther."

The barge passed through another few sections, and then they passed beyond the edge of the city.

Sam's breath caught.

She turned, looking to take in the city behind her. The canals created a sharp barrier. Where the canals ran, creating the islands that formed each section of the city, there was a distinct line. Beyond that stretched the swamp, a great section of seemingly impassable water, an expanse of darkness she'd never dared enter, even when she'd come upon it while some thieves in her pursuit to understand what Marin was up to. Why should she? Her canal staff would be of no use to her. Even with an augmentation, she wasn't sure there would be any way for her to make it through the swamp. It required transport by boat—by barge, it seemed.

Elaine nodded at the captain, and he signaled to his men to slow the barge.

They stopped in a reedy section of the swamp. Water stretched all around. The air hung with the stench. It was filthy, fouler than what she smelled even from the canals, and Sam wondered if there were eels even in here. The air was still and humid, and she wiped a sheen of sweat off her forehead.

"This is the assignment?"

Elaine grabbed her canal staff where it leaned against a rail. She stepped to the edge of the barge and flipped out over the water, stabbing down with her staff.

She hung on the end of the staff, holding herself in

place. As she did, she watched Sam, and then nodded. "Join me."

"Why? What is the assignment?"

"Join me," Elaine said again.

Sam looked at the captain. He watched her, and there was an unreadable expression on his dark face. The other two men held their long staffs, and Sam realized that the staffs they used to propel the barge were much thicker than her own.

She had a sense that if she didn't follow Elaine, these men, who were clearly stronger than she, would encourage her to do so.

What was this assignment? What did Elaine intend for her to do with her here?

She shook her head, stretched out with her staff, and jumped, pushing off the bottom of the swamp.

Holding herself balanced on the end of her staff, she turned to Elaine. "What now?"

"Now we return."

"What?"

Elaine flipped herself up and brought her staff back around, piercing the swamp again. She flipped like that, moving five feet or more each time, heading back toward the city.

Sam watched her for far too long. By the time she pulled her gaze away, she realized that the barge had departed, making its way westerly through the swamp.

She either had to follow Elaine—or swim.

UNDERSTANDING THE LESSON

The damned air was too thick. Sam swore to herself, cursing Kyza for placing her in this position. It wasn't the god's fault that she was here, but it *was* her fault that she hadn't found a way to get Sam help. All she wanted was some way to get out of this stinking swamp.

She managed to stay balanced on the end of her staff but hadn't been able to move more than a few inches. Elaine had long ago disappeared. Sam's arms quivered from the effort of holding on to the staff, and she knew that she needed to move, or she would soon be swimming.

An assignment, she thought to herself bitterly. This wasn't an assignment so much as it was a way to torment her. Maybe it was another *test,* but in this test, if she failed, she would end up in the swamp. She didn't know enough about it to know whether it was dangerous, but she had to believe that it wasn't safe. Clearly, it was one of the barricades that protected the city. To be an effective barricade, there had to be danger present for anyone who attempted passage. And right now, she was that person.

Sam had always been confident in her ability with the staff, but seeing the way the other Kavers managed to move on the staff, balancing as they went, she felt inadequate. She thought of Raylene and the way that she managed to remain perched on the staff, almost as if she were an acrobat. For Sam to get out of here, she would have to manage a similar technique.

But each time she attempted to flip forward on the staff, she managed only a few inches, just like in the practice yard. And with each attempt, she felt her strength wane.

Why would Elaine do this to her?

Was it her way of getting rid of her? Was it her way of proving that she didn't have what she needed to become the Kaver that the others were?

Fear of slipping down into the water had at least given her the ability to move somewhat, but it was a long way back and she didn't think she'd make it.

What was the key?

Once again, she tried to envision what she'd seen from Raylene. The woman used an entire contortion of her body as she flipped. Was that what Sam needed to do? She had tried it before, but without having an augmentation, she didn't feel like she had enough strength to do it.

How had Elaine disappeared so quickly?

It was possible that she had an augmentation, but Sam doubted it. If she *had* been augmented, she wouldn't have been able to torment Sam quite as easily about learning how to work without one. No, Elaine wanted to prove that she didn't need an augmentation in order for her to escape the swamp.

She closed her eyes, visualizing the way that Elaine had flipped her way free from the swamp.

It was a movement of her entire body. It required using her stomach and her arms and... everything.

Sam took a deep breath. She tightened her muscles, preparing herself, holding tightly on to the staff, and pushed off, flipping into the air.

Panic set in as she did, and she frantically worked to stab down with her staff, bringing it around so that she landed on the staff rather than in the water.

She managed to stay on the staff as she came around. Her body ached from the effort of the movement, but she was still above the surface of the water.

Sam let out a small whoop of victory.

She had moved, but how far had she gone?

And could she keep it up?

That was the bigger challenge. Now that she had done it once, could she do it over and over again long enough to escape from the swamp?

She had no choice. If she didn't, if she failed to make it across the swamp, she would end up in the water.

Something hit her staff.

It struck with force, and Sam slipped, only a little, but enough to make her sweat even more. What struck her?

The force with which it struck felt... thick. Fear coursed through her as she remembered a similar sensation when she'd fallen into the canal. Could the damned canal eels be out in the swamp too?

She saw no reason why not. The canals connected with the swamp. The swamp was yet another protective barrier to the city, so the Scribes probably made *sure* they were here, too.

She needed to get moving. Delay only weakened her, which would make each flip that much more difficult.

She contorted herself and flipped again.

This time it was easier. The movement felt more familiar. More than that, now that she had repeated it, her confidence surged and she knew she could keep going.

When she landed, the water splashed below her.

That wasn't the staff.

A face with sharp teeth appeared in the water.

Sam's breath caught again. It was the largest eel she had ever seen. Not that she had seen many canal eels, but this one was enormous.

Kyza!

How was she supposed to keep this up? Already, her arms were shaking, quivering with the effort of trying to hold her up, but she had to keep going.

And if Elaine could do it, Sam knew that she could. She had to.

She had no choice. The thought of that eel waiting for her to slip into the water actually gave her a surge of adrenaline. Fear can do that.

Another contortion, and she flipped again, heading toward the city. Each time she landed, she grew more confident. But she'd not escaped her tormentor. The eel seemed to follow her openly, swimming around the base of her staff, though it didn't smack into the staff again. Those in the city canals weren't nearly as aggressive—at least they weren't as willing to make their presence known. Why would the eels in the swamp be different?

But why wouldn't they? There was nothing here to

scare them away. There was no reason for them not to be fearless. Few barges made their way through here, and there weren't people to throw things at them, not like there were in the city.

Everything in the swamp would be prey to the eels.

Sam swallowed. Her mouth was dry and she was thirsty, but she didn't dare drink from this water.

She flipped again. The city didn't feel any closer, but it had to be, didn't it?

The eel stayed with her, swimming alongside almost like an escort… or a guard.

"Go away," Sam yelled. Her voice sounded weak, even to her. She wouldn't intimidate an eel, and certainly not one that was so daring as to swim next to her.

She flipped, again and again, losing count of how many times she did it. A few times, her hands slipped, and she had to push herself back up to the top of the staff. Every so often, she would pause and wrap her legs around the staff to give her arms a break. Balancing became easier the longer that she did it. The fear of falling into the swamp helped, though she would never admit that to Elaine. It had seemed like hours before the edge of the city finally came into view.

Her arms shook. Only a few more flips, and she would be able to reach it, but she feared she didn't have the strength. Not anymore. It was a matter of stamina. She had spent everything she had getting this far, and going any farther seemed to be beyond her.

Sam rested, keeping her legs wrapped around the staff, holding herself in place. She looked toward the edge of the city, where she would reach land. Her vision blurry, but she had expected to see Elaine waiting for her.

She wasn't there.

Could she have abandoned Sam to the swamp?

That was surprising. Why would Elaine have left her... unless she had presumed that Sam would make it. Or she knew that she would not.

Anger surged within her again, and she found the strength to flip a few more times, finally reaching the edge of the city. She fell onto the shore, collapsing in a heap. She clutched onto her canal staff and looked down at the end, fearing that the eel had taken a chunk out of the end, but there was no damage.

After resting for a while, she managed to pull herself to her feet. She looked out over the swamp, wondering how far had she gone.

Farther than she would've thought possible. But she had done it. Yes, her body ached, and all she wanted at this moment was to fall into bed and sleep. But she had made it. Had she been augmented, she would not only have made it across the swamp more quickly, she would have had no reason to fear the eel. Even if she'd ended up in the water, her strength would have allowed her to outswim the eel. And if Alec could have given her thicker skin—making her denser—the eel would have been unable to harm her. The augmentations could have helped her in any number of ways.

But no. Elaine needed to have her tormented. She needed to send her out into the swamp, to almost die.

And that captain had been a willing participant.

All of it made her blood boil.

She leaned on the staff as she headed back into the city. The air here was so much more humid than it was in the Caster section. It cooled off closer to the sea, but Sam was surprised how different it was here. She was surprised how different much of the city was.

Sam's strength returned now that she was back on solid ground. She moved quickly, heading back toward the palace. She was tempted to pause at the university, but anger propelled her forward, and she suspected that Elaine wouldn't even allow her to pause at the university. She had likely set some other barrier up to thwart her.

It was nearly nightfall by the time she reached the innermost sections of the city. The moon was high overhead, nearly full, and a few wispy clouds surrounded it. A faint breeze wafted through the city, cooling her. She would've liked that breeze when she had been out in the swamp.

When she reached the canal separating this section from the university, she paused.

Why shouldn't she go see Alec?

Now that she knew how to balance on her staff, and now that she knew how to cross through the swamp, why shouldn't she use those new skills to reach her Scribe?

Did she have the strength that she needed?

She didn't even know.

At least she didn't fear the canals here quite as much as she feared the swamp. She didn't want to end up in one, but if she did, she didn't think she would end up eaten.

She hesitated for a moment. She must stink, and she didn't want to go to Alex smelling like this. She could head into the palace and take a bath, but that meant she would have to confront Elaine, and she wanted to do that with a calmer head. Right now, she was simply too angry.

She found flowers and smeared them all over her, rubbing them into her cloak. If nothing else, she hoped the fragrance would distract from the stench of the swamp.

When she reached the edge of the canal, she stopped. Even if she reached the university, would she be able to find Alec? It wasn't as if he would be simply waiting for her, would he?

She didn't want to distract him from his studies. But could she pass up this opportunity? She only hoped she didn't find him with Beckah.

She faced the canal.

She jumped, flipping, and landed on her staff. She would not be kept from Alec any longer.

16

A FRIEND VISITS

I t was late, and the water lapped at the shore of the canal, its soft burbling the only sound that broke through the night's silence. Alec stood staring over the water, looking at the faint candlelight glowing in the windows of the palace. Longing filled his heart, and he wished he could cross, but when he'd tried, he'd been turned away. He needed to find Sam, to make sure she was okay. But had she wanted to come to him, to do something other than send word that she was well, she would have. And he knew that he needed to continue his studies. If he didn't, if he abandoned them, what use would he be to her?

A shadowed form moved on the other side of the canal. Alec watched, thinking that perhaps it might be Sam, but it appeared to be nothing more than one of the guards.

He turned. The canal was widest around the palace. It formed a barrier, a defense that other parts of the city did not have. It was more than simply the width of the canal

172 | D.K. HOLMBERG

and the physical barrier, it was the eels swimming within the canal. He didn't totally understand how the early Scribes had created this magical barrier that prevented the Thelns from reaching the palace. But he believed what Master Eckerd had told them.

There came a splash, and he scanned the water, thinking that perhaps one of the canal eels had broken the surface, but saw nothing.

"Are you waiting for me?"

Alec spun and found Sam standing behind him. She wore the dark, shimmery cloak that she had worn since he first met her, and the hood was pulled up, concealing her face. In her hand, she held her long, slender staff. It was a weapon, and it was something else. A means to freedom for her. It was something that he didn't understand, not well, but he knew it was important to her.

"Where have you been?"

"Alec—"

"No. I know that you've sent word. But the one time you didn't, I—"

Sam nodded. "I know. You placed an augmentation. I appreciate that."

"Appreciate? That's all I get?"

Sam sighed and took a step toward him. She smelled of a floral perfume, and a hint of mint was there with it. She approached slowly, with heat radiating from her body. "That's not all you get, but I've been kept busy. Elaine has been trying to train me, wanting me to know how to work without my augmentations."

As she said it, Alec could hear the annoyance in her tone. "I thought she had been doing that before."

"She had. And I've been training, but after the

attack... Well, let's just say that she had a renewed urgency after the attack. She thought I needed to be better prepared to handle myself if I was confronted by someone who had augmentations and I did not. Apparently, that's something all Kavers must do during their training."

Sam took a position next to him, and she stared out over the canal. Ever since he'd met her, she had done the same sort of thing, and he had always enjoyed standing next to her, looking out into the darkness, wondering what she was thinking. This time, he wished that she would share more than she usually did. He was growing tired of not knowing, and tired of worrying about her.

"We need to practice together," he said.

"Can we? How much paper do we have left?"

Alec thought about their supplies. The number of sheets they had remaining was dwindling, but still there was enough for them to practice, wasn't there? He could write small. The size of the writing didn't matter, it was the content.

"Enough to keep practicing."

Sam stared at him, and for a moment, he thought that she might share something, but she only sighed.

"I want to practice, too, but, though I hate to admit it, I think Elaine is right. We do need to know how to work without our augmentations. I need to know what I can do without enhancement."

"Is it because of what Marin was able to do?"

Sam's face darkened. Beneath her hood, it was difficult to tell, but he knew her too well. "Marin was able to counter me even without augmentations. She knows something, Alec."

"Then we need to find her. We can go after her, find where Tray has her, and—"

"Tray found me."

"What do you mean he found you?"

She sighed again and turned toward him for a moment. She couldn't seem to look him in the eye. Her gaze drifted out over the water and then down to the ground.

"What is it that you don't want to tell me?"

"That night when I didn't check in."

"Tray found you then? Is that why you weren't able to get to me? Oh, Sam, I didn't need to place an augmentation then. I felt so foolish doing so, and even Beckah thought I was overreacting."

"No. You weren't overreacting. I... I needed that augmentation. Without it, I would have been trapped."

Alec frowned at her. "Trapped? I don't like the sound of that."

Sam rubbed her wrists. "I didn't like the way it felt, either. I was following someone—"

"Tray?"

"Yes. I was following Tray, thinking that I could get to Marin. But Ralun caught me."

Alec blinked. He didn't know what to make of what she was telling him. Why wouldn't she have come to him when she found Tray? It was her brother, but she also knew how dangerous he was—how dangerous he had to be—especially given his heritage. He was half Theln and half Kaver. They didn't know what that made him, other than someone to keep an eye on. Other than that, what was he? Did he still share the same bond to Sam as he had before? Did he view her differently now since learning he wasn't her birth brother? Would he put her in danger?

That last was the one that he cared the most about. Alec knew what Sam would do, and he knew the steps she would take to avoid harming her brother, thinking that she could protect him from himself, but how well did she know him anymore?

He and Sam had spent significant time together before he left for the university, and during that time, she seen much of Tray. Because of that, how well did she know him anymore?

But it was what she said last that concerned him the most.

"Ralun? Isn't that the same Theln who poisoned the princess?"

"It is. Apparently, he's some high-ranking Theln, and Elaine was quite concerned by the fact that he returned to the city, and now she thinks…"

When Sam didn't finish, Alec frowned. "Now she thinks what? Is that why you're training as hard as you are? She thinks he's after you, doesn't she?"

Sam breathed out heavily. "That's what she's afraid of."

"Is that why you finally came to me? You wanted me to know that Ralun might be after you? I'm happy to place whatever augmentations you need to defeat him, Sam, but I need to know what's going on so that I can help you."

"That's not why I came to find you," she said.

"No? You would've kept that from me?"

"Only because there's nothing I can do about it. Elaine has made it quite clear that I'm not allowed to go after Ralun, and without the support of the Kavers, I don't know that it even makes sense for me to try. Besides, there's something else that is more important."

"Not the Book. We've already talked about it. You can't go after the Book, not without knowing more about it."

Sam glowered at him. "That's not what I was going to say, and you can't tell me not to go after the Book. It's the only hope I have of getting my memories back. But Helen believes that even destroying that page might not work. I need to know what Marin did so that I can remove its effects. I need to know more about what happened before I lost all of my memories."

"What will that change?" Alec asked.

She shrugged. "Maybe nothing. Maybe all it does is show me that I had a mother who cared about me, rather than this hard woman who wants nothing more than to train me and hone me into a Kaver so that I can effectively defend the princess. I need to know that there was something more once. If Ralun is in the city, and if he has access to the Book, I need to get to him so I can get my hands on it."

"I thought you said that wasn't why you were here."

"It isn't. Not totally. Listen, I don't know if there's any way for me to get to Ralun, but if there is, I'll need to be careful approaching him. I know better than to attack him without your support." She looked up at him before glancing back at the university. "But there is something else. The night I was attacked... When I awoke, bound to a chair in some strange room, there was someone there."

"Why do I get the feeling that this is someone I should be afraid of?"

"I don't know if *you* should be afraid of him, but he's a physicker. Marin's Scribe."

Alec's breath caught. "Marin? You were held captive by Marin's Scribe?"

Sam nodded. "It was the same night that I followed Tray. It was Ralun who captured me and took me to this Scribe. Tray was there when I was attacked, but for some reason, the Scribe didn't seem to know that we had lost Marin. He wanted me to bring her to him or maybe he wanted to take me to her, I don't really know, but either way, he didn't know that Tray had her."

"Why is that significant?"

"It's significant because Tray could have told him that he had Marin. But he didn't."

There was anguish on her face. Alec hated how much this was hurting her, and hated that he had to push, but they needed to know, especially as there were so many questions that remained with Tray and his involvement with the Thelns.

If it were Alec in a similar situation, wouldn't he want to know more about who he was and what it meant for him to be a Theln? He knew that he would, much as he suspected Tray did.

What would happen if Tray decided that he was pleased by what he'd learned? What would happen if he decided he wanted to work with and side with the Thelns?

How much danger did that put all of them in?

He knew that it would cause problems for Sam. She had a soft spot for Tray, regardless of how that had gotten there. He was a weakness, and maybe the only weakness Sam had.

"And when you escaped?"

"When I escaped, I didn't think about bringing him with me. I thought only of getting to safety."

"Which means that he got away."

"That's what it means. I went back after escaping, but he'd already disappeared. I don't know where he went or where Tray is now. I haven't seen him since that night."

"You want to find this man, and you think I have some way of doing so?"

"He's a Scribe, and he was wearing a physicker jacket."

"If he's a Scribe, it likely means he's a master physicker."

"That was my concern, but Elaine tried to convince me that would be unlikely."

"Why is that?"

"Because she thinks that all of the master physickers would have been screened, and that if one of them was working with Marin, they would have known about it."

"And you don't agree."

"I don't know if I should agree. Marin was able to deceive us—*me*—for an incredibly long time. Who's to say her Scribe isn't doing the same thing?"

Sam reached out and grabbed his arm, and Alec didn't pull away. He enjoyed the comfort of her touch, and as that realization set in, so did everything that Beckah and his father had been teasing him about. Could he allow himself to feel for Sam? Or was that dangerous, especially given their connection? Ruining that would only lead to problems. A Kaver and Scribe only connected rarely, and the fact that they had such a connection, and that they got along as well as they did, was something that he needed to treasure and protect not ruin by his foolish feelings toward her.

"Listen, if her Scribe was a master physicker, then you would need to find someone who has been away from the university for a while," Sam said.

"Are you sure about that?" Alec asked. "Marin was still active in the city. It only stands to reason that her Scribe remained active, which means he might still be at the university."

"Who do you think it might be?"

Alec tried to think of the different master physickers, wondering if any of them could be tied to Marin. There were quite a few he suspected to be Scribes, but that secret was kept from him. It seemed to be reserved for the master physickers, those like Master Eckerd or Master Helen, and not for any of the students with potential.

Could it be someone like Master Carl?

He didn't care for the man, but he had a sharp mind and would certainly have been skilled enough to be a Scribe. He had some political ambition also, and that seemed fitting with a Scribe, somehow.

"You have someone in mind?"

"I'm just thinking through the different master physickers and who it might be," Alec said. "Did you get a good look at him?"

"Only as I attacked him once you augmented me," Sam said. "He was mostly in shadows. When I broke free, the lantern broke, and I wasn't able to see him. I ran before I got a good look at him."

"That's unfortunate. If you had seen him, I could have brought you into the university, perhaps playing the part of someone with an illness, and maybe you could have identified him."

"I heard him talk. Would that help?"

Alec tried to think of a way that Sam might be able to recognize the voice of her captor, but struggled. There weren't many times when all of the master physickers came together, which made it unlikely that there would be an opportunity for her to identify him by voice.

"I could still come in and play the sick role," she said, covering her mouth and coughing forcefully. "See? And if you really needed to create something, you could use easar paper, and give me some mild illness that would be unexplainable."

Alec smiled to himself. That wasn't a terrible idea, if only because the easar paper wouldn't lead to a permanent deficit. It would be temporary, which was all he would allow Sam to have.

"Even if that worked, I doubt it would make a difference. When people come in sick, they're assigned a junior physicker, and it's only the illnesses that are more challenging that are given to a master physicker and the students. And since I don't know how the assignments are made, I wouldn't be able to ensure which of the master physickers you'd be assigned to."

Maybe it had something to do with interest, or maybe it had something to do with skill level. Some of the master physickers were more skilled than others, especially when it came to certain areas.

"Let me look into it. I can see if there's any way that we can come up with something that might work so that we can bring you in."

"I don't like waiting. If he's out there—"

"I'll work quickly," Alec said. "But I don't want you going off and doing something stupid in the meantime."

"Stupid?"

"You know what I mean. Without any augmentations, if there are Thelns in the city, you're in danger. Ralun was hard enough for us to defeat the first time."

"I know. I seem to remember being the one who had to combat him."

"And I seem to remember being the one who granted you the augmentations you needed so that you could." He stared at her. "Please, Sam. With you out there on your own, I worry about whether you're in danger or harmed or any number of other things that could happen. And as with your recent capture, I would have no way of knowing. My decision to augment you when you needed it was pure guesswork. Just... I know you have to go, but whatever it is you do, do me a favor and just be careful."

"Now you're starting to sound like Elaine."

"You're equating me to your mother?"

"Well, not necessarily my mother, but... Well, I suppose, Elaine *is* my mother, but not in quite the same way. We don't have that maternal connection, so to speak."

"Please, Sam. I don't like not knowing if you're in any danger. I can't help you if I don't know."

She sighed. "You're right. I will be careful. I promise not to go running into danger, if you promise to do all that you can to search for information about who this master physicker might be."

"And if he's no longer with the university?"

"If he's not, there has to be some record of him," Sam said. "And if he still is with the university, you need to search for who it might be. See if there is some way you can bring all of the master physickers together, maybe."

"I doubt that would be quite possible, but I can look

into who might have had a connection to a Kaver in the past." If only he could find Master Eckerd. If he could, then he might be able to discover who had that Scribe-Kaver connection. "And Sam?"

She turned back to him, arching a brow.

"Don't wait so long to come back and visit. I…" Alec flushed. Should he tell her what he was feeling? Could he not? It seemed that she deserved to know, but it also was difficult for him to be that honest with her. Then again, if he wasn't honest with her, would he miss out on the opportunity to do so? "I miss you," he said.

Sam watched him for a moment, and in that brief moment, fears rushed into Alec's mind, fear that she might be upset with him, or that she might disregard his affection, or countless other possibilities. He hated feeling that way. He was always accustomed to being in control of his emotions, of being the one who knew rather than feeling uncertainty. Even when he did face uncertainty, one of the things about healing that he loved was that he knew where to go to find answers. With Sam and his uncertainty about how he felt toward her, he didn't know where he could go or who he could turn to.

"I miss you, too," she said. "I wish… I wish we could go back to training together, rather than being separated, but I think Elaine is right. I think that I am too dependent on my augmentations, and I haven't taken the opportunity to discover what other talents I might have. And from what I am learning, there are other talents that Kavers possess, and if I can learn those, you and I can be more effective together. I'm hopeful we can work together again soon. That we can be together…" she said, her voice trailing off at the end.

Alec stood for a moment before rushing over and giving her a quick hug. He enjoyed feeling that closeness with her even if it was only for a moment, and even if it couldn't last. When she stepped away, she gave him a small smile, then turned and flipped out over the water, twisting her staff back down and hopping across the canal, never touching the surface of the water, all without an augmentation.

She *had* improved. That was something she never would have been able to do before, and he marveled at her skill, knowing that for her, he needed to improve. She deserved that.

And they needed to find answers. They would, working together. He would uncover who might be Marin's Scribe, and he would get that information to her so they could uncover whatever deception might exist within the university, if there was one.

Alec turned back to the university, smiling to himself. All it took was that brief time with Sam for him to feel better. Maybe Beckah and his father were right. Maybe his feelings for her were much deeper than he had acknowledged. And maybe Alec didn't care. If it meant that he could work with Sam, and that he could protect her, why did it matter?

17

THE ASSIGNMENT

The university was quiet, calm for this time of morning, and Alec clutched his set of journals to his side, not wanting to drop them. The journals were his most prized possessions. They held his notes from all of the sessions that he'd studied, lessons that he'd had from the various masters, and he dreaded losing any of them. He no longer felt comfortable leaving them in his room, especially since Beckah had played that prank on him. If she was willing to play pranks, and was willing to compromise the accuracy of his journals, he would need to keep them with him.

But there would come a time when his journals would be too heavy to carry with him. Eventually, he'd have to store them somewhere else, and he wasn't certain where he could store them safely.

"I'm not going to change do anything to your precious journals," Beckah said, glancing over at him.

Alec looked over at her, and he only shrugged. "That's

what you want me to believe. How do I know that you won't pull some prank on me again?"

"If I were going to play a prank on you, I wouldn't do the same one. It's only fun once."

"It wasn't funny the first time," Alec said.

"Maybe not to you, but I thought it was funny."

"Can you focus?" he asked.

"I am focused. Just because you're worried about this doesn't mean that I need to have the same concern," she said.

"If what Sam told me was true, then we all need to be concerned." Lowering his voice, he said, "If Marin has a Scribe in the university it puts us at risk."

"Have you talked to Master Eckerd?"

"I haven't been able to find Master Eckerd," Alec said. That bothered him, though he knew that it shouldn't. Master Eckerd owed him nothing, and as one of the master physickers, he would be free to pursue his own studies. There were other master physickers that Alec knew were Scribes, but he didn't know them well enough, certainly not well enough to question.

"Well, now is not really the time to try to find him," Beckah said. "If we are late to Master Carl's class, he's only going to be angrier at you."

"Only me?"

"He might be angry at me, but if I come in with you, he'll focus most of his attention on you." She smiled. "That's an added benefit of spending time with you."

"Great," he said.

"At least there *are* benefits to spending time with you."

"You don't have to. You're more than welcome to avoid me."

"If I did, I think you'd miss me."

They hurried along the hall and came to their classroom. Alec was surprised to see that Master Carl wasn't there, not yet. Where was he?

They took their seats, neither of them saying anything. A few others were present, but Master Carl's lectures were never meant for a large class. He preferred to keep his sessions more intimate, better for him to harass more students.

"Where do you think he is?" Alec asked.

"I don't know. Maybe we're early."

Alec arched a brow at her. "When have we ever been to one of these lectures early?"

"I seem to recall that you used to be early to most of them," Beckah said.

"That's true," Alec said. "That's what kind of a bad influence you've been."

"I think you are mistaking bad for entertaining."

"And I think you fail to know what entertaining means."

The door opened, and Master Carl swept in. He glanced around the room, and when his gaze fell on Alec, his expression soured. He clasped his hands behind his back, thrusting his belly outward. He stood tall, his back curved, and paced in the front of the classroom. "Today, we will be discussing techniques for assessing injury. I would have you all take out your notebooks."

Everyone quickly grabbed for a notebook. Alec already had his on his desk. Master Carl took a piece of chalk and began scratching on the enormous chalkboard that covered the front of the room. He drew a diagram of a body, with far more skill than Alec would have expected from Master Carl. It surprised him that he had such artistic ability. Then again, it shouldn't surprise him. Master Carl wasn't incapable.

"Now, let's discuss internal injuries. There are many theories about which internal injury would be the worst, if only because they're difficult to diagnose and subsequently treat. Which injury would you be most concerned about?"

Master Carl looked at Alec, practically daring him to answer.

He had read about internal injuries, but only recently. Working with his father, they hadn't had much time to study such things, mostly because if such patients came to the apothecary, his father sent them on to the university. There were limits to what his father could treat, the kind of limits that made him unwilling to attempt surgery with the breech delivery.

But Alec's interest in injuries came from his time working with Sam. So far, using his own skills and having access to easar paper had been enough. But if she were injured again—and he was all too certain she would be— he wanted to be able to help her quickly, and he couldn't do that without being able to assess the nature of her injuries. It forced him to explore the various types of injuries that she might sustain. He hoped he'd never have to bring her to the university in the event her injuries were beyond his abilities, but that concerned him. The more that he learned about her role as Kaver, the more he wondered whether or not that would be possible. With the right master physickers, she could come to the university and be healed, but there were times when that might not be possible, and when questions might arise, espe-

188 | D.K. HOLMBERG

cially if she went off on her own, searching for Marin and information about her.

"No one cares to answer?" Master Carl asked.

Barnath stood, drawing attention to him. He was slightly older than Alec, and quite a bit heavier, and Alec had no problem with him other than the fact that he seemed to lack a spine. "My research has shown that a kidney injury would be the most devastating."

Beckah snickered. Barnath shot her a hard look, and she only shrugged. "A kidney injury could bleed, and it can be painful, but it's not typically fatal," she said. "Not like an injury to one of the upper organs, like the liver or the spleen."

Master Carl glanced at Alec before answering. "Very good. I can tell that some of you have been reading."

Beckah grinned at the compliment. Getting one from Master Carl was rare, and Alec knew she was deserving of the compliments.

"And yes, Ms. Reynolds is right. Such injuries often are worse than a kidney injury, especially as they can be difficult to diagnose. There is often pain, but occasionally, it is not the type of pain you would expect." Master Carl turned to the chalkboard and began drawing, detailing pictures of the internal organs. As he did, he pointed to some of the upper organs, the liver and the spleen, and placed a large X over each of them. "Without these, a person does not survive, at least not for long."

Alec bit back a smile. He had seen otherwise. Not losing a liver—that seemed to be a crucial organ—but he had seen people survive a spleen injury. From what he could tell, it was an unessential organ.

"Mr. Stross. Do you have something to say?"

Perhaps he hadn't bitten back his smile quite as well as he thought he had. "No."

Master Carl studied him for a moment, his glare lingering before he finally turned away and began to lecture, droning on about the various organs and their functions. Alec was able to tune him out, focusing on trying to think through how he was going to approach Sam's request. Most of this information was not new to him. He had read about the known physiology, and his father had quizzed him, ensuring that he did know what the various organs were for.

When the class got out, Master Carl left first, as was his habit. Most of the students waited for Master Carl to depart, not wanting to follow him too closely. If they did, they ran the risk of him asking additional questions, something that few students wanted, especially from Master Carl.

"What was that about?" Beckah asked.

"What was what about?" Alec said.

"Your lack of interest in this talk today. Normally, you're taking notes. Normally, you're one of the more engaged, asking questions. But today, you just sat there, staring blankly. So, what was it about?"

"It wasn't about anything," Alec said. "I... I'm distracted, that's all."

"I can see that you're distracted, I'm just asking why."

"You know why."

"I know you're concerned that there is something you don't understand, but that's not the same as you losing focus during a lecture. You're usually the first one to speak up, and one of the first to ask questions. So, for you to be silent... I think you might have made Master Carl happy, but I'm not sure that was your intent."

"I'm just troubled by what Sam told me. If there is anything going on with the master physickers, and if the Scribes have hidden their presence here, I think we need to be more concerned about what they might be after."

"Which is why you need to go to Master Eckerd. He's shown that he's willing to listen to you. More than anyone else, I think he would be the one to talk to about this."

"And I told you that I don't know how to find him. The one time I tried, I..."

Alec flushed. He hadn't told Beckah about that.

"What do you mean you tried?"

"I went to the masters' quarters," Alec said, lowering his voice. They were in the hall and kept some distance between themselves and the other students. "I was looking for Master Eckerd, but he wasn't in his rooms. Instead, I found Master Jessup."

"That was lucky," she said.

"Why?"

"Only that Master Jessup is probably as good an instructor as Master Eckerd. Both are only slightly below Master Helen."

"Do you know Master Helen?" Alec asked.

"No more than anyone can know her."

"Other than Stefan."

"Well, Stefan is a unique case. Grandma does tend to give him quite a bit of attention," Beckah said.

"Maybe I should be going to Stefan to see what Grandma Helen might be able to do to help with this."

"Do you think she would help?"

Alec shrugged. He didn't know. When it came to the masters, it was difficult to know what they might be willing to do. Master Helen would be among the more difficult ones to know. He hadn't spent much time with her, not the way that some had, and even though she was Stefan's grandmother, she was still a mystery to him. And there was her connection to the princess, who was also a Scribe.

Beckah grabbed his sleeve and pulled him along the hallway. Alec followed, knowing that when she got something into her mind like that, she wasn't easily deterred. And he wasn't sure he wanted to deter her. He considered speaking to Master Jessup, but he didn't know if he was one of the Scribe physickers, and he knew that Master Eckerd and Helen were.

They reached the student section. Beckah guided him to Stefan's room, and they knocked. They waited for a while, but there was no answer.

"Maybe he's down in the wards," Alec said.

"Stefan? He doesn't go down to the wards unless he has to."

"He was down there with me the other day," Alec said. "He has been working with Master Jessup, so I think that he might be there now."

"First you and now Stefan working with Master Jessup? I'm beginning to feel like I've been pushed out."

"You could ask to work with him," Alec said.

"No. You know they don't like it when we make requests like that. They consider it being too forward. It's better for me to stay with Master Isabel, and eventually, maybe I can ask to study with Master Jessup." She glanced over at Alec and arched a brow. "Or maybe I could even ask about Master Eckerd. I bet he'll get to a point where he's tired of explaining things to you."

"Be my guest. I will tell you that he can be demanding."

"More demanding than Master Carl?"

"I'm not sure Master Carl is—" Alec hesitated, realizing that there was someone behind them.

He turned and saw Master Carl standing in one of the side hallways. "Do go on, Mr. Stross. Tell me what you are not sure Master Carl is."

Alec flushed. "I was just going to say that I'm not sure Master Carl was finished teaching us everything about internal injuries."

"Is that right? Are you so certain that you know my teaching method?"

"I wouldn't dare question your teaching methods," Alec said. "All I'm trying to say is—"

"I know what you're trying to say," Master Carl said. "I've seen it from you too many times. You come in here thinking that your time with your father has made you equal—if not superior—to any of our students, but it does not. That's not to say, were you to apply yourself, that you couldn't be incredibly skilled. I won't deny a bright mind when I see one, and if you were to take some time and apply yourself, you might make something of yourself here."

Master Carl watched him, and Alec said nothing. There didn't seem to be anything he could say, and certainly not without offending Master Carl. He turned and strode off, leaving them alone in the hallway.

"That was strange," Beckah said.

"The fact that he complimented me?" Alec asked.

Beckah shook her head. "No. If you pay attention,

you'll notice that Master Carl can be much kinder than you realize. He's a blowhard, but he means well, at least, most of the time."

"What was strange, then?"

Beckah looked along the hallway, and Alec followed the direction of her gaze. There were a few other students out here. Many were going in or out of their rooms, and considering the size of the university, and the number of students who studied here, it wasn't all too surprising that there would be so many people here.

But there were only students.

"Why would Master Carl be in the student section?" Beckah asked, putting words to his own confusion. She had noted the oddity of the master's presence far more quickly than he had.

"There are lots of reasons that he could be here," Alec said.

"Really?" She turned to him, crossing her arms over her chest. "Lots of reasons for a master to be in the student section?"

Alec shrugged. "There would have to be. I saw Master Jessup come through here, using this as a sort of back access to the wards."

"He did that?" She smiled. "I could see Master Jessup doing something like that. He probably thought to take a shortcut."

"He said that it was nostalgic for him."

Beckah shook her head. "If I ever get nostalgic for these quarters, I want you to hit me."

"What makes you think I will still know you when you're a master physicker."

"You don't think you will still be speaking to me then?"

Alec shrugged. "I don't know. Maybe you'll have grown tired of me by then."

"I think I'm tired of you now."

Alec smiled, and he couldn't shake the same concern that Beckah had, the same question she had about why Master Carl would have come through here. It could be something innocuous, but given what he had heard from Sam, he was on edge. Nothing was innocuous, not anymore. Now everything that master physickers did needed to be questioned.

"Let's find Stefan and see if we can't see what Grandma Helen might have told him," Alec said. "Maybe he can help us get an audience with her."

"Is that really something you think you want to do?" Beckah asked. She clutched her arms around herself and shivered. "That woman terrifies me."

"She makes me uncomfortable, too. The last time I saw her, she basically told me I needed to return to the university and stop wasting time."

"The last time? Where was it that you came across her?"

"At the palace," Alec said.

"Master Helen was at the palace?"

"I get the sense that she is working with the Anders family. She's been working with Sam, trying to help her with her memory loss."

Beckah's eyes widened slightly. "She's a Scribe. Which means—"

"Which means nothing. It could be that she was there only because she was summoned by the royal family to answer questions. It could be that those who know about the Kavers and Scribes called her over."

"It could be that she's someone's Scribe," Beckah said.

Alec had thought about it, but had discarded it. If she was someone's Scribe, wouldn't she have been over at the palace more often?

But then, wouldn't he be over at the palace more often, since they were now aware that he was Sam's Scribe?

It was even more reason to find Master Eckerd.

If only he could figure out where he'd gone. Why had he disappeared?

Given what Master Eckerd knew of Alec, and vice versa, he thought the man would have stuck around to help Alec understand. To provide the answers he needed. Because he'd expected his help, the master physicker's disappearance left him unsettled.

Beckah watched him and nodded. "Come on. Let's get going and see if we can't get some answers for you so that you can stop looking at me like that."

"Looking at you like what?"

"Like you aren't certain what to make of me."

"I'm pretty sure I know what to make of you. It's the master physickers that I'm still not able to figure out."

"Then let's find a way to figure it out."

18

TREATMENT PLAN

"What is your assessment?" Master Harrison asked. The students were arranged around a cot in the hospital ward. It held an older man, and he had yellowing to his face and arms. There was a strange, almost fetid odor. Alec held his nose, though he had dealt with similar stench in the past. This one didn't bother him nearly as much as some.

"Jaundice," someone called from the back of the bed.

Master Harrison grunted. "Perhaps we can get something that is a bit more detailed than that?"

"Jaundice like that is typically related to inflammation in the bile connections," Alec said.

"Very good, Mr. Stross. What more can you tell me other than what you read in the surgical journals that Master Eckerd has allowed you to study?"

Alec frowned. Were all the masters going to pick on him for his connection to Master Eckerd? He didn't think that was something he deserved, but he recognized the irritation. It wasn't as if he had demanded that Master

Eckerd include him, but then, he hadn't complained when he was pulled into the surgical suites.

"There are different types of inflammation that can contribute to jaundice," Alec answered. He started thinking about what his father had taught him about this kind of jaundice. Many of them were surgical cases, though there were some that were not, and those were the ones that he hoped to treat. Those that were surgical would often be fatal, especially since so few would be able to afford the treatment at the university. This was even more reason for Alec's bewilderment that his father had been unwilling to perform any surgeries. "We would first need to know if it was painful or painless."

"And why would that make a difference?"

"The presence of pain often indicates the need of a master physicker, and the patient would likely need to be treated here at the university."

"And considering that you are here at the university, why should that matter?"

Alec flushed. "Because there are various medicinal approaches to jaundice which could be diagnosed and treated by others. Even those who appear to be untreatable can be targeted with the right combination of medicines and show improvement."

Master Harrison considered him for a long moment before nodding. "That is acceptable. Though I would say that your knowledge is rudimentary. I expected more from you, especially given what I've heard."

Alec flushed again. It felt as if he was being targeted, and he thought that was unfair, especially since he hadn't done anything to deserve the attention. All he wanted was a chance to prove himself, and to learn, and if the physickers were going to continue to target him because he spoke up, maybe he shouldn't. He needed to learn how not to draw additional attention to himself. He couldn't risk not being allowed to learn from them.

Master Harrison continued his lecture, talking about various treatments, and Alec barely paid attention. He knew that he should focus better, and he knew that ignoring him would only anger Master Harrison, but he preferred to focus on what Master Harrison might know about the Scribes. It was possible that Master Harrison was the very Scribe that Sam wanted him to search for.

Beckah nudged him, and he glanced over. "Aren't you going to pay attention?" she whispered.

"I am paying attention."

"But you're not speaking up," she said. "All of this is very much unlike you."

"I'm trying to keep an eye on things," he said.

"You can't really believe that Master Harrison might be—"

"Master Harrison might be what, Ms. Reynolds?" Master Harrison asked.

Beckah flushed. "Nothing," she said. "I was just trying to see if Mr. Stross might help me better understand this jaundice that you're demonstrating to us."

"Indeed? Well, if that's the case, then perhaps Mr. Stross can share with us what he knows. I would be most curious to hear about what he has discovered."

"I haven't discovered anything," he said, shooting Beckah a hard glare. What was she thinking drawing attention to him? Did she want to get him into trouble with Master Harrison? "Only that a combination of epson roots and tearath leaves might be effective with treating this type of jaundice."

He said it without thinking too much, though he knew it was correct. It was the kind of treatment he would have suggested to his father, though there, he wouldn't have had the same concern about what response he would get by suggesting it.

Master Harrison watched Alec for a moment. "Is that right? And by what mechanism would you feel these combinations would be effective?"

Alec sighed. He was growing frustrated and knew that he shouldn't, but he couldn't help it. "The epson root will help absorb some of the toxins that cause the jaundice. The tearath leaves will help restore the individual."

Master Harrison tipped his head in a slight nod. "That would be an interesting combination. Is this something your father helped you discover?"

"This is something that my father has done before."

"Yes, well he always was quite the expert with knowing his medicinal uses, wasn't he?"

Alec could only stare. There was no sarcasm in his tone. No biting jab about his father being just an apothecary. It was said as a statement of fact. It was the first that he'd heard of his father being renowned for his knowledge of medicinal uses of different leaves and other treatments. He knew that his father was quite skilled, but hearing about it from a master physicker at the university was surprising.

Master Harrison made a few notes, and then he guided the group of students away from the jaundice man, heading to another station. Alec paused and reached for the record to see what Master Harrison had documented.

He scanned the page and was not surprised to see that his notes reflected what Alec had said, but he was surprised to see that Master Harrison had included a notation that Alec had been the one to suggest it.

"What is it?" Beckah asked.

"It's nothing," Alec said.

"It's something—"

Beckah looked over his shoulder, and when she saw the notation, her eyes widened. "You should be pleased."

"I don't know whether to be pleased or concerned."

"Why would you be concerned?"

"Not concerned, but..." Alec looked around. "I'm not trying to draw additional attention to myself."

"You're not trying, but you do it so well."

"That's just the problem. I don't *want* to do that well. I want to help people, and I don't have any problem with the knowledge that my father taught me being used in that way, but I feel like I'm not getting the kind of attention that I should be."

"What kind of attention do you think you should be getting?"

Alec didn't know. "We should move on. We can't linger. It's just one more way to draw the wrong kind of attention."

Beckah smiled. "Well if you wouldn't keep letting your mind drift off, maybe that wouldn't be a problem."

"My mind is not drifting off, but what if Master Harrison wants me to draw attention?"

"You can't believe that Master Harrison is involved in this."

Alec shook his head. "As I said, I don't know what to

make of anyone anymore. It could be that any one of the physickers could be involved."

"How will you figure it out?"

Alec frowned to himself. "Somehow, I have to find a way to get them together, that way Sam could sneak in and maybe listen in. She said she thought she would recognize the Scribe's voice."

"Your plan is to bring the masters together and see which one she recognizes?"

"If I can't figure it out otherwise, maybe I will have to."

"We still haven't found Master Helen. Maybe she can help us still."

Stefan hadn't been able to provide any answers, or arrange for them to meet with Master Helen. He wasn't exactly close to his grandmother, not in the way that would allow him to bring his friends in front of her to ask questions.

"Maybe."

As they headed on to the next person, Alec nodded to Master Jessup as he brought in his group of students. The man smiled widely, wrinkling his bushy eyebrows, and led his students to the far side of the room. If only Alec knew whether Master Jessup was a Scribe or not. If he was, he could ask what he knew about the other Scribes. Without knowing, he couldn't risk asking, and was left with more questions.

19

CONFRONTING THE KAVER

The inside of the palace was dark. Anger still rolled through Sam, and she knew that she needed to control it, but after what Elaine had done to her, she found that more difficult than she thought she would have. But her anger was tempered by the fact that she had actually learned something during her horrific experience, and as a result, she would no longer be trapped on this island. Now she could flip her way to freedom. Even without an augmentation, she could balance her way across the canal.

When she reached Elaine's room, she pounded on the door.

Elaine pulled it open and nodded. "You survived."

"That's all you have to say to me?"

"I had no doubt that you would survive, Samara. Had you not figured out how to make your own way back, the barge would have picked you up and brought you here," Elaine said. "What more did you want me to say?"

"The barge left."

"The barge would not have left. You might not have seen it, but they were there in case you failed."

"And what of the eels?"

"The eels avoid the swamp," Elaine said.

"Not the one that followed me," she said.

"You must be mistaken."

"Mistaken? I think I'd recognize an eel."

"It's unlikely that you would have even seen an eel," Elaine said.

"Seen an eel? The damned thing watched me! It swam alongside me as I was flipping my way back to the city. Why wouldn't it have followed me? It probably saw me as lunch."

Elaine was silent for a moment and then she sighed. "You were in no danger."

"No danger? I have felt the bite of an eel before," Sam said.

"And I'm telling you that you were in no danger."

Sam pushed her way into Elaine's room, and Elaine closed the door behind her. It was a simple room. A thick rug covered the floor, a simple table and chair sat in a corner, and a narrow bed rested along one wall. It was the kind of room that appeared to be more for utility than for comfort. Sam hadn't spent much time in the room, though partly because she had avoided Elaine as much as she could. She was willing to train with her mother, but she didn't want to have any sort of relationship with her, especially given that Elaine was reluctant to have one with her.

"The eels would not have bitten you," Elaine said.

"And I'm telling you they have in the past, and they would again." Sam glared at Elaine for a moment. "Why are you so determined to tell me what the eels would and wouldn't do? Why is it that you think you know everything about them?"

Elaine shook her head. "It's nothing."

"It's something, otherwise you wouldn't appear so confident about it."

"I'm glad you made it back. You have proven that you now have the ability to cross the canals without an augmentation. Now, your training can begin in earnest."

"My training? You would have me believe that all of this was about my training?"

Elaine crossed her arms over her chest. "Tell me, Samara, did you not just successfully cross the swamp with only your canal staff? Were you able to do that without an augmentation?"

"I'm here, aren't I?"

"Yes. You are here. As I've said, you managed to cross a section of the swamp with only your staff. Eventually, you will be able to cross the entirety of the swamp with only your staff."

Sam's eyes widened. "The entirety of the swamp? And will you let me have augmentations then?"

"Why would you need augmentations when you can do this without them?"

"Because the augmentations make it easier."

"Easier doesn't mean that it is better or even right. Easier only means that you have given up on using your own gifts."

"And if I cross the swamp and have no strength to fight if necessary?"

"If you are able to cross without the benefit of augmentation, it means you have the strength and the ability on your own. That same strength would see you through any possible confrontation." Elaine paused, watching Sam for a long moment. "I have made that crossing many times. Only once have I ever used an augmentation, and that was when Thelns were chasing me. Trust me when I tell you that you do not need your augmentations."

Sam breathed out heavily. Elaine had crossed the swamp many times? Even the small section that Sam had gone across had been difficult, she couldn't imagine making that crossing multiple times. And to do so without augmentations?

She had challenged Elaine's method of "training," but maybe there was more to what she was trying to get Sam to learn than what she was giving her credit for. What else might there be that she didn't know? What else might there be that she needed to learn so that she could be a more effective Kaver?

Wasn't it the same reason that Alec wanted to stay at the university? He knew that there were things they could teach that he couldn't learn otherwise. That was the very reason he had gone to the university in the first place. There were things that Sam couldn't learn any other way than training with other Kavers. That was why she was here.

"What now?" Sam asked.

"Now your training will continue. It does not get any easier, Samara. Do not think that I will take it easy on you because you are my daughter. I can't."

"What do you mean that you can't?"

"I can't be perceived as favoring you, and giving you an easier pathway to understanding your abilities than anyone else who has come here to train. There are few enough of us as it is, and we must be challenged so that we can be as skilled as we possibly can. The threat is real —and significant. We must be ready to oppose it."

Sam didn't know what to say. Instead, she simply stared. These were the things that Marin knew, and the things that Sam did not yet know. She had defeated her once, but had it only been because she was lucky? If she didn't train and learn what she needed to know as a Kaver, would she ultimately end up on the wrong end of one of Marin's attacks?

She needed to prepare.

"What about Marin and the Thelns? What about Ralun?"

"Do you see that you're not ready?" Elaine asked.

"I don't see anything other than that there are answers I want that I can't get. You aren't telling me anything."

"Do you think that you are the only one who has questions that have gone unanswered? Do you think that you're the only one who has been wronged in all of this?"

"Why can't you be more forthcoming with me?" Sam said. She wanted answers, and Elaine was not giving them to her.

"Get some rest, Samara. Your training will continue tomorrow. And as I've told you, it will not be any easier."

Sam stared at Elaine for a moment before finally sighing and turning away. There wasn't anything else for her to say.

As Sam walked out the door, frustration surged through her. Elaine wasn't going to share anything more than she already had, and it annoyed her to no end. But even the little her mother had shared made Sam finally admit to herself that she knew even less than she thought, and that she needed to listen to Elaine and be willing to follow her lead. Sam wanted to know more about what Marin's Scribe might be after, but it was clearer than ever that she wasn't prepared to face Marin, not without help.

The door closed behind her, and Sam debated going to her room, but she didn't think she could sleep. Her mind was racing, and all she could think about was what she had experienced.

A part of her wanted to go back to the university and to speak with Alec, but even that wouldn't be appropriate. He needed to have time on his own to study, and she'd already tasked him with something that hopefully would get her more information.

There had to be something she could do. If she couldn't sleep, and if she was no longer confined to this island, what should she do?

She stopped outside the palace grounds, staring up at the moon. It was late, a time of night when she was accustomed to sneaking. She tapped her canal staff on the ground, enjoying the way that it rang out, a soft sound that was muted by the night.

Taking a deep breath, she glanced up at the palace and the lights glowing inside. Did Elaine know that she had departed the palace?

Sam wouldn't put it past her to keep tabs on her, but what did it matter if she did? Once she left this section, there wouldn't be quite the same ease for Elaine to track her.

And though she might not know nearly as much as

Marin, that didn't mean she couldn't collect information. It didn't mean that she had to be reliant upon Elaine to provide her with what she wanted to know. She could go off on her own, to the place where she might learn some of the answers she sought.

But would Bastan help?

20

AN OLD FRIEND

"You never came back."

Sam stared at Bastan. His gray hair was slicked back, and he was dressed well in a black jacket and pants, clothing that would fit in any highborn section. Where had he been? Papers were stacked on his desk even higher than they had been before, and he shifted a page, as if trying to conceal something from her. Typical of Bastan.

"It was Tray."

"I know it was Tray. But you were supposed to do something for me."

"Your contact was dead." Sam didn't want to tell him that it might have been Tray who had been the one to take out his contact. Or it might have been Ralun, though neither explanation made a whole lot of sense. She still didn't know how Bastan had known where to find Tray and didn't know why Ralun would have a shared interest in the contact of Bastan's.

"So I've heard. My sources of information out of that section now are limited."

"I doubt that's true. I suspect you have multiple contacts there."

"I have a few," Bastan said.

Sam shook her head, laughing to herself. "You have a few. Knowing you, you have more than that."

Bastan clasped his hands on the desk, looking over at her. His eyes hardened slightly, and his gaze swept over her, taking in her cloak and her staff. He looked like he wanted to say something, but bit back whatever it was.

"What is it?" Sam asked.

"It's you," Bastan said.

"Yes? And what about me?"

"You and your disappearance. You've been gone, and I don't care for it. I don't like worrying about you."

Sam chuckled softly. "You don't have to worry about me. I know how to take care of myself."

"I understand that. But I've grown used to keeping tabs on you."

"You've been keeping track of me all this time?"

"Not this time. You're silent to me in that section."

Did he know how much time she'd been spending in the palace? Knowing Bastan, he likely would try to use that, thinking that Sam could help him somehow, and knowing her, considering how much Bastan had helped her over the years, especially lately, she would feel compelled to at least consider helping him.

"I don't like not knowing what's happening with you."

Sam started to smile, but she saw the irritation on his face, and her smile faded. She'd always known that Bastan had a soft spot for her. He used her for some of the best jobs, and though he had forced her to work for him, she also knew that he was responsible for keeping her safe.

There had been plenty of times over the years when she could have been in much more trouble, had it not been for him. It was known throughout Caster that Bastan always made sure to protect her, and that fact kept her safe from other unsavory types in the city.

"I've been fine," she said.

"All I need to know is that you are well, Samara. Whatever else happens, just make sure that you send word to me."

Sam frowned. She had to send word to Alec, and now she would have to send word to Bastan? "I haven't exactly been able to get away before now."

"Are they holding you against your will?"

"I think it was more of a training exercise," Sam said. "It appears I have passed, so I'm hopeful that things will get better."

"So why have you come to me now, Samara?" Bastan asked.

"I'm hurt that you would think I'd hold off on coming to you," she said.

"I doubt that you're hurt. There's only been one thing that I've seen hurt you in the time that I've known you, Samara." When she shot him a look full of irritation, he waved his hand. "You do understand that your feelings for Tray are transparent?"

"I want to do whatever I can to help him," Sam said. "I don't know if he knows what he's gotten himself into."

"Do you understand what he's gotten himself into?"

"Maybe better than Tray does."

Bastan stared at her for a moment before sighing. "What do you need from me?"

"A favor," she said.

"What kind of favor? And why do I have a feeling that this favor is going to benefit you far more than it will benefit me?"

"What if I could make certain that it would benefit you?"

Bastan leaned back in his chair and put his hand up to pinch his chin thoughtfully. "That might be worthwhile," he said. "But it would have to be something that would make sense for me."

"You trade in information, Bastan. All I'm asking is that you be somewhat free with the information you have."

"You want to know what I've heard about Marin."

The fact that Bastan knew what she was looking for shouldn't have surprised her. He had an uncanny knack for knowing such things. It was how he was always one step ahead. He made certain that he was prepared, knowing in advance when people might be coming to him, and for what reason.

"I was hoping you might have heard something," Sam admitted.

"I shared with you what I knew before, and you didn't complete the job I asked you to perform in return."

"The job was wrong," Sam said.

"Wrong? You wanted to know about your brother, and I gave information about where to find him."

"The information that you gave me ended up with me being attacked, Bastan. Is that what you intended?"

He stared at her for a long moment before shaking his head. "You know that it wasn't."

"What happened?"

Bastan breathed out. "I don't know. It shouldn't have happened that way. I have connections there that should have prevented such a catastrophe."

"Losing a contact was a catastrophe?"

"Yes. Almost as much as nearly losing you."

That surprised Sam. Bastan had never struck her as someone who was particularly sentimental, and maybe it wasn't that he was sentimental as much as the fact that he valued his contacts because of the information they provided. Yet Bastan treated Sam with kindness, and there was a part of her that wondered if perhaps she misread Bastan and misread his intentions.

"Who was this contact to you?"

Bastan stared at her for a moment. "She was a friend."

A friend. Bastan didn't admit to having too many friends, so for him to say that told Sam this person had been more than just a contact and meant much more to him than he had let on. "What if I told you that I knew something about what happened to this friend of yours?"

"I would tell you that was valuable."

"The person who is responsible is dangerous, Bastan."

"You don't think that I'm dangerous?"

"You're dangerous, but this person..."

Bastan smiled. "This person what?"

"This person is probably more dangerous than you." When he frowned, she shrugged. "I'm sorry. I know you take pride in your position, but there are some things that even the great Bastan isn't equipped to handle."

"And you are?"

"Maybe not yet. Not the way I might need to be. But I'm getting there," she said. She would continue to train, because that was what was needed for her to understand her Kaver abilities, but her desire to continue to train was about more than that. It was about being able to defend herself, and being able to counter Ralun if he were to attack again. Now that he knew more about her, she suspected that he *would* attack.

And what role would Tray have in that?

Sam didn't like to think about her brother being involved with Ralun, but what better way for him to understand his connection to the Thelns than going to someone like Ralun? And what did his connection mean?

Those are questions that she would have to save for Marin if she could ever find the woman.

That was why she needed Bastan. She needed information. Not only about Tray—and Bastan would be able to help with that, she suspected, but also about Marin and this Scribe.

For her to get Bastan's help would require Sam to reveal information. That was how it worked with Bastan. He needed an equal exchange.

"Tray took Marin somewhere. The man I believe attacked your contact—a Theln—is working with Tray."

"I remember you mentioning something about Thelns before. You said they were dangerous."

"They're very dangerous."

"And they were responsible for destroying my first tavern?"

"As far as I know," Sam said.

"Do you know that we heard nothing after that attack? There was no reason for it. There was no word about the intent behind it. There was simply the explosion in the city and the nothing more. It's unusual. Typically, if someone were to come at me, they would continue to come at me, but these people did nothing other than destroy my tavern. And you know something about it?"

"I know that they attacked you because they were trying to get to me."

"Interesting. And what about now?"

"Now might be the same. Especially now that he knows that I'm here."

"From the way you describe the last time you faced him, he was aware of you, and came after you in particular."

"He did, but he also did so back when I knew nothing."

"And now you know something?"

"More than I did before."

"And this is why I should help you?"

"If you want to get revenge for your friend's death, you should help me. Listen. I don't know exactly what purpose he has in coming back to the city. From everything I've heard, there should be no reason for him to be here, but he is. So—"

Bastan leaned forward. "But you say he's here because of you?"

"I don't know."

Bastan watched her for a moment. Sam did her best to hold his gaze. She'd known Bastan a long time and had been on the receiving end of that accusatory stare before, but even after all these years, it was hard not to look away. There was an intensity to his gaze, and something like compassion. That last part was what troubled her the most. It unsettled her to have Bastan looking at her with anything bordering on compassion.

"There is some rumor of movement near the northern

edge of the city," Bastan said, shuffling some papers on his desk. "Typically, something like that wouldn't gain much attention, but considering what happened, and the way that my last contact disappeared"—he looked back up at her, an unreadable expression on his face—"I question this one a little bit more. I intend to go and look into it myself."

Sam frowned. "You're going to go yourself?"

"Shouldn't I?"

"If it's this man, then you absolutely shouldn't."

"If it's this man, then I absolutely should," Bastan said.

"You don't understand, Bastan."

"What I understand is that whoever this man is has you scared. I understand that he might be the one who hurt someone I promised to protect. And I understand that you are keeping something from me, and whether it's because you think to protect me or for another reason, I don't particularly care for it." He glanced back down to his pages. "Now, if you are interested in finding out what's going on, you're welcome to come with me."

Sam blinked. That was perhaps the most unusual part of this entire conversation. She had often done jobs *for* Bastan, but she had never worked *with* Bastan. He must have taken jobs on his own at one point, but as long as she had worked for him, she had never seen him do so. The way that some people talked about him indicated that he had some skill, and Sam wouldn't be surprised to find out that he was a skilled thief, but going after a Theln? Even with augmentations, Sam wasn't sure that was something that she wanted to do.

"Bastan—"

"Sam." He looked up, his hands resting crossed on the

desk. "As I said, you're welcome to come with me, but don't think I'm going to provide you any details otherwise. This isn't a job that I'm going to assign to you. If you want to know more about what I might have heard, you will have to come with me."

"Even if it means placing yourself—and me—in danger?"

Bastan studied her for a long moment. "How do you think I've risen to my position, Samara? Do you think that I've done it by avoiding danger?"

"No, it's just—"

"It has taken me being willing to put myself into harm's way. Sometimes, I do so knowingly, and sometimes, I run into unanticipated challenges. Either way, I'm not necessarily afraid."

"When it comes to the Thelns, you should be."

Bastan studied her for a moment before offering a slight shrug of his shoulders. "You decide whether you intend to come with me, Sam. I suspect that I will leave soon."

What choice did Sam have? She wanted to learn more about what Marin might be doing, and where Tray might be holding her, and that meant finding Ralun and figuring out what he was after. Everyone seemed to think he was after Sam, but she doubted she was enough of a threat to draw him into the city. That meant there was something else that he was after.

What was it? And how was he even here? If the canals were intact—if the attempt to poison the eels had failed—how had Ralun and the Thelns reached the city?

But of greater interest to her was the Book. If she could find the Book, she could finally begin to understand something about herself. She might finally understand what happened to her and where she came from. And why Marin had used her.

"Fine. I'm coming with you."

Bastan nodded as if it had never been in question.

21

LATE NIGHT IN THE LIBRARY

Beckah pointed to the side of the hallway, pushing Alec over there. It was dimly lit, a single lantern near the end of the hall the only light at this time of day, and otherwise empty. It was late enough that they were the only ones wandering about. Were they discovered, they would have to answer questions about their presence, questions that wouldn't necessarily have easy answers.

"Are you sure you saw her come through here?" Alec asked.

"I already told you that," Beckah said, annoyance in her voice.

Stefan shook his head. "My grandmother wouldn't come to the library. She would have books brought to her. You don't understand what she's like."

"I understand her by her reputation," Beckah said. "Just as I understand that even people who we don't normally see in the library often wait until it's empty, and then they will when they have free rein within it." She looked over at the two of them, frowning. "And if you don't think your grandmother goes to the library, then you haven't been paying attention. I've seen her there several times. She never stays in the common section, always going back to the area exclusive to the masters, but she has been there, especially lately."

Stefan frowned. "Lately? What would have come up for Grandma Helen to have decided to go to the library? It's not as if there's anything there she needs to be researching."

"That's where I think you're wrong," Beckah said. "She's working on something. Regardless of whether you know it or not, there is something there that she is looking into."

"Why do I get the sense that you're intending to see what she might be after?" Stefan asked.

"It's not for me. All of this is for Alec and his issue."

Stefan looked at Alec. "Why again do you need to find Master Eckerd?"

"Let's just say that I think that Master Eckerd can help me explore my studies better." He hadn't decided how much to share with Stefan, and he didn't like the idea of keeping things from him, but there didn't seem to be much of a choice. If he could get them to Master Helen, then she could decide how much to reveal. Until then, Alec didn't feel comfortable revealing anything to anyone else. Had Beckah not already known, he would've kept it from her.

"You know, we don't have to be so careful heading into the library. Just because it's late doesn't mean that were not allowed to go there," Stefan said.

"We're not disallowed, but it would raise questions," Alec said without thinking. He should have known better.

"Why would it raise questions?" Stefan asked.

Beckah pushed him. "Only because Alec is being ridiculous. I think he's nervous about the attention he's getting from various masters."

"I would think he would be happy with that attention. It's because of that attention that you've been allowed into the surgical suite. You even got Master Jessup talking about you, and I can't remember the last time he's spoken so highly of someone."

"That's the kind of attention I don't want to get," Alec said. "It gets people talking about me."

"People were talking about you even before," Stefan said. "You might as well enjoy it."

Alec sighed. "I don't know that there's anything I can enjoy, not when it comes to this."

He looked at the door to the library, and he made a decision, pushing it open. Beckah followed him, with Stefan only a little behind them.

Once inside, they found the library darkened. Alec wasn't surprised by that. It was well beyond the normal time for students to use the library, and anyone coming after hours would likely be one of the masters, not someone who would require the librarian's assistance. He turned the brightness up on one of the lanterns and looked around. It was strange being in the library with it completely empty.

"Where did you hear her—"

Alec cut off when he heard voices near the back section of the library. They came from the masters' section, and he motioned to his friends, pointing for them to follow him.

He was sure Beckah had said she'd seen Master Helen come here by herself. Would she have been meeting someone else at this late hour?

As he leaned in, he recognized one of the voices.

It was Master Carl.

He couldn't hear what he was saying, only the mumbling tones of the way he spoke, and Alec sensed some agitation in it.

Stefan prodded Alec. "That's Grandma Helen," he mouthed, not speaking anything over a whisper.

At least Alec knew that the other voice was Master Helen. "Why would she have come here with Master Carl?"

Beckah smirked. "I can think of a reason," she whispered.

Alec wrinkled his nose. "That's awful."

"Maybe for you, but they knew each other before. Who's to say that isn't the reason he's here?"

There was movement near the door, and someone shuffled closer.

Alec motioned for them to move out of the way, and they all ducked behind stacks.

The door opened, and Master Carl popped out.

Alec froze in place. They had left the lantern lit. If Master Carl paid attention to it, he would realize that someone had come in here after he had come, and Alec certainly didn't want to be caught by Master Carl observing his and Master Helen's quiet tryst.

Master Carl hurried past them without even a glance, He left the library, closing the door behind him.

Alec breathed out heavily.

He looked over at his friends, and neither of them moved.

The door to the masters' section opened again, and there was the shuffling sound of Master Helen as she appeared. She paused, looking around the library. Alec could see just the top of her head as she studied the library.

"You may step out."

Alec swallowed, and Stefan started to move, but Alec grabbed him by the sleeve and held him in place. He raised a finger to his lips and stepped around the bookshelf he'd been hiding behind. "I only came to research—"

Her gaze flicked to the lantern. "Research at this time of night?" Master Helen asked. She frowned, and her graying hair was frazzled, but otherwise she looked just as stern as she usually did. There was something about her that intimidated Alec, and he didn't know whether it was her intellect—rumored to be the greatest of any of the masters at the university—or her age and experience.

"I'm looking for something on referred pain. I thought that I would try to demonstrate to—"

"Yes. I understand that you would like to prove to Master Carl that you know more about abdominal ailments than a master physicker."

Alec flushed, hating that he believed he did. "It's not that I know more than a master physicker, it's just that I have read through several journals with reference to various ailments, all of them indicating that there was such a referred type of pain."

Master Helen nodded. "Indeed. I'm sure more than a few of those were mine."

Alec's eyes widened. "Yours?" He thought of the tight script and tried to remember what he had read of one of the illnesses. It was described as a shoulder pain, but the source was the abdomen rather than the shoulder. It was an interesting presentation, but he wouldn't have expected that to have come from Master Helen. Wouldn't she have labeled her journals differently? These had been only initials, and he didn't recall them being her initials.

"Tell me why you're really here, Mr. Stross. First, I see you at the palace. Now, I find you here, in the library, well beyond normal student hours, when you must have observed me coming in. Are you attempting to harass me?"

"Not harass. I'm only trying to understand a few things."

"And what are you trying to understand?"

He glanced back toward the shelves, where Stefan remain hidden. He had to be careful with how he approached this, since Stefan didn't know about the Kavers and the Scribes. If he said too much, Stefan might begin to ask questions. It wasn't that he was trying to hide anything from his friend; it was that he didn't want to pull Stefan into a situation where he could end up in trouble.

"I want to know how many have knowledge about documentation."

That seemed to be sufficiently vague and might avoid too many questions from Stefan, though Alec suspected he would have *some* questions. It was a risk that Alec would have to take.

Master Helen narrowed her eyes. "Am I supposed to understand what you mean?"

"I think you do know what I mean. I've been looking

for Master Eckerd, and I would ask him, but I haven't been able to find him for the last week or more."

"No? And why would you think to look for Master Eckerd?"

"Because I have questions, and he had been answering them for me until he went missing." Alec no longer lowered his voice as he knew he should. He knew he needed to be more careful, especially with Stefan, knowing that his friend had a quick mind and would surely ask questions later, but now that he had an opportunity to have Master Helen in front of him, and now that he knew he needed to gather the masters together, maybe there was something she could do to help.

"It's more than that, isn't it?"

"It's more than that," Alec agreed. "There is a master physicker that I need to find."

"Which master is that?"

"I don't know." When Master Helen frowned at him, Alec shrugged. "I don't know because I don't know who he is. My... friend... had an encounter with him, and she would recognize his voice, but we don't have any other way of finding him other than by his voice."

Master Helen studied him, and then her gaze looked behind him. "Your friend had this experience?"

"Yes, and she would like to know who to thank for it."

Master Helen frowned. "There are several dozen master physickers. I think to find this person, you will need to be a little more explicit."

"I would love to be," Alec said, "but as I said, I don't know much more than what I've told you. We thought that perhaps a gathering of the master physickers would allow her to identify him by voice, and if she could, then she could offer her thanks for her experience."

"Her thanks?"

Alec nodded.

"There are few such occurrences. The only time the master physickers gather is at the promotion of another master."

"That's the only time?"

"Yes. There is an expectation that all master physickers attend the promotion. It is a time of celebration."

Alec hesitated before asking the next question. He thought he knew the answer, but he needed to ask anyway. "When will the next such promotion take place?"

"There are no promotions planned."

"None?"

She shook her head. "None are planned, Mr. Stross. I'm sorry, but I think your idea of having your friend come to a gathering of masters will be ineffective. Now, if that will be all, I think I take my leave and go to my quarters."

He sighed. How else could he gather the masters together?

He had one other question, and he wasn't sure whether Master Helen would answer or not, but at this point, he decided it couldn't hurt to at least ask. "Master Helen?" She hesitated, and turned back to him. "Would there be any record of all the master physickers who are at the university?"

"All master physickers are recorded in the record of promotions."

"The record of promotions?"

She nodded. "I'm sure that my grandson would be able to show you. Isn't that right, Stefan?"

Alec hoped that Stefan wouldn't reveal himself, but he stepped out from around the row of shelves and looked at his grandmother. His face was pale, and he trembled slightly. "I can show him, Grandmother—I mean, Master Helen."

"Very good. I don't know how much good it will do you, but if you intend to survey the records and see who is here and whose name you recognize, that would be a place to start. Perhaps you could use that record to determine whether there is anyone here that might have *helped* your friend."

Alec nodded. "Thank you."

"If that will be all, you should both head to bed, and perhaps you could take Ms. Reynolds with you," she said.

Beckah stepped out from behind the shelf, and she was as quiet and somber as Stefan. "Thank you, Master Helen," she said.

She glanced at the three of them. "You three have bright futures ahead of you, but if you continue to attempt to dig into things that are outside of your level of understanding, your futures may be much dimmer than they appear at this time." She fixed Alec with a hard expression as she said it, and he knew she was speaking primarily to him.

With a nod, she turned and departed the library.

Alec looked at the others. "I'm sorry."

"This is about finding who helped your friend?" Stefan asked.

"It wasn't someone who helped her. This was someone who harmed her," Alec said.

"Harmed? And this is a master physicker?"

"As far as we know."

"Why didn't you just tell my grandmother that one of the master physickers had harmed your friend?"

Alec glanced at Stefan and then looked over to Beckah. "Because I didn't want her to think that I was going to do something to one of the master physickers."

"Do something? What kind of thing would you do?" Stefan asked.

"I don't know, maybe challenge him with why he would harm my friend."

"I hadn't considered the record of promotions," Beckah said. "That would make sense, especially considering it would have a listing for every master physicker that has been promoted over the years. All we have to do is figure out timing, and we should be able to determine which one might have been here at the same time."

"The same time as what?" Stefan asked.

Beckah found the record of promotions and set the book out on the table in front of the stack where she'd found it. She glanced at Alec briefly before turning her attention to Stefan. He had been watching Alec, and there was a growing irritation to the way that he did. Was he angry that they weren't sharing with him? Or was it simply curiosity?

"What do you think?" she asked Alec.

"I think that it's late and we need to return to our rooms."

"I thought you wanted to go through the promotions and see if there was anything that might trigger something for you," she said.

"At this time of night? I don't know that it makes sense

to do it." He was getting tired, and if they were going to be of any use to Sam, then he needed to get some rest.

"We can always return later…" Stefan said.

Beckah lifted the book of records and she clutched it to her chest. "I'm ready," she said.

"Beckah—" Stefan began.

She looked over at him and shook her head. "What? If Alec isn't going to stay here, we're going to take this with us so that we can continue the research that we need."

Stefan reached for the book, shaking his head. "That's supposed to stay in the library."

"There will be other copies," Beckah said. "Besides, it's not like anyone else is coming here looking for the record of promotions. We're probably the first people to come looking for it in years." She held out the book and pretended to wipe dust off the cover. "Are you going to move out of my way or do you really intend to block me from getting through? Because if you are, I will push through you."

He looked over to Alec, beseeching him to help, but Alec thought Beckah had it right. If they could take the book, they would be able to search through it at their own pace, and wouldn't be dependent on having access to the library—or drawing any attention while they were here.

"I think we take it," he said.

Stefan looked from Alec to Beckah and threw his hands up. "Fine. You do what you want, but I'm not going to be a part of it." He stormed out of the library, closing the door firmly behind him.

Beckah watched him go. "Do you think we made a mistake?"

"Maybe. But knowing Stefan, he'll get over it pretty quickly," he said.

"I don't know. I've known Stefan a long time. I'm not sure he will—at least not too quickly. First, we used him to get to his grandmother, and now, we are taking this book from the library that he doesn't think we should."

"I could go talk to him," Alec said.

"And tell him what? Would you reveal to him what a Scribe is? Is that your intention?"

"No, but—"

Beckah shook her head. "Then I don't think it will help if you go to him. Let it blow over, and then we can see if we can't help him."

She hung on to the book as they departed the library, and Alec took a moment to dim the lantern, casting the library back into darkness. He thought he saw shadows move, and he shivered before hurrying after Beckah.

22

THE APOTHECARY'S SECRET

"I'm not seeing anything here," Alec said. He stared at the record of promotions, scanning the pages but coming up with no answers. Most of the names over the last few years were physickers that he knew, if only vaguely. There were names of other master physickers he came across that he didn't recognize, but they were older names.

"I think we need to keep looking," Beckah suggested. She sat at the table in her room, and her hair hung over her face as she leaned over a section of the records, pressing her shoulder against his. They had been sitting like that for hours, poring over the book, and had come up with nothing, at least not anything that would be of use.

"Without having a master physicker to help, I don't know what use anything here is going to be," Alec said, taking a moment to look around Beckah's room. It was better decorated than his own. She had a few hand-drawn pictures hanging on the walls and had somehow managed to procure a thick carpet. Most student rooms were bare, and colder because of that. Not Beckah's room. Hers was warm, almost inviting. "I don't know that we thought through this plan all that well."

She arched a brow at him. "Are you blaming me?"

He sighed. "I'm not blaming you. I'm just saying that everything we've been searching for here has been pointless."

"Not pointless. If you look at this, you can see which master physickers were promoted around the same time. That has to be valuable."

"We already knew that many of these master physickers were promoted at the same time." He hadn't known that Master Jessup had come up after Master Carl and Eckerd, but he had suspected that Master Helen was the oldest of them, which the record of promotions revealed.

"We knew that, but now it's been confirmed."

Alec shook his head. "I didn't realize we needed that kind of proof."

"If we're going to make an accusation against someone, we will need proof."

"No, what we need is some way of bringing all of the masters together."

Even if they did that, it would also require that they brought Sam into the university to identify the voice of her captor, and he knew she would be willing to do that, but would her mother allow her?

Alec leaned back, pushing himself away from the table, and breathed out. The room smelled of flowers from the vase that Beckah kept sitting on the table. She had lilacs and daisies jammed into it. The aroma was almost overwhelming. "I think we need to return to our studies," he said.

"Why?"

"Why? Because that's why we're here at the university."

"Maybe that's why I'm here, but I don't know that you need same focus. Most of the time, when we're going through these lectures, you already know everything that the master physicker is teaching."

"Not everything."

"Fine. You don't have the same experience with the surgical suite, but not all masters spend time there. You wouldn't even need to spend time in the surgical area to be a master."

"That's not entirely true," Alec said.

"But it is. There are quite a few masters who don't spend any time in surgery. Look at Master Harrison. I don't think anyone has seen him in surgery in decades."

"Just because he doesn't go to surgery doesn't mean that he couldn't. I mean, my father has more knowledge about the medicinal treatment of illnesses than many of the master physickers, but he isn't a master physicker."

"Have you ever wondered why?"

"I wonder that all the time," Alec said. Even more now that he was at the university, and he saw how much his father had been able to teach him. If his father was here, and had that level of knowledge, why wouldn't he have accepted a promotion?

"How long has he been in his section of the city?"

Alec shrugged. "I don't know. Ever since my mother passed. I don't know if he was there before that. I was too young to know."

"Hmm."

"What are you getting at," he asked.

"I'm not getting anything, only that I think there are questions you need to ask your father."

"My father doesn't talk about his time at the university. Gods, had the shop not exploded, I don't know that he ever would've told me."

"You don't think he would have eventually? Was he planning on keeping you from the university?"

"I don't know if he wanted to keep me from the university as much as he wanted to protect me. I've told you how his approach to treatment is different from what's found here."

"You've told me that he doesn't charge for his services," she said, her mouth screwing up as she did.

Alec grinned at the reaction. It was a very highborn reaction to treatment. The more time he spent with Sam, the more he was aware of the class distinctions, and it was something he had never given much thought to until working with her, but she was right about the university being set up to treat the highborns and not others.

"He only felt that everyone was worthy of treatment, regardless of their ability to pay."

"But if they can't pay, how can the university keep open?" she asked.

Alec drummed his fingers on the table. He wasn't interested in having a debate about this with Beckah. It wouldn't be valuable to either of them. He understood the reasoning behind the masters' approach to encouraging payment, but he didn't have to like it.

"I think I need to head back to the wards."

"I thought you wanted to study and prepare for our classes," she said.

He threw his hands up. "I don't know what I want to do. Looking at this book has been useless. More than useless. All we're learning is what we already knew."

"I don't think it's been useless. Besides, it has given us a chance to sit and chat."

He looked over at her, arching a brow. "I don't—"

Beckah laughed, a sharp and biting sound. "You keep thinking that I'm trying to proposition you. When are you going to get it through your head that while you're a handsome man, that's not what I'm interested in?"

"I thought that at one point." She forced a smile, and Alec thought that maybe she was not being completely honest with him. "You could come with me to the wards," he offered, trying to change the subject.

"For what reason? There's nothing there for us to study," she said.

"There's always something there to study. I learn the best from the people that I've treated, using them to help me understand what illness they have, and what needs to be done to help improve their situation. It's so much better than learning from books."

"You go. I'm going to continue looking through this to see if there's anything I can come up with."

"You don't need to do that. I understand that this is more for me than it is for you."

"Is it? If we don't find what happened to Tray, I won't ever be able to understand what it is for me to be a Scribe."

Alec sighed. "You're right. I keep forgetting that, and I shouldn't. I know how hard it would be if I didn't have any way of working with Sam and trying to continue to master my abilities."

She turned her attention back to the record of promotions, and he left to head to the wards. He passed through the student section, moving quickly, avoiding the questioning glances of a few of the other students. Some of them gave him a knowing smirk as he left Beckah's room.

Great. Now, he was going to be the subject of a different sort of rumor. It was bad enough when he was the topic of conversation because of what he'd learned from his father. He didn't need to be again because of a presumed scandalous relationship with Beckah.

And he knew she didn't necessarily care. It wasn't as if she was worried about the perception of others about their friendship, but she didn't need any perception of impropriety. Maybe they should have continued to meet in the library rather than anywhere else.

He would have to worry about that later. He hurried down to the wards. He hadn't been deceptive with Beckah. There was value to him spending time in the hospital, learning from the sick. That was how his father had taught him, so that was how he felt he learned the best.

It was early in the day, past lunchtime, but still well before the dinner hour. Several of the junior physickers weaved around the room, pausing at the records as they made their notes, or possibly looked at notes made by the master physickers, and looked after the patients. These were the sickest of the sick, the people who came to the university with the most need. And this was where he felt compelled to spend more of his time. He glanced around, looking to see whether there were any master physickers and their cadre of students, but there were not.

One of the physickers looked over at him and

shrugged. Alec was a familiar enough sight here; the physickers didn't mind his presence, especially as there were times that he had left notes in the records that had been helpful. He didn't even attempt to gain recognition for it. It wasn't the reason he had left a note. It was better that the people here got the help they needed.

Alec paused at the cot of a young woman he had seen a few days ago. He glanced at the records, skimming the page, looking for any information about how she might be doing. They had continued with the treatment, and she had been making steady progress. It certainly seemed as if she was breathing easier, as if her overall coloring was better, which put him at ease. It was better that she had gotten help, regardless of how she had come to it.

He moved on, looking over at the man a few rows over. The jaundice had receded, and he lay on his side, clearly having moved himself. That was progress for him as well.

"Are you checking on the master physicker's work?"

Alec turned and saw a junior physicker that he knew. "I'm not checking on anything, more just looking to see if those I've seen have improved," he told Matthew.

Matthew tucked his hands inside his gray physicker coat. He looked down at the man. "It was good that Master Jessup identified the proper combination of medicines for him. I don't think we would have thought of it."

Alec only nodded. Would Master Jessup have come up with the treatment had Alec not come here? Probably, and it was likely that Master Jessup had only been testing him, rather than delaying treatment. There would be no value in that.

"Are there any other interesting illnesses here?"

"All of these are interesting," Matthew said. He scratched the scruff on his chin. He was older than Alec, but not by much. He had managed to grow a thin layer of beard, something that Alec had noted many of the junior physickers did, thinking that it gave them an appearance of age. "Some are sicker than others. And there are a few that we simply can't help."

"Which ones can't you help?"

Matthew gave him a quizzical look. "You think that you know better than the master physickers?"

"Not at all," Alec said hurriedly. "It's only that I think I can learn more from those patients that are the most challenging."

That was what his father would have asked him to do. He had long ago moved past the more basic treatments and needed to focus more on the obscure, not only to test his knowledge, but to develop a deeper understanding of illness and the way the body worked.

"Be my guest," Matthew said. He stepped aside and continued to make his way through the room. Alec had thought that perhaps Matthew might lead him to some of the more complex cases, but he didn't.

Alec sighed. It wasn't that he wanted to offend the junior physickers, and it wasn't that he was trying to challenge them and what they knew, but they thought that way. Would there come a time when he didn't feel persecuted for his interest in healing?

And why didn't they share it? If nothing else, they should have the same interest in trying to understand illness and to develop the same breadth of knowledge, but not all of them felt that way. Matthew was one of many junior physickers who didn't see serving as a physicker as a calling as much as a way toward something else. Maybe it was respect and a lifestyle that serving as a physicker granted. Maybe he was like Master Carl, someone who hoped to eventually move into politics, wanting to take the level of physicker and use that to give him a sort of credibility.

And then there was Alec. Didn't he have ulterior motives for serving as a physicker? Wasn't his interest now something other than only healing others? Everything he did, and everything he saw, he applied to his connection to Sam and how he might better be able to augment her. Maybe he wasn't so different from Matthew and some of the other junior physickers.

He paused at a thin older woman. She had bulging eyes, and a sheen of sweat clung to her. Even without doing more than a cursory examination, he recognized a glandular issue. It was the same as what he'd seen from Mrs. Rubbles when she had been sick. He had healed her with the easar paper, but there were other treatments. He had known of those treatments even when he had been with his father, and now that he'd been at the university with their access to the library, Alec had learned of even more possible treatments. He flipped open the records, scanning what they'd tried, and his breath caught.

What were they thinking? This wasn't simply old age claiming her as one note suggested, and there was no evidence of infection as another claimed, not from what he saw in the notes. Yet that was what the junior physickers were attempting to claim. So far, it didn't appear that any master physickers had reviewed her case.

Alec looked around to make sure none of the junior physickers were watching, and he scrawled a quick note, trying to mimic Master Jessup's handwriting. If nothing else, he would see if he could get this woman a different type of help.

He set the records down and started away. If he'd had access to medicines, he would've mixed them and attempted to administer them himself, but the university worked quite a bit differently than his father's apothecary. His father would have rows and rows of medicines, while the university had a massive supply cabinet where they kept their medicines. As a student, and without a master sending him, Alec wouldn't even be allowed in. It would take reaching junior physicker level before he would be granted access.

When he paused at the next cot, he started to examine the person. There wasn't anything obviously wrong, which was his favorite type of illness. It was the mystery that he enjoyed. He reached for the record, wanting to see what this man had presented with, when he heard the booming sound of Master Carl's voice.

Alec froze. He didn't want Master Carl to see him here, not without his master physicker and other students.

But it was too late. Master Carl entered, a group of students in tow. When he saw Alec, he headed his way, an angry look on his face. "Mr. Stross. And why are you here?"

"I just was checking on the progress of a few of the people that I've seen."

"Indeed? Have you decided that you are a junior physicker now?"

The students arranged around Master Carl watched with widened eyes. They were all newer students than

Alec, though he recognized Jen from his earliest days at the university. Alec had come in at the same time as some of them—particularly Arnold, a pudgy highborn who snickered behind Master Carl at the uncomfortable way that Alec shifted his feet.

"I haven't decided that I'm a junior physicker. I'm simply wanting to see what progress the people that I had seen before have made."

Master Carl looked down at the man on the cot. He grabbed the record from Alec and scanned it. "I don't see any record of Master Eckerd having seen this individual." He looked up, and Alec wanted to shrink away from his stare. "Tell me, Mr. Stross, do you believe you are more talented than the junior physickers here?"

Alec glanced around. He saw Matthew standing near the woman whose records he'd just made notes on. She was sick with a glandular problem, and it was advanced, but it had been overlooked by the junior physickers. He didn't know how many had studied her, or how many had overlooked the nature of her illness, but he did know that they were wrong in their treatment.

"I wouldn't say that I'm more talented, but I would say that I have a different background."

He needed to choose his words carefully. Master Carl already didn't care for him, which put him in a difficult spot. How would Alec ever reach the level of junior physicker if Master Carl wouldn't support it? It took the support of all master physickers for students to take the next step.

"A different background is right. You are an apothecary. If you ever want to be anything more, you will focus your studies, and you will stop setting yourself apart from the university training. There is a purpose to the way we do things, Mr. Stross."

"I understand that, Master Carl."

"I don't believe that you do. When Master Eckerd returns, I think that perhaps I will discuss this with him."

"Do you know when he will return?" Maybe some good could come out of this confrontation. He didn't like the idea of facing off with Master Carl, but if he could learn where Master Eckerd had gone, it would be useful to him.

Master Carl's brow furrowed. "Do I look as if I keep track of where each of the master physickers spends their time?"

Alec flushed. This wasn't what he wanted. He didn't need a confrontation with Master Carl, and he didn't need to raise his ire any more than he already had.

"I'm sorry. I'll be going."

Master Carl looked down at the man. "Tell me, Mr. Stross, did you come up with a treatment for this man?"

Alec looked at the man. He had normal coloration, and his breathing was regular, and when he had done his brief examination, he had noticed that his heart rate was regular. He hadn't seen anything wrong with him, at least not so much that he could tell.

"I hadn't taken enough time to fully assess him," he admitted.

Master Carl sneered at him. "Fully assess? Now you would like us to think that you can examine as well as a physicker?"

"My father taught me—"

Master Carl cut him off. "I'm aware of what your father taught you. Just as I'm telling you that if you are training at the university, you need to practice the way that we teach, not the way that an apothecary would practice."

"Again, I don't mean any offense, Master Carl. I was only trying to say that I hadn't taken the time to complete my examination. I was trying to see what he presented with so I could better understand why he came to the university for healing."

"You can't determine that by examining him?"

Alec kept his gaze fixed on the patient. "I could try, but it would be easier if I knew why he came, so I could have a better understanding as to how I might be able to help him," he said.

"If you intend to be a master physicker, you should know that no diagnosis is necessarily easy."

"I know that. I was just saying—"

"I know what you're saying."

Alec looked at Master Carl, unsure why he was escalating this encounter, rather than simply ordering Alec to leave the ward. Why was he pursuing this so vehemently? Master Carl watched him, and there was irritation on his face, but there was something else, an expression that Alec didn't think was warranted, but it seemed Master Carl felt it, regardless.

Hatred.

He looked around, wanting nothing more than to retreat. When he did, he saw Beckah standing near the entrance to the wards, watching. Her eyes were wide, and she nodded to him, trying to motion him over.

"I… I will be going," Alec said.

"What? You don't want to stay and prove how brilliant you are, Mr. Stross?"

"It's never been about proving brilliance, it's about helping these people," Alec said softly.

He hurried toward Beckah, not giving Master Carl a chance to say anything else. As he did, he could feel Master Carl's gaze burning on his back. Alec ignored it and fought the temptation to turn back, and to see what he might do—or say.

When he reached Beckah, she looked over his shoulder. "What was that?"

"That was Master Carl making it clear how he feels about me."

"I'm not surprised."

Alec looked at her, but she grabbed his sleeve and took them along the stairs, heading back toward their rooms.

"Why aren't you surprised?"

"Because Master Carl and your father were here at the same time."

"So? There were lots of people who studied here at that time, I imagine."

"And your father was promoted to master physicker long before Master Carl."

Alec stopped and turned to Beckah. "What?"

She nodded. "It's what I found in the record of promotions. Your father was promoted before Master Carl. That's probably why he doesn't like you."

"My father was a master physicker?"

Beckah shook her head. "Your father *is* a master physicker."

23

A FATHER'S GRIEF

Alec pulled on the door to the apothecary, listening to the faint jingling of the bell as he entered. It felt strange entering today. There had never been a time when he had hesitated coming back to his father's apothecary, certainly not as he did now, but after learning that he was a master physicker, Alec was filled with a certain trepidation.

Would his father even be here? It wasn't a given that he would. There were times when his father disappeared, often for days at a time, usually to go out harvesting, though that wasn't always the case.

The shop was empty.

Alec shouldn't have been surprised, but he was disappointed. He needed to talk to his father, if only to better understand why he had left the university after becoming a master physicker. Why would he abandon such a prestigious post? Was it because he felt that people didn't need to pay for his services? That seemed a fairly strange reason for him to abandon the university altogether, espe-

246 | D.K. HOLMBERG

cially as there were other ways to work around it and still help people.

There had to be some other reason.

He wandered the shelves. There was something familiar and reassuring about walking along the shelves with their rows of cataloged leaves and roots and oils. Everything was neatly organized, and everything was where he remembered it. He smiled to himself. It might be easier for him to return to serving as an apothecary, at least then he wouldn't have to deal with the physickers, and he could use his knowledge to help people. Wasn't that what he wanted?

But if he did that, he would miss out on what it meant to be a Scribe, and what it meant for him to be connected to Sam. That was the benefit of staying at the university and continuing his studies there.

The cot at the back of the room was empty. A few bloody towels were near it, so Alec suspected someone had been here recently and had required minor stitching for wounds. A needle with thread still attached was poked into a cushion nearby.

All of this that he had once considered normal, his father simply being a skilled apothecary, but his father had been more—so much more.

The bell over the door jingled, and Alec turned.

"Alec."

His father approached. He appeared tired, and his eyes looked almost haunted. He wore a heavy robe over his jacket, and dirt stained certain sections of it.

"Father. Where have you been?"

"I didn't think I needed to answer to you now that you've gone to the university."

"You don't need to answer to me. I just wondered where you've been. You look as if you've been harvesting."

His father sighed. "Harvesting, in a sense. It's not always the easiest task."

"What isn't?"

His father sighed again, then reached his hand into his pocket, clutching something. "It doesn't matter. To what do I owe this visit?"

"A question."

His father paused before one of the shelves. "What sort of question?"

"Why would you have not told me that you were promoted to master physicker?"

His father's eyes changed, shifting. "I hadn't thought it necessarily important."

"Not important? Why wouldn't it be important for you to tell me that all of your knowledge was acquired at the university?"

"You already know that. Why would you need me to tell you again?"

"It's not that I need you to tell me again, it's just that…"

"It's just nothing," his father said. He moved past Alec and made his way toward the back of the shop where he had a locked cabinet. He pulled a key out and opened the cabinet, then reached into his pocket and pulled out a small jar. It was filled with a strange yellowish liquid, nothing like Alec had ever seen before. His father put it inside the cabinet, then closed the door.

"What is that?"

"That is what I just completed harvesting," his father said.

"And?"

His father met his gaze. "And I told you that there were ways I served the palace that I can't always explain to you."

"It seems there are many things you can't always explain to me."

"Because I want to protect you."

"Protect me from what? How does keeping me unaware of your connection to the university protect me? Why wouldn't you share with me that you were a master physicker? And how does that have anything to do with what you've collected?"

"I told you that there are certain parts of my responsibilities that aren't always the most... savory."

"You haven't exactly told me much, Father. What is that?"

"It's eel venom," he said.

"Eel? As in the canal eels?"

His father nodded. "As in the canal eels. There venom is valuable for many purposes."

Alec frowned. "How would you harvest eel venom? *Where* would you harvest eel venom?"

"The canals are filled with the eels," he said.

"They are, but you would draw attention to yourself if you were seen collecting eel venom in the middle of the city."

"There are parts of the city that I can go where I don't necessarily draw attention," he said.

"Can I see it?" Alec nodded toward the cabinet.

His father studied Alec for a long moment before breathing out. He reached into the cabinet and handed over the jar. "You need to be very careful. There are times when this can be beneficial, but for the most part, it is incredibly toxic."

"Then why do you have it..." Alec frowned to himself. His father had made it clear that he wasn't always doing things that he was proud of, and that there were requirements placed upon him by those in the palace, but he had never thought that his father would use his knowledge in ways that could be harmful to others.

Was that it? Was he using his knowledge of healing to harm someone else?

"Do you intend to allow someone to use your knowledge to hurt someone else?"

"I intend to use my knowledge to help protect the city," his father said.

"And if that entails killing someone?" Alec held up the jar of eel venom, and he shivered. It was slightly warm and it seemed to have an oily consistency. He shook it and watched as it coated the sides of the jar. He could easily imagine one of the eels clamping down on its unsuspecting prey, allowing its venom to seep into their bloodstream. Sam had described her experience with the eels in the canal, and he had never given her enough credit for what she had experienced. Maybe he had been mistaken.

"If that entails someone dying so that others may live, that is the price I must pay."

"Is that what you wanted me to be? Is that why you didn't want me to go to the university?"

His father motioned for Alec to sit, and he did, taking a seat on the cot. His father pulled a chair around the table and sat across from him. "I've always known that you would need to go to the university. It was the only place that you would gain the additional knowledge you needed to complete your training. I thought I might expedite it by teaching you myself."

"All that's happened is that I've upset a significant number of master physickers."

"Because they don't care for me," his father said.

"Why? Is it because you were promoted before they were?"

His father snorted and waved his hand in the air. "There wasn't quite as much competition for promotion as some would like you to believe. There is some of that, but it has never been about who was promoted before who."

"Then why does Master Carl dislike me so much?"

"He dislikes me. And because of me, he dislikes you."

"Why does he dislike you?"

"Because I thwarted his political ambitions."

Alec sat there, staring at his father. The door to the apothecary opened, with the bell jingling, and his father raised a hand, motioning for him to stay there, and he hurried off. Alec heard him speaking softly to someone before making his way along the shelves to find a collection of healing medicines, and then the door opened again with another jingling of the bell. When his father returned, he set a few copper pennies down. Likely, it wasn't enough for the services his father had provided, but it was also likely that it was all the person was able to pay.

"How did you thwart his political ambitions?"

"Master Carl thought to use connections within the university to gain power. He thought to heal only those who could help him. When I called him out on it, there was enough of an uproar that..." His father shrugged.

"After that, his political ambitions were quenched. The university has always been about profit, but they at least paid lip service to the idea of healing everyone equally once they reached the university. If they had the ability to pay, anyone would be offered the same treatment. Carl made a mockery of that."

"Is that why you left?"

"I left because of your mother."

"Mother wanted you to leave?"

"No, your mother was perfectly content to stay at the university." His father met his gaze, and tears welled in his eyes. "It's not easy to talk about, even after all of this time. I... I wish it were."

"What happened?"

"You happened."

"Me? What you mean?"

His father sighed. "What I mean is, when she was pregnant with you, you were a difficult pregnancy. There was a disagreement among the master physickers at the time about how best to proceed with the delivery. I pushed, thinking that I knew better than several other master physickers, and eventually, they acquiesced. Because of that, I lost your mother."

He looked down, staring at his hands. "What did you do? Did you try to have her deliver me naturally?"

He shook his head slowly. "I tried to force surgery," his father said. He looked up, and tears fell down his cheeks. His father wiped them away and swallowed. "I thought the only way to save both of you was to put her through surgery. It was dangerous, and I knew it, but I thought I knew better than several others who had much more experience with surgery than I did. We had you, but they couldn't stop her bleeding." His voice trailed off at the end, becoming little more than a whisper. "After that, I left. It was shame that pulled me away. My shame. My arrogance. I settled out here, thinking I would attempt to repay that debt, that I would use my knowledge to help others, that I could find some way of making amends."

Alec didn't know what to say. The fact that his father was a master physicker had been surprising enough, but learning that he had left the university because of a decision he'd made that had gone awry was even more surprising. That didn't fit with what he knew of his father. He was a proud man and incredibly intelligent, but he had never been the kind of person to run away from a mistake.

"You can go back," Alec said.

"Oh, I suppose that I could. Once you've been promoted to master physicker, the rank can never be stripped from you. But I don't know if I could ever practice in that environment again. Besides, there is value to my work out here. And I have a different responsibility, one that isn't entirely linked to healing." His gaze drifted back to the cabinet where he'd returned the eel venom. "That is another part of my penance. Beyond my service to these outer sections, I thought if I could help protect many, it would somehow makeup for the one that I couldn't protect."

They sat in silence for a long time. Thoughts raced through Alec's head. What would his life have been like had his father made a different decision? What if his father had allowed the other master physickers to make the decision about the delivery rather than his father? What would it have been like to grow up with his mother?

To have had her in his life through everything he'd experienced?

All he'd ever known was life with his father. It was comforting, but there was a void.

"Is that why you came?" his father asked.

"I came for answers. I guess... I guess I have them now."

"Are they what you wanted?"

"They are what they are. I wish they were different," Alec said. "But I... I appreciate that you told me."

"You deserve to know. It has been long enough."

"What other secrets are you keeping from me?"

"Nothing else. There would be nothing else to keep from you."

"Even your role as an assassin?"

His father looked up, and his gaze became harder. "I am not an assassin."

"If you're using your knowledge of medicines to harm others, that is what you have become."

"And what of you? You have used your knowledge of healing to aid your friend as she attacks. Does that make you any different?"

Alec sighed. It didn't. And he knew that it didn't. Somehow, it felt different, if only because he wasn't the one doing the direct attack. Even though it was Sam, did that absolve him? If he was using his knowledge to help augment her so that she could harm someone else, wasn't he still complicit?

"The person who destroyed your shop is back in the city," Alec said.

His father's gaze drifted to the back wall. "So I have heard."

"And that's why you've collected the eel venom?"

"There has been a request."

"Who makes such a request?"

His father fixed him with a hard expression. "That, unfortunately, I am not privileged to share with you."

"Because you want to keep me uninvolved?"

"Because I have committed to secrecy."

Maybe there was another way his father could help. If he was a master physicker, and he knew enough about the Scribes, maybe he could provide answers that Master Eckerd could not in his absence. "Sam was attacked. She claims that a Scribe—someone who was likely a master physicker—is the one who attacked her."

His father frowned. "There has been some suspicion that the university was compromised."

"Suspicion?"

"Nothing more than that. Only a suspicion. It could be nothing more than a misdirection. The Thelns would like nothing more than to create a diversion, to try to find a way to cast suspicion on everyone."

"The way you said it suggests to me that you believe those suspicions."

"I do."

"Sam didn't get to see him. She thinks she would recognize his voice."

"And you would like to find a way to get all of the master physickers together so that she could identify him?"

"It seemed a reasonable idea, and just the fact that you came up with it just now tells me it's not too far-fetched, but Master Helen tells me the only time that all of the master physickers come together is at the promotion of another."

"That would be one time when all of the master physickers come together."

"One time?"

His father shrugged. "There would be another time, but it has been rare enough that it has hardly ever happened."

"What is it?"

"A student may request testing for promotion to physicker."

"Students can request testing?" Alec hadn't heard of that. As far as he knew, promotion required that students pass through a series of classes and experience with patients on the ward. Considering his experience with Master Carl, Alec didn't like his chances of promotion anytime soon.

"As I said, it's not common, but it has happened. When a student makes a request, the master physickers all gather for the testing. That's why it rarely happens. Few students are confident enough in their abilities to force the testing. Fewer still are skilled enough to be promoted in such a way."

The bell above the door jingled again, and his father stood and made his way to the front. He said something quietly to whoever entered, and then returned. "Alec, I'm afraid that this will take me a bit longer. You are welcome to remain, but my visitor requests privacy."

Alec looked toward the front of the shop, but saw no one. It was unusual. His father usually was willing to include him in all treatments. Maybe this person was the one who was involved in the use of the eel venom.

"No. I'll be going," Alec said.

His father studied him for a moment, but said nothing. He clasped Alec on the arm as he passed, and when Alec reached the rear door, he glanced back, looking to see if there was any sign of the other person in the room, but wherever they were, they had elected to remain hidden. Out of sight.

When he stepped out, he took a deep breath. He now knew another he could gain access to the master physickers, but doing so would be risky. And he didn't know anything about what would happen if he failed. Would they expel him from the university? Or would he simply return to his position?

For Sam, he would risk that. Didn't he have to?

4

BASTAN'S TEST

Water lapped along the canal. It was a moonless
light, and few lanterns were lit, their reflection
off the water not offering nearly as much light as Sam was
accustomed to. She crept silently along the street, padding
as softly as she could over the stones. She kept her canal
staff gripped in hand, her other hand slipped into the
pocket of her cloak, fingering the vial of her and Alec's
blood. She had a scrap of easar paper, hopefully enough
for her to add an augmentation were she to need it. She
didn't want to need it, not if she could help it, but she
feared that she might.

Bastan guided her, moving with more confidence than
what she felt. He was dressed in all black and carried a
sword as well as a crossbow, walking with a swagger that
would scare anyone else away. Sam smiled to herself as
she watched him. If nothing else, having an opportunity
to observe Bastan was as valuable an exercise as any other.
She knew so little about how he operated. All she knew
was that he had some skill. But even with a sword and a

crossbow, it mattered little against Ralun. And the three armed men with him would probably be of little help, either.

Sam glanced at those men. She recognized one of them. Colin was a solid man. He had a sharp chin and deep-set eyes, and she knew he was somewhat skilled. She'd seen him tossing people from Bastan's tavern often enough to know that he was strong, but against the Thelns, strength often wasn't enough. The Thelns were naturally strong, and they were fast, but they had some magical ability, as well. That was something that Colin was unlikely to counter.

The other two were more of a mystery to her. They were of average height and build, and they had cloaks that were somewhat like hers, with the same shimmery fabric that seemed to deflect the light, wrapping shadows around them. For that matter, Bastan was dressed in similar fabric. Neither man appeared armed, though she hadn't examined them thoroughly. There was something almost unremarkable about both of them.

Sam wasn't familiar with the sections of the city they were going through. They had used the bridges as they crossed, Bastan having some way of getting them past without raising question. And most of the bridges had been unguarded, something that was unusual at this time of night. She suspected he had connections that he'd used, and that the guards who normally would be here had been turned away. She couldn't deny how impressed she was that they moved so easily from section to section.

Normally, Sam would be forced to jump the canals. It wasn't something she minded, especially now that she knew how to flip across the canals, but regardless how they crossed, their presence would still raise questions. If Bastan was connected to the guards, they would be less likely to raise those questions.

Sam tried not to think about what would happen if Elaine caught her out here. How angry would her mother be if she discovered Sam working with Bastan, trying to find out information about Ralun, something she had expressly told her not to do?

Did Sam even care?

If it meant that she would be able to help Tray, she didn't.

They passed a series of empty shops. None of them were remarkable in any way. One looked to be a seamstress from the sign hanging outside the window, but the others were less obvious. Farther down the street, homes rose on either side. The air was still, and it held the typical stench of the canal, but nothing else. Sam expected something of filth, especially in an outer section like this, but there was none. This place was likely lowborn, but it didn't feel lowborn.

"How much farther?" she whispered.

"Quiet," Bastan said.

Sam leaned toward him and tried to catch his eye, but Bastan made a point of keeping his gaze fixed straight ahead of him. Sam had tried to figure out where they were heading, but had not been able to discover anything. They headed in a generally northerly direction, crossing nearly a dozen sections on their way. Eventually, they would reach the edge of the city—and the swamp.

As they trailed along the canals, Sam could make out the distant sight of the edge of the city. It had come upon them much faster than she expected. They reached the

260 | D.K. HOLMBERG

swamp, and paused along the shore, staring out into the darkness. The canal that circled around the outer edge, that formed the farthest barrier here dumped into the swamp.

Humid winds gusted out from deep within the swamp. They carried the now-familiar odor, that hot, bitter scent that reminded her of her escape just days ago, and the torment of the eel as it chased her.

Sam shivered.

Bastan looked over at her. "I would never have pegged you as someone afraid of the swamp."

"I thought you wanted me to be quiet."

"Now that we're here, we have less need of complete silence," Bastan said.

"Why the swamp?"

"Because this is where there was rumor of activity," Bastan said. "It's not passable—at least not easily passable. Only a barge can cross through here."

"Not only a barge," Sam said.

Bastan frowned. "There's only one way to get through the swamp, Samara."

"Trust me when I tell you there is another."

"Trust you? You haven't necessarily given me reason to trust you."

Sam shook her head. "Fine."

She screwed the two halves of her canal staff together and flipped out over the canal, ignoring one of the men's shout for her to stop. When she landed, she balanced on the end of the canal staff. She hesitated and then launched herself up, pulling the staff free and flipping it back out, heading across the canal. She made a small circle before returning to the shore and landing next to Bastan.

She tapped the water free of her staff and fixed him with a hard gaze.

"Training?"

Sam nodded. "Training."

"Well. That was... unexpected. How many are able to travel quite like that?"

"More than you would expect," Sam said.

Bastan frowned, staring out into the water. "That answers a few questions for me."

"What kinds of questions?"

"The kind that would be answered by someone able to perform some acrobatic maneuvers as they jump across the canal." He looked over at her. "How far out into the swamp can you go?"

"I haven't tried to see how far I can go, but I've heard from someone who claims they can cross the entire swamp."

His eyes widened slightly. "The entire swamp? The thing stretches for leagues, Sam."

Sam shrugged. "I'm not saying that *I* can, only that I know of someone who claims that they can."

"And who is this someone?"

She smiled at him. Should she tell him that it was Elaine? He already knew that she was a Kaver, and it wasn't that she didn't trust Bastan. Well, it wasn't that she didn't trust him completely. She trusted him, but he had his own motivation, and as long as she was aware of that, she was able to work within his expectations. She had no interest in revealing more than was necessary. With Bastan, any knowledge was power, and she needed to ensure that she didn't give up too much power to him.

"What activity did you hear about in the swamp?"

"Only that there have been smugglers moving through here."

"Smugglers? That's what you've heard about?" She laughed, but the sound faded as it drifted into the swamp.

"I fail to see your humor."

"Only that I find it interesting that you're offended by the idea of smugglers moving through here."

"You understand what impact smugglers might have on my business?"

"I understand that you would like to be in control of every person who moves in and out of the city. I also understand that it's an enormous city, and your influence goes only so far."

"Does it?"

She frowned. "How far does your influence reach?"

"Far enough that having smugglers in my city runs the risk of impacting me and my business."

"That's all this is about?"

"Not all. It's the fact that they are moving through the swamp that intrigues me the most," Bastan said.

"Because the swamp is unusual?"

"Most things move in and out of the bay, so having something coming off the swamp is unusual. It attracted my attention, which means that it raises questions. If someone's willing to risk coming across the swamp, and risk the highborns identifying them, I would like to know why. I would like to know what they think to find risking this."

Sam could think of many things that would prompt someone to risk coming across the swamp. But it was something Elaine had said that made her most suspicious.

If the Thelns were found on the other side of the swamp, this might be where they were coming through.

But Sam wasn't entirely certain that was what would be found on the other side. She didn't know enough about where the Thelns came from or how they even reached these lands. What if there was another way that they came? What if there was some other access?

And how would the Thelns have suddenly been able to cross the swamp?

"What kind of smugglers have you been hearing about?"

"As I've said, the kind that influence my business," Bastan said. "It's enough of an impact that I need to involve myself."

She could tell from the way he said it that he wasn't accustomed to involving himself in this way.

"You know what they're moving?"

"No. And that frustrates me even more," he said.

"Why all the muscle?" Sam asked, looking at the other three with them. They had stood off to the side, giving her and Bastan space as they talked. There was something almost coordinated about the way they stood away, almost as if Bastan had warned them about getting too close to him. But why?

"The muscle, as you say, is because I intend to move on the source of the rumors."

"You know of this place?"

"There is one place that seems to be the epicenter of most of the activity."

"And where is it?"

"In another section nearby. I wanted to make sure that you were ready before we moved on."

Sam frowned at him. It was more than him wanting to make sure she was ready. He had convinced her to come, and he wouldn't have shared with her any of this had she not come with him, but a part of her felt as if he had manipulated her into coming. Why would he have done that? What would it benefit him?

"You already knew that I could cross the swamp," she said.

Bastan grinned.

Sam suddenly understood why the others were standing off and away from her. Bastan had advised them to do so.

"I heard of a girl appearing in this section. She came in off the canal, and there was nothing with her. There was no sign of a barge, nothing that would explain where she might've come from." He fixed her with an amused expression. "Most interestingly, she was carrying a long staff. When I heard this, I knew that it had to be you—or someone like you. And if there is some way of navigating the swamp without drawing attention, I thought I should know. Hiring a barge to cross the swamp is not easy, even for me."

"Which is why you brought me here? You wanted me to demonstrate what I can do?"

"I wanted to know if that's what you've been learning. And it seems that I was right to do so."

"You're a bastard."

"No. I only wanted to make sure that you weren't getting into the wrong kind of trouble."

"Why? Because you'd rather have me getting into the right kind of trouble?"

"Because I'd like to know what sorts of things you're

learning over *there*." He said it with enough of an inflection that Sam knew he was fully aware of where she trained, and likely aware of what she was learning.

How connected was Bastan?

She'd never given it much thought, and maybe she should have.

Yet she wasn't surprised that Bastan had manipulated her to discover that secret. It was information. He wanted to know what she was capable of doing, and now that he did, it was likely he would attempt to use that information in some way.

"Now that you've gotten what you wanted, are you going to show me what you heard?"

Bastan smiled again and nodded. "Now I will."

He turned, and they started down the street, moving away from the swamp and back toward a more central section. They still ran along one of the main canals, one that was wider here than it was in many other places. Every so often, she heard splashing in the water, and she resisted the urge to look over to see what might be moving there. If it was the eels, as much as she hated them, she now knew they were beneficial.

Bastan watched her, almost as if reading her thoughts. "Still don't care for the canals? I find that interesting, especially as you are so willing to jump over them."

"It's not the canals that I don't like, it's what's in them."

"The eels?"

She nodded. "The damn things tried to eat me more than once."

"The eels don't attack people, Samara."

"Are you sure?"

"I've been in the city a long time. I've never heard any reports of eels attacking people."

"How many are swimming in the canals?"

"What you mean?"

"How many people swim in the canals?"

"The canals aren't for swimming. There are too many barges moving through here, and the water..."

"It's because of the eels," she said. "You can tell me all you want that there's another reason, but people don't swim here because of the damned eels." Bastan didn't know the other purpose of the eels, and she wasn't about to reveal that to him. He didn't need more reason to raise questions. Understanding the purpose of the eels would invite many more questions than what she was interested in answering. "How much farther are we going?"

"I thought you wanted to get answers?"

"I *do* want answers, but given that you think you will use this as your own way of gleaning information from me, I'm thinking that perhaps I want to be a little more careful than I have been with you."

"That hurts."

"You'll get over it."

They crossed another bridge, this one again with no guards. She glanced over to Bastan, and he only shrugged. What must he have done to have manipulated the guards to avoid placing people at any of these crossings? How much power did Bastan actually have?

That might be the most important question for her to get answered. She had known Bastan had connections, but she hadn't known that he had such power before. Now that she knew, what did that change?

Nothing.

All that it did was leave more questions in her mind.

The most troubling one for her was why Bastan had been so involved in her upbringing. The more she thought about it, the more she understood what he was after, the more she was forced to question why he was involved in helping her survive. Not only survive, but thrive. He had been responsible for ensuring that she was protected and well fed. In some ways, he had even kept her away from Marin.

She watched him as they made their way along the streets. Had he known about Marin's involvement with the Thelns?

She didn't think so. Had he known, the information about the Thelns wouldn't have been such a surprise to him. Neither would the fact that she knew how to cross the swamp using only her canal staff.

There was another possibility, but it was one that left her even more troubled.

Could Elaine have known that Bastan was essentially raising her?

Elaine and the princess had made it seem as if the palace hadn't known where to find her, and that Elaine had not known where she ended up, but could she have somehow influenced events, somehow encouraging Bastan to keep track of her, training her so that she would gain some of the Kaver skills without even knowing that was what she was doing? Sam couldn't deny the fact that everything she'd learned from Bastan had some applicability to what she now needed to know as a Kaver.

Bastan didn't look at her, and now wasn't the time to ask.

He made a motion to silence her as they hurried along the street.

Sam looked around, not recognizing the section.

That wasn't entirely surprising. There were plenty of sections of the city that she had not spent much time in, but she was surprised that Bastan moved so comfortably between them.

They paused at a small building. Bastan moved them to the side, and he pressed up against the stone facing of the building. He nodded to it. "In there," he whispered.

"What will be in there?" Sam asked.

"If I'm right, violence."

Bastan unsheathed his sword and kicked open the door, storming inside.

25

THE ATTACK

S am swore to herself, gathering the ends of her canal staff. She reacted a step slower than the other three. They must have anticipated what Bastan intended, and stormed in after him. She heard shouts and debated reaching for her easar paper, thinking of making an augmentation, but there wasn't time. Had she attempted an augmentation, she would have been delayed entering, and Bastan needed her help, whether he knew it or not.

She took a deep breath and hurried inside.

A battle spread out in front of her.

Sam took a quick survey of the room as she screwed the ends of her staff together. It was a wide-open space, thankfully not tight quarters. It would be easier for her to fight using the entire length of her staff, as she could get more speed on it as she flowed through the movements. Bastan was engaged with a massive man near one corner, and she saw the other two men—the unremarkable ones —fighting hand-to-hand combat with three others.

They were a revelation. They fought quickly, almost a

blur, and she suddenly understood they were much more dangerous than she had expected.

Colin used his brute strength, bashing in a man's head as he fought his way through the room.

What was this?

Why would Bastan have come here ready for such violence?

Sam didn't have a chance to think about it. Someone appeared in front of her, and she swung her staff around, catching him on the side of the head, knocking him down. Another person appeared, coming down stairs that she hadn't seen off to her left. He was larger, but not quite Theln size. She spun her staff around and swept his legs out from underneath him, dropping him to the ground. She jammed the end of her staff into his sternum and then smacked him on the side of the head.

The heavy sound of boots over wooden floorboards came from above her.

Sam glanced back at the room. The others were all preoccupied, which meant that she would need to investigate.

She unscrewed the ends of her canal staff and stepped onto the staircase.

It was dark in here, and she waited a moment for her eyes to adjust. While she waited, she quickly pulled out the scrap of easar paper and the vial of blood ink, dipping her finger into the vial. She scrawled a few words on the page, again thinking of how less effective her own writing was compared to what Alec would be able to do, but it was all she had. Hopefully, this time she wouldn't make a mistake, wanting only to add strength and speed, again thinking that she should ask Alec about enhancing her eyesight, or her hearing, or any of her other senses.

With one last flourish, she decided to add a brief line about thickening her skin.

It may not work. She wasn't sure that she used the same technique that Alec did, but if she did encounter a Theln, she wanted to be prepared so that she could avoid a bolt going through her again. Without Alec nearby, she wasn't sure she would survive the poisoning.

She started up the stairs.

At the top, she paused, poking her head around the corner. There had been sound here, at least one person. If there was only one, she thought she could handle him. If there was more than one—and if they were Thelns—even augmented, she would likely fail.

She saw nothing.

Sam stepped out.

Someone clubbed her from behind. She staggered forward, sprawling across the floor. She twisted as she fell, trying to bring her staff around, when someone kicked her from the other side.

Kyza!

That last one hurt, but she rolled across the floor, twisting so that her staff could slam into the side of her attacker's leg. She missed, catching only air.

Sam continued to roll, pushing off with her staff as she flipped into the air.

When she landed, she skittered off to the side, avoiding an attack.

She looked up and saw her attacker.

Ralun.

"You came looking for me?" he asked. He darted

forward, nearly too fast for her. His foot swung up in an arc, and his arm came down at the same time. She flipped herself up, pushing off with her staff, and avoided his kick, but not the entirety of his arm. It hurt, but not as much as it could have.

Whatever she done to thicken her skin seemed to have worked.

How long would the augmentation last? Did she have enough time to defeat him?

"Where is my brother?"

Ralun grinned at her. He ducked underneath her swinging staff, the smile never leaving his face. "Your brother. A most interesting individual. I find it interesting that you would have a connection to someone like him. Even more interesting is that he has a connection to someone like you."

Sam frowned, and that hesitation was a mistake.

Someone caught her from behind.

Sam rolled, not surprised to see another Theln behind her. A part of her feared that it would be Tray, but it wasn't. It was an unfamiliar face. She spun her staff around and cracked the Theln on the side of his head. He was thrown back, but only staggered, not knocked out as she had hoped.

"Why don't you stupid Thelns fall easier?"

Sam hurried back, putting her back to the wall, needing space more than anything else. She faced two Thelns. It was hard enough with her augmentations, but she knew they would fade soon. And if she didn't defeat Ralun, and if he escaped, then how would she ever learn why he was in the city and what he was after?

She would have to press the attack.

Sam spun her staff, flicking around in a hard arc. She caught the first Theln, sweeping his legs out from him, and jabbed down, but he rolled off to the side.

Sam ducked, avoiding Ralun and his attack, but only barely.

"You've improved," he said.

"Yeah. I hate to disappoint you. I don't think I'll be quite as easy for you to hurt this time."

"Perhaps not. But I think that without a Scribe, you will find it is more difficult than you realize."

There was movement on the stairs, and Colin barreled into the room, crashing into Ralun.

The Theln spun and slammed his fist down on Colin's head, crushing it.

Sam swallowed. His head had exploded. She wasn't sure that she had solidified herself enough to withstand something like that.

Kyza!

If Alec were here, he likely would be able to add an augmentation that would support her, but without him... she wasn't going to be fast enough or strong enough.

Ralun shifted his attention back to her, casually tossing Colin's body off to the side. "You brought help. It's unfortunate that you brought this help, as I doubt they will be of much use to you."

"Why are you here?" she asked.

"Here? Isn't coming after you reason enough?"

"You're not after me. There's something that you want in the city."

"Want? Do you believe you know me so well after our single encounter?"

"I think I know the kind of person you are. You

wouldn't risk coming back to the city without a reason. Is it for Marin? Did you come to rescue her after you attempted to poison her?"

Ralun frowned. "I think you have the events mistaken."

"Then why don't you enlighten me."

Sam swung her staff and jabbed into the other Theln. It caught him in the stomach, and she swung it back around, connecting with the back of his head. He staggered forward, falling. She tried jumping forward, to finish him, but Ralun positioned himself so that she wasn't able to do so.

"I don't think so. It's far more interesting to me to have you questioning."

"I *will* stop you."

"I believe that you would like to stop me, but I don't believe that you have the necessary skills. You caught me off guard the last time, I'll admit that." Ralun slipped forward, his fist balled, and caught her in the stomach.

Sam fell backward. It hurt less than it would have without enhancements, but more than it had before.

Her augmentations were fading.

Ralun watched her, and the widening of his eyes told her that he realized the same.

"Dare I say, little one, you seem to have overestimated your augmented abilities."

He started forward, but a thudding on the stairs pulled his attention back.

He swung around, and the two other men with Bastan darted toward him.

"Djohn. You brought djohn with you."

Sam didn't know what to say. She didn't know what a djohn was, but they faced Ralun fearlessly and attacked in unison, sliding forward, moving faster than she could follow, managing to force him back. Ralun swung and caught one of the djohn on the side of the head. The man flipped up in the air, but landed on his feet.

Ralun grunted.

Sam had some of her augmentation left. She slipped forward, slamming her staff down in an arc, hoping to connect with the top of Ralun's head, but he simply grabbed the staff and swung it around, knocking both of the djohn back.

Sam was empty handed. Ralun held her staff and faced the djohn.

"Perhaps not as foolish as I thought," he said, stalking toward the nearest djohn. He brought the staff up and swung it down, colliding with the man's stomach.

He turned, facing Sam for a moment as he readied to smack the other djohn.

"How were you able to hire them?"

"You first. Why are you here?"

Ralun grinned at her and slammed down the staff into the other djohn. "Seeing as how your augmentations have faded, I doubt that it matters if I tell you. You would like to believe that you're the reason I'm here? Is that it?"

"I believe that you're here for a reason. Others would like to have me believe that you're here for me, but I don't think that's it."

She backed away as he stalked toward her.

"No. If not for your unfortunate bonding, I could care less about you. What does one more Kaver matter to me?"

What was that supposed to mean? "Then why are you here?"

He leered at her. "There is someone here that I will

return to my lands. He is more valuable than you can ever know."

It hit Sam suddenly. Ralun's earlier comments made much more sense. She understood why Ralun was here, and what he was after.

The Thelns wanted Tray.

Could Ralun know that Tray was part Kaver? Could he know that he'd already found his Scribe?

It was likely that he did.

Was that what Marin had revealed to the Thelns before she was poisoned?

Why would she have poisoned the canals? Not to protect Tray. Unless she was doing it for a different reason.

Sam's head spun as she tried to sort through everything that she had experienced. How much of it was because of Marin and everything that she had done? How much could Sam change?

"You won't get him."

Ralun came close to her. She could smell the sharp bitter stink of his magic. It radiated from him, wafting toward her unpleasantly. "And who do you think will stop me? You? You will fall before you have a chance to stop me."

Sam ducked beneath his attack and rolled forward, trying to keep clear of him, but Ralun caught her hard with a booted foot.

The pain from the attack was enormous. She could barely move, and could barely take a breath. Sam tried rolling out of the way so that Ralun didn't catch her with his foot again, but she couldn't move.

Pain nearly blurred her vision.

Ralun approached slowly, sneering at her. "Did you honestly think you were capable of stopping me?"

"I will keep you from getting Tray."

"No. You won't."

He brought his staff around, and Sam braced for the brutality of an impact, but it never came.

Something cracked against him, and Ralun went staggering forward.

Sam looked up and saw Elaine facing off against Ralun. Before she could process what she was seeing, another Kaver came in—Raylene. Together, they attacked with their canal staffs, driving Ralun back.

"You came yourself. Interesting. I would've expected you to send someone else."

"Why would I send someone else? Why would I have needed to?"

"You regard me so highly?"

"Don't try to play this game with me, Ralun. I know exactly what you are, and who you are."

"Do you? Let me tell you what I know. I know that this one means something to you, or else you wouldn't have come yourself. I will find out what that is. And when I do…"

Elaine swung forward, catching him with her staff, driving him back a step.

Ralun grinned.

"You're done." Elaine said.

"Am I? I'm not nearly as done as you would like to believe," Ralun said.

He turned and sprinted toward the far wall, crashing through it.

Raylene went after him, and Elaine rushed over and crouched down next to Sam.

"What were you thinking coming here yourself?"

"You knew where he was?"

"We've been monitoring this area. Do you think that so much happens in the city that we are not aware of?"

"Where's Bastan?"

"Bastan is unharmed," Elaine said. "And you were foolish to have involved him in this."

"He involved me."

"Only because you went to him. You know how much he cares about you."

Sam laughed bitterly. "Bastan? He doesn't care about me. He cares about profit and information and—"

Elaine leaned close, close enough that Sam could smell her breath. "Bastan cares about you. Don't mistake his business interests for anything else. Why did you involve Bastan?"

Sam tried to move, but her body didn't respond. Pain enveloped her, and she bit back a scream. She needed to get to Alec, anything so that she could recover, but she wasn't sure she would be able to move on her own.

Elaine seemed to notice Sam's pain and shifted her cloak so that she could examine Sam's injuries. She did a cursory evaluation, nothing like what Alec would do, and nodded to herself, seemingly satisfied that Sam was mostly unharmed.

"He's after Tray," Sam said, biting back a painful moan.

"I know."

"You know? I thought you said he was after me."

"I said that for the others' benefit."

"It's because he's half Kaver and half Theln, isn't it?"

Elaine licked her lips. "It's a dangerous combination. I don't know what Marin was thinking when she allowed herself to be used in such a way, but…"

Elaine shook her head and spun.

Sam glanced over. The two djohn were getting up off the floor, and though they looked beaten and injured, they still managed to stand. How that was possible after the way Ralun had pummeled them both, she didn't know.

"Why are you in the city?" Elaine asked them.

The nearest man looked at her with a blank expression. "We were hired."

"Bastan?" Elaine asked.

The man nodded.

"You know the terms of the agreement," Elaine said.

"And you know the terms of our contract. We are not excluded from the city if hired for a task like this."

Elaine breathed out heavily. "It's good that you are here. Now go grab your employer and leave."

The djohn looked around and grabbed the fallen Theln, carrying him with them.

That surprised Sam. Why would they want to take the fallen Theln? Was it for Bastan? More questions for later.

When they were gone, Elaine shook her head. "It was a mistake hiring them," she muttered.

"Why?" Sam asked.

Elaine sighed and turned her attention back to Sam. "The djohn have an agreement with us. It's one that's built on mutual interest, but there has never been anything but animosity between our people."

"Our people?"

"The Kavers and the djohn. They would like to control

the city, but they have been disallowed. There is an agreement in place that prevents it."

There was so much that Sam didn't know. How was it possible that she knew so little?

"He can't get Tray," Sam said.

"No, I don't believe he can."

"Why haven't you shared what you know about Tray with the princess?"

Sam couldn't imagine keeping anything from Alec, at least not anything so important. For Elaine to keep something like that from her Scribe, it was surprising.

"If they knew what your... Tray... is, they would want to destroy him."

"But they already know that he's at least part Theln."

"But they don't know that he is Kaver, do they? And that he has found his Scribe?"

Sam's breath caught. "You know?"

"It is my job to know. How else can I protect the city if I don't know everything that might put them in danger?"

"What now?"

"Now? You return to the palace and your training. You continue doing what you've done. And you will stop attempting to meddle in things that you're not prepared for. In time, you may gain enough information to be valuable, but right now? Now you're a danger. You come in unprepared, you put others in danger, and you draw Bastan into events that he should not be a part of."

Sam sighed. As much as she wanted to be a part of things, she was sure Elaine would do everything she could to prevent it. And she couldn't even argue against it. She hadn't proven that she was capable. She'd proven that she was incapable. That any attempt she might make to participate would only lead to her making mistakes, and even putting others in harm's way. And now Ralun had escaped again.

"If I train, and if I'm willing to do everything that you say, can I be a part of his capture?"

"Ralun or Tray?"

Sam stared at her for a moment, as what Elaine said sank in. Could Elaine really intend to capture Tray? She wanted to find Marin, but Tray had done nothing that warranted capture.

"Both."

Elaine sighed. "I will consider it."

That seemed all Sam could hope for.

26

A REQUEST TO THE MASTERS

"I don't think you should do this," Beckah said, grabbing onto his sleeve as they made their way through a hall in the university.

Alec glanced over at her. She had a look of worry on her face, a pained expression that told him that she feared what he intended. "This is the only way that we have. If I intend to get the master physickers together, this is the only way that I can do it. There aren't any promotions coming up, so there's no other way that we can gather them all together. And if what Sam said is true, and if a master physicker is Marin's Scribe, I need to do this."

"I'm not saying that you *can't* do it, I'm saying that you *shouldn't*. Do you know what happens to people who fail the requested testing?"

Alec shook his head. "I don't know." They paused in the hallway near a lantern. On the wall near it was a painting done by one of the ancient physickers. It depicted the canals, and there was splashes of color within the water, and he wondered if they were supposed to represent the eels. Maybe whoever had painted it was a Scribe as well as a master physicker.

"You will be seen as arrogant."

"The master physickers already see me as arrogant."

"That's not what I'm trying to say. What I'm trying to say is that you would be seen as someone thinking to move too quickly. As someone who doesn't understand his limitations."

"I understand my limitations."

"I know you do, but if you demand testing like this, it puts you in a different place. If you don't get a unanimous vote—and you fail—you will be expelled."

"Are you sure?"

"Ever since you told me your foolish idea, I've been researching it. What other choice did I have? If you're going to do this—and I've seen that look on your face before, so I know you are committed to seeing this through—I wanted to know everything I could about what you were planning and what implication it might have."

"And what did you find?"

"In the record of promotions," she said, "there is documentation of others who have tried to gain promotion this way before. There haven't been many. It was difficult to find any reference, and the most recent I could find happened some thirty-five years ago, and though the person succeeded and was promoted, those I found listed prior to that one were not successful and were expelled."

"Who was it? The one who gained promotion?"

"I couldn't tell. The writing is old and faded, and..."

She shrugged. "But don't you see? If you fail at this, you will be expelled from the university."

Alec swallowed. "If I don't do this, then Marin's Scribe will continue to wander free. The attack they intend on the city will go unopposed. We need to know who it is so we can prevent him from harming the university."

"Then take it to one of the master physickers."

"I would take it to Master Eckerd, but I haven't seen him." Alec was hopeful that in placing this request, Master Eckerd would appear, and he would be able to discuss with him his reason for requesting the testing. He wasn't sure there would be time for quiet conversation. But he was hopeful that doing this would at least give him that audience. "And Master Helen wasn't interested in help-ing." He had wished she would have been more willing to listen. He knew she was a Scribe, but didn't know much more than that about her.

"Alec, I don't want you to risk this and be expelled."

"What if I'm not expelled?" He didn't know what the testing would entail, but he thought he had enough knowledge to at least reach the level of junior physicker—especially having seen what they know. But depending on what testing they demanded of him, it was possible that he didn't.

And then there was the one person that Alec wasn't sure he would be able to convince. Master Carl would be the most difficult, if only because he didn't want Alec to move on.

"How do you intend to get your friend in here if you do this?"

"You don't think they will allow her to observe?"

"I don't know what they'll allow, all I know is that you doing this is putting you in danger."

Alec started off down the hall again. "Sam has been in danger for this, without any help from me. It's time that I risk myself."

Beckah looked over at him, but she didn't say anything as they hurried along the hallway. They reached the stairs to the masters' quarters, and headed up. Now that his decision was made, Alec wanted to act quickly before he lost the nerve. He feared that happening. It wouldn't be too much of a stretch for him to decide not to do this, and to look for another way, but how?

When they reached the top of the stairs, Alec paused. He didn't know if there was a procedure of some sort to make this request. All he knew was that he needed to tell someone his intention, but how?

There were no master physickers here.

This wasn't the place to do it, Alec suddenly realized.

He turned, heading toward the back stairs.

"Where are you going?" Beckah asked.

"I'm going to the wards."

"Why to the wards?"

"Because that's where I need to go to make this request." It was early enough that there were bound to be master physickers making the rounds with students at this time of day.

Beckah sighed and said nothing as she kept pace with him. He had worried that she would resist him, and though she had tried to argue against him doing it, she at least hadn't resisted him any more than that.

He paused briefly at the student section, glancing down the hall. A part of him wanted nothing more than to return to his room, to sit down at his desk, to his journals, to study what he had observed here, but he needed to take action. He needed to risk himself the same way that Sam had risked herself.

Alec took a deep breath, steeling himself, and headed down toward the wards.

Three master physickers were present, and nearly a dozen students with them altogether. He saw Master Jessup with his group of students, and there was master Harold, an older master physicker who leaned on a cane as he hobbled around the wards, and there was Master Carl.

It was almost enough to make him turn back.

"You don't have to do this," Beckah said.

"I *do* have to do this."

Alec stepped forward. He started toward Master Jessup. He knew him the best and thought that he might be the most accepting of him, and that he might be willing to work with him and perhaps guide him on the steps necessary to making the request. Instead, Master Carl looked over and saw him. He stepped away from his students and headed straight toward Alec.

"Mr. Stross. I don't see Master Eckerd here, so there is no reason for you to be on the wards." He looked over to Beckah. "And you, Ms. Reynolds—"

Alec closed his eyes, taking a deep breath, and opened them, fixing Master Carl with the hardest expression that he could. "I have come here to demand testing to physicker."

Master Carl blinked before clasping his hands behind his back, his belly thrusting forward in that way he had.

"You have what?" he asked, a hint of a smile crossing his face.

"I have come here to demand testing for promotion to physicker."

Master Carl leaned close. "Mr. Stross, you are making a grave mistake."

"According to the charter of the university, I have the right to request testing."

"What is this, Carl?"

Alec looked over to see Master Jessup approaching. He frowned, his bushy eyebrows creating shadows over his eyes.

"This is Mr. Stross coming to the wards to request testing for promotion to physicker."

There was always a playfulness about Master Jessup, but it faded immediately. "Request testing? Something like that has not happened in—"

"Many years," Master Carl said.

"I request testing to promotion to physicker," Alec said again. He tried to put more force into his voice, wanting to sound more confident than he felt, but he wasn't sure he had succeeded.

"Mr. Stross," Master Jessup said, stepping close, putting himself between Alec and Master Carl, "it's not too late for you to withdraw this request. I can smooth things over with Master Carl, but—"

Alec looked over to Master Jessup. "No. I don't want to withdraw the request."

"You understand the consequences of failure?" he asked, glancing over to Master Carl.

"I understand," Alec said.

"You haven't been here long," Master Jessup said. "Certainly not long enough to understand exactly what you would be missing if you were expelled, but trust me when I tell you that you have potential. You will become a master physicker in time, but please, take that time."

Alec looked over to Master Jessup. He appreciated the man's interest in him. "I need to do this. I need to be tested."

"It is decided," Master Carl said. "Mr. Stross has demanded testing, and testing will be provided."

He turned away, heading toward his students, whistling as he went. There was an eagerness to his step, and Alec had a sinking feeling that he had just made a significant mistake. Even if he answered all of Master Carl's questions correctly, could he still choose not to promote him?

"Why did you do this?" Master Jessup asked.

"I needed to," Alec said.

Master Jessup studied him for a moment, then clasped him on the shoulder before returning to his students.

"Well," Beckah said, "I guess now it's time for you to prepare."

"How long do you think I have?"

"I don't know. The records aren't clear about the timing of the request and the testing. I imagine it will be a few days, but maybe it will be less."

Alec looked over to Master Carl. He suspected that if Master Carl had anything to do with it, it would be less, likely much less.

And that would be okay with him. He wanted to get this over with.

First, he had to talk to Sam and tell her what he had done, so that they could prepare. That meant returning to the palace, and if he did, would he be granted entrance? Would she be able to see him?

Hopefully, he could send a note ahead of him so that she understood the significance of meeting with him. Now that he had committed to this, he was determined to see it through.

27

LAST VISIT

Alec approached the palace with caution. He couldn't stop thinking about the last time he'd come, and the admonition that Master Helen had given him, warning him away. A part of him feared that he might encounter her again, and if he did, what would he do? He would have to press on, especially considering his recent request. After all, she'd be at the testing, too. Didn't he need to show his resolve? His commitment and confidence?

The guards at the bridge allowed him to cross. Why hadn't they let him cross before? The ring *should* have granted him access, and the fact that it hadn't before meant someone wanted him to stay away. Had it been part of Sam's training? Now that she could jump the canals without augmentations, they didn't need to keep the two of them apart?

Would he have any difficulty getting to Sam?

Would she even be here? When he'd last seen her, she was returning to the palace for continued training, but that didn't ensure she'd be here now. If she wasn't here, Alec wasn't sure how else to find her. He'd sent a note ahead, hoping to at least send word to her that he was looking for her, but hadn't heard anything back.

His testing was now only one day away.

That hadn't surprised him. Rather, he suspected it was all Master Carl's doing, forcing the issue, and maybe even making certain that it happened during a time when Master Eckerd was still away from the university. Alec still hadn't seen any sign of him, and hadn't heard anything about him returning, so he didn't know if Master Eckerd even knew about his request.

How many master physickers would be there for his testing?

The clatter of wood against wood drew his attention. There was movement near an open courtyard, and it was a part of the palace grounds that Alec had never seen before. When he reached it, he paused, amazed at what he saw. Two people—a man and a woman—faced each other, staffs spinning so rapidly that they had to be augmented. They were smacking them off of each other, flipping into the air and spinning back down, the staffs a whiz of movement. Alec struggled simply to follow them.

Kavers training.

Was this what Sam was learning?

He had seen her fight before and had been impressed by it, but these Kavers were moving with even more fluidity than what Sam had managed with his augmentations. He looked around the courtyard, looking for evidence of their Scribes, but saw no one. Maybe they were connected to a Scribe at the university, a master physicker, but these two were young. Typically, the

Kaver-Scribe pairing was two people similar in age, and he didn't know anyone at the university who would be age-matched with them.

Maybe they hadn't found their Scribes yet.

Then again, Alec didn't know all of the inside details about the connection to the Scribes. Many of the master physickers were Scribes, but he suspected other physickers were Scribes also. They had to be, especially considering the number of Kavers that Sam said trained here.

He saw someone sitting near a wall, slumped forward, staff leaning against the wall, and Alec frowned. The dark hair was familiar to him.

"Sam?" he asked, approaching.

She looked up at him. "Alec? Why are you here?"

"Didn't you get my note?"

She breathed out. "I've been a little preoccupied," she said.

"What happened?"

"I went to Bastan, and he led me to Ralun, and..."

"And what?"

"And I nearly died."

Alec crouched down next to her and reached for a scrap of easar paper that he kept with him.

Sam shook her head. "I've been healed. Elaine made certain to heal me, though I think she wanted me to suffer. When I was in too much pain to even move, she was forced to do something."

"You don't look as if you're completely healed."

"Because I've been training. Raylene is a brutal master, and she is trying to demonstrate what I can do without augmentations." She looked past him, and Alec turned to the pair still fighting with their staffs.

"That's without augmentation?"

"Apparently," she said.

"Can you do that?" Alec asked, turning back to her.

"Not yet. Elaine is convinced that I can, and she wants me to learn so that I don't end up nearly dead again."

"I would agree with that desire," Alec said.

He took a seat next to her and leaned toward her. There was something comforting about sitting next to Sam, and he breathed in her scent, wanting only to remain near her.

"Why have you come?" she asked.

"I found a way to get the master physickers together."

Her eyes widened. Alec told her of his plan and what he had done.

"Let me get this straight. If this fails, you will be expelled from the university?"

Alec nodded. "And Master Carl doesn't care for me, so it's possible that I will fail."

"Why doesn't he care for you?"

"It has something to do with my father. I learned that he was a master physicker but left the university after my mother died."

"He *what*?"

Alec sighed. He still didn't know what to make of that information. "All this time I thought he was nothing more than a very skilled apothecary." He shook his head. "But that's not why I'm telling you this. Apparently, my father prevented Master Carl from moving up in the political ranks. I think now he's holding that against me because of what my father did to him."

"Do you think he could be Marin's Scribe?"

"I think anyone could be. Master Carl certainly is smart enough, but I don't get the sense that he is a Scribe."

"If he's treating you this way, maybe he knows about us. Maybe that's why he's doing this and not because of your father."

"I don't know."

"Describe him for me." Alec did, and Sam frowned. "I don't know. With those augmentations that you gave me, I had such strength that I tore doors off the wall. It's possible I wouldn't even have noticed how large the man was. And the deep voice fits."

"If it was Master Carl, I'd be happy for you to beat on him again."

"Are you sure that you want to do this? I thought there might be an easier way to get the master physickers together. I didn't think you would be forced to risk yourself like this, or risk your future with the university. We might need you to continue training there."

"I've thought about it, but I think this might be the only way we can make this work," Alec said.

"I don't like it," she said.

"I don't like it, either, but that's the plan, and now, we need to figure out a way to get you in."

"That might be harder than it once was," Sam said. She glared at the other Kaver, the one she called Raylene. "Elaine has me training with Raylene constantly. She knows that Ralun is in the city, and"—Sam turned to Alec and lowered her voice—"Elaine is afraid of what might happen if anyone else learns that Tray has both Kaver and Theln in him."

"How would they not know that? They know that he's Marin's son."

"I think the belief is that he is mostly Theln. Apparently, such pairings have been attempted before, and none of them have been successful. The offspring have always been either Kaver or Theln, never both."

"And Tray?"

Sam shrugged. "You're the one who proved that he has Kaver potential."

It wasn't Alec, but Beckah. "What does it mean?"

"It means that Ralun came to the city searching for Tray. I had been afraid that Tray was already working with Ralun, but that's not it. I think he's trying to figure out where he fits and what he's meant to do."

"You still want to help them."

"I have to. He's my brother."

"So first, we find Marin's Scribe, then we stop Ralun, and then..."

"Then we find where Tray is keeping Marin," Sam said. "Then both of us can get some answers."

"That's not all you want."

"It's not, but I don't know if Ralun even has the Book with him. If he did, you'd think he'd have used it against me before now."

"Maybe he can't use it against you."

"Why would you think that?"

Alec stared out over the courtyard. From here, he could see the edge of the university rising above the palace wall. In another direction, the rest of the city spread out, though it was peaceful here. Quiet. He could understand why Sam enjoyed her time in the palace.

"What if there is something in your Kaver blood that allows you to be protected?"

"The Book *was* used on me, Alec. That's why I lost my memoires. And why wouldn't it protect Scribes?"

"I don't know. We know that it doesn't, especially given that the princess nearly died from being poisoned. But maybe he can't use it against you. It seems as if he fears you more than he lets on."

"I don't think he fears me. Kyza knows he almost killed me. My augmentation wore off before I had a chance to even hurt him. If it weren't for Elaine and Raylene appearing…"

Alec didn't like to hear that, and was thankful that Elaine had arrived in time to help Sam. "I'm glad they were there."

"There was something else," Sam said.

"What is it?"

"Bastan had hired a couple of men, not locals. They have some strange ability that allows them to confront the Thelns."

"Who else could he have hired?"

"They weren't Kavers. Ralun called them djohn, and they were able to fight in ways that I've never seen. I don't know if they had similar augmentations, or if it was some natural ability, but whatever it was…"

"I'm glad Bastan thought to hire them."

"Yeah, but why did he think to hire them? And how did he know to hire them?"

"Haven't you always told me that Bastan is well-connected?"

"There's well-connected, and then there's whatever

this was. This is more than just being well-connected. This is understanding the limitations of the Thelns."

"Maybe Bastan is more involved in this than you realize."

Sam frowned. "Maybe."

"The testing is in a day, maybe a little more. If you could be there…"

Sam looked over at him. "I'll get there. I think I can sneak away. And now that I don't need augmentations to cross the canal, I should be able to reach you more easily. I think I can sneak in unnoticed. Do you know where the testing will be?"

Alec shook his head. "I don't know. I can send word once they tell me when and where it will be."

"You think they'll give you enough time to send word to me?"

"Hopefully. I might have to send Beckah."

Sam's mouth twisted in a sour expression.

"She's been helping me. She wants to find Tray almost as much as you do."

"I doubt that."

"She does. She wants to know what it's like to be a Scribe and have an opportunity to work with her Kaver."

"I don't like the way she acts around you."

"And how is that?"

"She's so *clingy*."

"You don't have to worry about Beckah. Nothing's going to happen between us." Alec flushed as he said it, but he looked at Sam, meeting her eyes. His heart fluttered, and he worried that she would reject him.

Instead, she took his hand. Her hand was so small around his, but she had quite a bit of strength as she squeezed. He enjoyed the way his hand felt in hers, and they sat for a long moment.

"What now?" Sam asked in a whisper.

"Now, we need to do what we've been talking about," he said. "We need to stop Ralun so that you can be safe. We need to see if we can't uncover the Book. And we need to find the Scribe."

"No. What now with us?"

Alec turned toward her, and slipped his hand out from hers and pulled her into an embrace, hugging her tightly. Sam squeezed back. Holding her felt... right. He enjoyed the connection, and it felt as if they were meant to have found each other. "We'll get through this together," he said.

"I know," Sam said. "Make sure you pass your test."

"I'll do my best," Alec said.

"I mean, you know more than most of the physickers there, don't you?"

"I know enough."

"Enough? That doesn't give me a lot of reassurance," she said, pushing back from him. Alec let her go, thankful that they'd had that moment. Would they ever get more moments like that? What would it take for them to have time together when they didn't have to worry about attacks and their roles as Kaver and Scribe?

"I'm not so sure that it's all about what I know, but more about getting the master physickers to allow me to be promoted," Alec said.

"And this Master Carl?"

"Master Carl might choose this as a way to deny me the opportunity." Alec thought about how happy Master Carl had been when he had requested testing. He had been practically giddy. That didn't give him a lot of hope that he would succeed. "And I'm not sure that it matters. As long as you're there and you can pick out which Scribe held you captive, I think that's all that matters."

"Then I'll be there."

She looked over his shoulder and nodded.

Alec turned and saw the other Kaver approaching. She held her staff casually, glancing from Alec to Sam.

"It is time," the woman said.

Sam smiled at Alec. "It looks like it's time for me to beat up on Raylene again." The other woman frowned at Sam, and she only shrugged. "Fine, maybe it's time for Raylene to beat up on me. Either way, it's time for something."

Alec watched Sam as she moved to the center of the courtyard and began to battle with Raylene. As he watched, it was obvious that she had improved. She was even more skilled than when he had seen her fighting with Marin. Alec watched for a while before getting up and making his way back to the university. It was time for him to prepare for his testing.

SEARCH FOR THE TRAITOR

A knock came at Sam's door, and she looked up.

When the door open, she recognized the pretty woman who entered. "Beckah?" she asked.

Beckah nodded and pushed a strand of hair back behind her ear. Sam hated that she looked pretty even doing that. It had helped that Alec had reassured her that there was nothing between them, but she couldn't help still feeling a little nervous about it. Regardless of what Alec said, she had seen the way Beckah looked at him.

"It's time," Beckah said.

"The testing?" Sam got to her feet and grabbed her canal staff. She looked around and grabbed her cloak from off her bed and threw it over her shoulders.

"They summoned him early this morning."

"And you're only coming to me now?"

"I'm only coming to you now because I couldn't get away before now."

Sam resisted the urge to smack Beckah. That wouldn't do anything other than make her feel better.

"How long is the testing expected to last?"

"I don't know. I haven't been able to figure it out. He was summoned, they took him to a room where they questioned him, and now they've moved on to the ward."

"The ward?"

"It's the hospital in the university. It's where the sickest go for treatment."

"Are all the masters there?" Sam wasn't sure how much Alec had told Beckah, but given her connection to Tray, she suspected he had shared everything with her. And why wouldn't he? If Beckah was meant to be a Scribe, there would be no reason for him to conceal anything from her.

"I watched them all go. That's how I knew where he was."

"Kyza!" Sam hurried out of her room and raced along the hall. Beckah kept up, and Sam was glad she didn't have to encourage her to move more quickly. "What's the easiest way to get to the ward?"

"I will lead you."

"What if I don't want you to lead me?"

Beckah grabbed for her sleeve, and Sam turned toward her, but neither stopped walking. "I want to help Alec the same as you," Beckah said. "I don't want him expelled from the university any more than you do. Probably less."

Sam glared at her. "I'm not sure that's true."

She saw Raylene at the end of the hall and hurriedly turned a corner, ducking down a back staircase. She didn't need any of the Kavers trying to grab her to train. If she was missing, at least there would be an excuse.

Beckah kept pace, and they reached the outside of the palace neared the bridge.

"Go ahead and cross the bridge. They won't let me go across."

"Who won't?"

Sam nodded to the guards stationed there. "The guards. I imagine Alec gave you his ring to warn me?"

Beckah glanced down at her hand where she still held the ring. "He did. He said I'd need it to come across here."

"No. It's good that he did. Otherwise, you would have been prevented from crossing over to the section. But they won't let me across."

"How will you get across then? Alec won't be able to place an augmentation on you."

"I don't need augmentation to cross the canal."

"But it's so wide!"

"Go. I'll meet you on the other side."

Beckah hesitated, and Sam waved her away. She stepped up to the shore and looked around. Seeing no one there, she screwed the ends of her canal staff together and flipped out into the water. She landed on the staff, balancing as she had managed to master, and flipped her way across the water. When she landed on the far shore, she unscrewed the ends of her staff and quickly tucked them beneath her cloak. On this side of the water—near the university—there was no reason for her to have the canal staff so obvious.

Beckah reached her a short while later. "How?"

"I'm a Kaver." She waved her hand. "Are you going to show me where the wards are?"

Beckah looked across the canal for a moment before nodding and leading Sam into the university. She followed carefully, keeping her cloak wrapped around her shoulders, not wanting to draw attention, but if she did, she didn't want to be recognized, either.

It was dark inside the university, and Beckah started off at a confident pace, knowing where she was heading. Sam followed slowly, carefully. It took a moment for her eyes to adjust, and when they heard voices along the hall, Beckah took a different path, leading them deeper and deeper into the university.

The canal staff pressed against Sam's leg, and she debated finding a place to hide it, but she didn't like going without it. There was a certain reassurance in having the canal staff with her, even if there was nothing that she could use it for here. She crept along the halls of the university, following Beckah, hating that she was reliant on this woman of all people to help Alec.

Then they reached a set of stairs, and she went down.

"He'll be in here," she said as she paused in front of a set of double doors.

Beckah pushed open one of the doors and slipped inside. Sam followed, keeping her cloak wrapped around her, her hood up to cover her face. They clung to one of the walls, and Sam hurriedly wrapped the cloak around Beckah so that she could conceal the other woman in it with her.

"What are you doing?" Beckah hissed.

"Quiet. The cloak will help conceal us."

Sam looked out from under the hood. Where they stood had enough shadows that she thought they might go unnoticed. At least here, she could look out over the ward and see exactly what it was that Alec was experiencing.

It took a moment for her to find him. He stood in the

middle of the room next to a row of beds. A dozen—maybe more—people were arranged around him, and they were asking question after question of him.

"Is this the testing?" Sam asked.

"I don't know. I haven't seen a testing before. I thought it was only questions, and was surprised that they brought him down to the ward," Beckah whispered.

They were too far away for Sam to easily hear. She started forward, pulling Beckah with her. Beckah tried to resist, but Sam shoved her along, not letting her slow her down.

Thankfully, everyone's attention seemed to be focused on the center of the room—and on Alec.

When they were closer, Sam ducked down, getting beneath one of the cots. From here, she could listen. She wasn't able to necessarily see everything, but if she could hear the voices, she was hopeful she could identify which one was the man that had captured her.

"Tell me, Mr. Stross, what do you know of this person?"

It was a woman's voice.

"This was a glandular issue. I simply made a few suggestions in the record."

"*You* made some suggestions?"

Sam couldn't tell who spoke, but there was definitely irritation in the voice. It seemed to come from someone near Alec, and she risked poking her head up to see. When she did, she identified Master Carl immediately. He was enormous, and he stood exactly as Alec had described, with his hands clasped behind his back, his belly thrust forward. He glared at Alec, but there was an almost eager expression on his face.

Sam dropped back down.

"I made some suggestions. They were treating this as an infection when it's clearly glandular."

"What made you think that it was glandular?" This was from the woman again.

Sam poked her head up, recognizing the voice. It was Master Helen. Her hair was done up as primly as it always was, and she stood with her arms crossed over her chest, her lips pursed, and she questioned Alec.

"I have seen glandular illnesses before. It's the protrusion of the eyes. There is a sheen of sweat over the body. There is the swelling in the neck. If you listen to her heart, you will hear a rapid heart rate as well."

"That could be dehydration," another voice said.

"It's not simply dehydration, not in combination with the other symptoms the woman presents."

Sam was proud of Alec. He was confident in his knowledge. That didn't surprise her. She had seen that confidence before, but she wasn't sure how he would react to being tested in this manner. Hearing him gave her hope that he might succeed. If he could manage to withstand the questioning, she was optimistic that he might be able to prove himself worthy of promotion to physicker.

And while he was being tested, she needed to complete her task.

She motioned to Beckah, indicating that she should stay near the cot. At least where she was, she was hidden and didn't risk discovery. Sam needed to creep around and see if she could get close enough to hear better.

She moved silently, trying to use every bit of her training as a thief. Never had the stakes been quite like this. Never had she needed to move around so many people who could catch her. And if they did? What would the consequences be?

Likely severe. There would be Scribes among these master physickers, and they would get word back to Elaine, and then what? What would Elaine do to her?

Sam didn't want to think about it.

"What of this one?" she heard. They had moved on, switching places, now standing before a different cot and a different person.

Sam struggled forward, trying to see if there was any way to inch even closer. All she needed was some way to get close enough to see—and hear—who was testing Alec. So far, she was certain that it wasn't Master Carl. With the irritation he displayed toward Alec, she thought she would have recognized that tone used on her, and she hadn't. That meant there was someone else at the university not in attendance today. There had to be.

She had to find him.

"This is a more basic infection," Alec was saying. "With the fever and the rapid heart rate, as well as the cough, I suspected a lung infection, and would treat with…"

Sam moved, less concerned about trying to listen when Alec was doing the talking.

"That is an interesting choice," someone said. This was a woman, and though she had a deep voice, it wasn't the same person that had held Sam captive. "Typically, one might try pastin oil for such an infection."

"You certainly could, but when I studied under my father, we found that oil was difficult, and often times quite a bit more costly than using something that was less expensive. Less expensive doesn't necessarily mean it's less effective, from what I have observed."

"No," Master Helen said. "But there is something to be said about the perception of value."

"I think the perception of value is only critical if you think people doubt the master physickers are capable," Alec said.

Sam popped her head up, looking for Alec, tempted to try to catch his eye, but now she was blocked by the line of master physickers.

If this started early this morning, and he was still going at it, how many questions was he subjected to? He seemed to give good answers, and she suspected that they had to believe he knew what he was talking about, especially considering what he'd told her about the junior physickers, and that few of them seemed to know everything. They relied on the master physickers to guide them still.

"Next," came a deep, rumbling voice. This was from a bearded man, and he was solid, muscular, but didn't seem to have the same tenor to his voice as the man who'd held her.

"This was a complicated fracture," Alec said. "There would be several options for treating this, but I think that setting the bone and giving it time would be the best option."

"What other options would you consider?"

Sam couldn't tell who was talking. The voice was soft, but it didn't sound quite right. How many had she heard speaking? Maybe half a dozen. Still, none of their voices were familiar. She had to find Marin's Scribe.

"There would be a surgical option, but it would be difficult and would raise the risk of ongoing infection."

"Some would argue that with the nature of this injury,

an infection is all but guaranteed," someone said. Another soft voice. A woman. Sam looked around and spotted a very slight woman. She had thick glasses and a drab dress that hung all the way to the floor. Surprisingly, a flower was tucked behind her ear.

"That's true," Alec said. "An injury like this, especially when the bone pierces the skin, is often infected. It's good that this person was brought to the university in time to be treated. There are a variety of compounds that all would help reduce the likelihood of infection, but of greatest importance is splinting in such a way that there is no long-term deficit."

"And how would you splint this?"

"Strips of cloth caked in hardened sand is often used, but even that would not necessarily be critical. You could use any one of the pre-formed metal splints, wrapping it with cloth. At least that was what we used to do when splinting this kind of injury."

"Archaic," Master Carl said.

Alec looked over to him. "Not archaic. The metal was easy to clean and unlikely to contribute to infection. The cloth could be steamed to ensure cleanliness, adding to the process, and limiting the likelihood of infection."

"Very good," someone said.

Sam poked her head up. There was something about that voice that was familiar.

She saw a man with bushy eyebrows and a slight smile to his face. No. That man seemed too happy. It was almost as if he beamed at Alec, as if approving that he had come for testing. Whoever had abducted her would have been upset by him doing this.

"Moving on," she heard. It was Master Carl again.

Alec coughed. Sam poked her head up and could see his face flushing. He was uncomfortable, but why?

"This one is a little more challenging. I had asked Master Carl about his presenting symptoms, but he did not reveal anything."

The others in the room all turned to Master Carl, and he only shrugged. "If he wants to be a physicker—even a junior physicker—then he needs to make a diagnosis based on the facts available to him."

"And if the facts included a presenting complaint?" Master Helen asked.

"That's not always the case."

"But in this case, it was." She turned to Alec and thrust a notebook into his hands. Alec flipped it open and scanned the pages, nodding to himself. He removed the sheet covering the man and shifted the gown to perform a visual assessment. "Yes. It appears he came in with shoulder pain and was dosed with a sedative."

He started listening, leaning his head down to the man's chest, before shifting to listen to his lungs and then to his stomach. He moved again and pressed on the man's stomach. The man moaned.

Alec leaned over the cot and traced his fingers over something on the man's stomach.

What was it that he observed?

Sam wished she had a better view, wishing there was a vantage from where she could see exactly what Alec saw, but doing so would only put her in view of the master physickers, and she didn't want to draw attention to herself and distract from Alec's testing. If she were caught, and if it disrupted his testing, she worried it would cause more problems for him.

"The shoulder pain could be referred from the stomach," Alec was saying.

"And I have told you that such a referred pain as you call it is unlikely. This is most likely an infection in this man's shoulder. We found a puncture wound on the skin of his back near the shoulder," Master Carl said.

"There might've been a puncture, but I suspect that was misleading," Alec said. "This would be an abdominal source. You see this bluish discoloration on his belly?" Alec asked. He grunted as he attempted to twist the man. "And the bruising along his flanks. This all signifies a fairly severe infection in one of his upper abdominal organs. Unfortunately, there's not much that can be done for such an infection."

Alec's voice trailed off toward the end, and Sam could tell that admitting that bothered him. If Alec had his way, he would use easar paper to heal as many people as possible, but there was a limit to its availability, so there was a limit to how many could be helped.

"Those weren't evident when he presented," Master Carl said. "It's likely from the aggressive palpation of the junior physickers. And he has improved."

Alec tapped something on the notebook. "I don't know that he's improved, only stabilized. It has been my experience—"

"Your experience as an apothecary? Or your experience as a student at the university?" Master Carl asked with a sneer. "If it's the latter, you have very little experience. You have not been here long enough to gain the adequate experience, which was why your requesting this testing makes this entire day a farce."

Sam watched as Alec controlled his breathing. "My

experience as an apothecary has placed me in a great many situations where I get to observe the body's response to treatment. Unfortunately, there are far too many times when treatment fails. This is one of them."

Sam started to move, shifting around to improve her view, when she felt a hand across her mouth.

She tried to bite, tried to kick, but someone held her tightly and dragged her from the room. She shook her head, trying to twist away, but the person who held her did so with much more strength than she had, at least without augmentation. She was dragged from the healing ward, and out into a hallway, away from Alec and Beckah.

The person carried her down a set of stairs and then into darkness. A door opened and she was thrown inside.

"What do we have here?"

The voice was familiar. This was Marin's Scribe.

He must've seen her.

"It seems as if your Scribe is distracted at the moment. I doubt there will be any escape this time."

Sam shivered.

"And now, you will help me find her."

29

RECAPTURE

A lantern flicked on, and Sam craned her neck to see the master physicker with the bushy eyebrows staring at her. The playfulness to his expression was gone. Now, he glared at her with a hard-eyed stare, his mouth pressed together in a tight line.

She was in an otherwise empty room. She suspected he had brought her deep into the university, far enough away that she wouldn't be able to make enough noise to draw anyone's attention. Her only hope was that Alec would realize she had been there—and was now missing. Would Beckah be able to help?

First, she would have to want to help, and Sam wasn't sure that she would.

"Who are you?"

"I think we've already discovered our roles."

"No. Who are you here?"

"Here?" He raised his hands and smiled. It was strange the way that his features shifted, the edge disappearing, replaced by something that almost appeared happy. Were it not for the darkness on his face only moments before, it would've been believable. "Here I am known as Master Jessup. Your Scribe has confided in me far more than I expected. I'll admit that he was easy to manipulate into such a daring request. I thought it would be more difficult to get him expelled from the university. Then again, I thought it would be more difficult to capture you, especially after you escaped from me the first time."

"Even if Alec is expelled, he will still continue his training."

"Perhaps, but he will do so without any formalized education about what it means to be a Scribe. And he will do so without his Kaver."

"Why do you think that I know where Marin is?" Sam asked. She needed to buy time. Every minute that passed was one minute closer to his testing being over. One minute closer to Beckah telling him she'd been there but had disappeared. She needed to believe Beckah would want to help her. Hadn't she risked herself by coming across to the palace?

"I was there when you defeated her. I know that Trayson carried her away, and I know that he must've done so under your direction."

"I can take you to Tray," Sam said.

"Oh, I know you can—and will," he said.

"What's your intention with Tray?"

"My intention? I will let Marin decide what happens with him."

"Do you know who he is?"

"Who? She would have some believe that he's her son, but..." The man grinned, shaking his head. "As it no longer matters that you know, I suppose it doesn't hurt to share with you that he is not Marin's son."

Sam swallowed. If he wasn't Marin's son, then she had continued to deceive Sam. How deep did Marin's deception go? What would be the point of raising her with one lie—that Tray was her brother—and then presenting yet another lie, calling him her own son?

"No? Then who is he related to?"

"You already know that he is part Theln."

"That would be obvious just taking one look at him," Sam said.

"It's the other part that is less obvious, isn't it? It's seeing the Anders in him that makes it more challenging."

Anders? If true, that meant that Tray was related to one of the royal family. But did she dare believe this man? Why would he tell her this? How could it even be true?

But then, it would make sense why Elaine was so intent on finding him now. It would make sense that she had pursued him the way that she did. And it would make sense why Ralun wanted him.

Not because he was part Kaver and part Theln, but because he was related to the royal family—and part Theln.

That made far more sense than any other information she had been given about her brother.

"I know someone who might have information about him."

"You know someone? I'm afraid that is of little value to me. Now, on the other hand, if you knew where to find him…"

If only she did.

Where was Alec?

She needed to get free of here, and she needed to get an augmentation, but since Alec likely presumed she was at the university, watching his testing, he'd have no reason to think she was in any danger.

She jerked at her bindings, trying to get herself free, but they were tight, even tighter than they had been the last time he had bound her, confining her to a chair.

He grinned at her, darkness on his face. "Marin will be most pleased that I managed to capture you."

"Marin the deceiver?"

"You know so little," he said.

"I know that you have betrayed the Scribes. I know that you have betrayed those who you vowed to work with. I think that's enough."

"No," he said. "What you know is only the edge of the truth. You know only that the Kavers and the Scribes have battled with the Thelns, but you know nothing about that battle, nothing about the history behind it, and you know nothing about the reason that we are isolated here, hidden away from the rest of the world, only those with permission granted access to the city. Have you ever thought to question?"

Sam stared at him. She hated that he was making sense, but she couldn't deny that there was something to what he was saying. The city *was* isolated, and she didn't know anything about why the Kavers and the Thelns were at war. Of all the things she had learned from Elaine so far, that was not one of them.

"What is it? Why are they at war?"

"It might be too bad that you won't live to have that question answered."

She jerked on her restraints again, trying to loosen them. Could Alec get free and place an augmentation?

But he couldn't. They hadn't drawn any blood from each other in days, possibly even longer. Even if he discovered that she was missing, there was nothing he could do to help her. She was truly trapped.

And here, within the belly of the university, with only Alec and Beckah knowing where she was, she didn't even have the hope that someone else could rescue her. There was no chance of Elain coming to her rescue this time. There was no chance she would be saved.

30

TESTING

A lec looked around the board. He wiped a bead of sweat from his brow, trying to ignore the nerves, but it was difficult, especially with the way the masters—especially Master Carl—peppered him with questions.

They had come to him far too quickly, and he hadn't been able to send word to Sam, but he was hopeful that Beckah had realized he not in his room, or any of their usual study places. Would she presume he'd been summoned for testing? Even if she was aware that the testing had begun, it might already be too late.

He looked down at the young man on the cot. This was the same one that he had seen when challenged by Master Carl, and he feared this would be the reason he failed his testing. The diagnosis was not straightforward. At least Master Helen had pressured Master Carl to reveal the presenting symptoms. Without that, Alec would have had even less of an idea about what he needed to do to treat this individual.

And he tried to remain confident, but that felt forced.

He motioned to the discoloration on the belly. There was a bluish hue, and his father had taught him that such markers indicated a significant abdominal illness. He rolled the man and saw bruising along his flanks.

When he saw it, he knew immediately that this man was beyond his help.

"I don't think there's anything that can be done for him," Alec said.

He tried to ignore the excited look on Master Carl's face. It was an expression that told Alec that Master Carl believed he was wrong. It was an expression that made Alec question, if only for a moment. *Could* he be wrong? He didn't have a lot of experience seeing illness like this, but certainly enough that he recalled a conversation with his father that there was only so much that could be done for someone in this condition. It was a conversation that had taught Alec that there were limitations to his father's abilities. He recalled all too well how he learned that day that there were times when his father's knowledge failed him.

And his father was a master physicker. Whatever else Master Carl might claim, Alec had been learning from a master physicker his entire life.

Alec looked out around the collected master physickers. It would have been helpful for him to have had at least one friendly face. Master Eckerd was not present, and Alec still didn't know where he had gone, and why he had failed to return for Alec's testing. At least Master Jessup had provided some reassuring nods, but where was he now?

"We will move on," Master Helen said.

"I think we have seen quite enough," Master Carl said.

Alec squeezed his hands together, wringing them beneath his jacket.

"You would call for a vote?" Master Helen said.

"I think we have all seen enough from Mr. Stross to make a decision," Master Carl said.

Alec looked at the other masters. There were many familiar faces—many of the master physickers that he had spent quite a bit of time with during his time at the university—but only a few that he could say with certainty might favor him. Far more likely were the number of master physickers who regarded him with skepticism. Master Harrison and Master Helen were among them. Without having an advocate, how would he fare when it came to a vote?

"We will call the vote," Master Helen said. She turned to Alec. "Mr. Stross. You may remain in the hall outside. We will call you when we have finalized our vote."

Alec nodded, feeling numb.

All of this had been designed as a way to give Sam a chance to listen to the master physickers, and it appeared that he had failed at that. He hadn't been able to get word to Sam in time.

Now, likely because of Master Carl, he would be expelled from the university.

His testing was a failure on all counts.

It hurt more than he thought it would.

Getting expelled didn't mean he would stop attempting to learn, and it didn't mean he would stop trying to heal, using his knowledge and gifts and training to help others, but it made it more difficult. He could return to his father, and he suspected that his father would work with him, but his time at the university had been a failure. Alec was not accustomed to failure.

He made his way out of the ward and paused once out in the hallway. When he did, he let out a deep breath, sighing heavily.

"Alec," someone hissed from down the hall.

Alec glanced back and saw Beckah. "What are *you* doing here?" he whispered.

"I brought Sam to see if she could hear which master physicker might've been the one who held her after she was attacked by the Thelns."

Beckah had come through. "Do you think she heard who it was?"

"It doesn't matter."

"It *does* matter. If we can't figure out which master physicker was involved, then—"

"It doesn't matter because I saw him. It was Master Jessup. He grabbed Sam and dragged her from the room when everyone else was distracted."

"You *saw* this?"

Beckah glanced over to the ward, her eyes wide. "Sam had hidden me beneath one of the cots. She had moved on, trying to get a better vantage, when she was grabbed. Master Jessup pulled her down, and pulled her from between the cots, keeping her out of sight." Beckah shivered. "I still can't believe that Master Jessup would do such a thing."

"Maybe it isn't what it looks like."

Beckah arched a brow at him. "Isn't what it looks like? It looked like he was covering her mouth so she wouldn't scream and had his arm clamped around her so she couldn't fight."

"But Master Jessup?"

"I don't know what to tell you, other than the fact that I know what I saw. He's the one who abducted Sam. I don't know where he took her, but..."

Alec's mind raced. "He won't be able to be gone long," Alec said. "Which means he couldn't have taken her very far."

"He wouldn't need to be present at the vote," Beckah said.

"He wouldn't need to be, but his absence would raise questions, especially among those who know the Scribes. He had been one of the master physickers who supported me, if only peripherally. His absence would be noticed."

And Alec thought he knew where to look. Master Jessup had shared it with him, maybe without meaning to.

He glanced over at the closed door leading into the wards. If he left now, he wouldn't know the result of his testing.

But if he didn't, he would run the risk of something happening to Sam.

"Can you stay here and watch? If they come out for me, let them know..." Alec tried to think about what he would have Beckah tell the master physickers. What was there to say that would be unlikely to raise the wrong kind of questions? There wasn't anything. His absence alone would raise questions. "If they come for me, let Master Helen know that I haven't abandoned my testing."

"Alec—"

"I need to do this. I might be the only one who can help her now."

Beckah glanced over at the ward before nodding. Alec hurried off, heading to the end of the hall and then down the stairs. Master Jessup had mentioned having a place where he had gone when he had been a student, a place that was a storeroom that he and his friends had gone to study. It was the kind of place where Alec suspected he could take Sam.

He tried to remain hidden as he went, prepared to duck off to the side and hide if he saw any sign of movement. At one point, he thought he did, and he slipped into a doorway, waiting. A moment passed, and then another, and as he was ready to step back out, someone hurried past.

Alec waited, counting silently until he reached ten, before poking his head out.

Could that have been Master Jessup?

If it was, he didn't have much time. He raced along the hallway and slowed as he studied the doors. This was a remote part of the university, and hidden deep enough that noise wouldn't carry beyond this floor. He listened, focusing on where he might find Sam, but didn't hear anything.

Worse, he didn't have any access to a combination of their blood to help her. So, he couldn't even try to augment her remotely.

That had been a mistake. When he saw her last, he should have collected more from her so they would have been prepared for this. Now, he had to find her in order to help her. If there was anything—or anyone—with her, he knew he wouldn't be able to help free her. He had no natural fighting ability.

He began opening every door along the hallway.

Most of them were storerooms, and he was able to

ignore them quickly. As he neared the end of the hallway, he began to lose hope. Maybe he'd been wrong.

And then he found one that looked like it had been used, and recently.

When Alec pushed it open, the room was dark. He hesitated in the doorway and tried to peer through the darkness, before it cleared for him.

Someone was sitting in a chair.

Not only sitting in a chair, but tied—restrained—in a chair.

Alec hurried forward, and crouched in front of Sam. He removed the gag over her mouth first. "What happened?"

"Alec? I thought you were being tested?"

"It was over."

"And you left?"

"To find you. Beckah said that you were with her, and she saw Master Jessup drag you away."

"Bushy brows. Yeah, he pulled me away. That's Marin's Scribe."

"Are you sure it's the same person?"

"I didn't recognize his voice, not at first, but there is an edge to him. He hides it well."

Alec didn't want to believe that Master Jessup could do that, but perhaps that was the point. It was a clever deception, and had kept Alec from questioning too much.

He untied the bindings around her wrists and ankles, and she jumped up.

"You have a knife?"

Alec frowned. "Why?"

"I want us to be prepared. Do you have a knife?"

Alec slipped a small knife out of his pocket. He kept a pair of vials with him, but hadn't expected to need them. It had become habit having them on him. She held her palm out, and he jabbed at it gently, drawing enough blood to halfway fill each of the vials. He did the same to himself, wincing at the pain as the tip of the blade poked him. There had to be an easier way to use their magic, but they hadn't discovered it.

Sam glanced at the vials, and Alec handed one of them to her. A relieved smile crossed her face. "I'd rather have you be the one doing the documentation, but if something happens and you're not with me…"

"What might happen?" Alec asked.

"I don't know. It wouldn't even have mattered this time. This Master Jessup—bushy brow—didn't give me a chance to react. I wouldn't have been able to make any notes."

"But I could have," Alec said.

Sam looked over his shoulder. "We need to get you back to your testing. If they finish and you're not there…"

"I know what might happen," Alec said. "It was a risk I was willing to take."

Sam stepped in and wrapped her arms around him. "Thank you for coming for me."

"You had to know that I would."

She stepped back and breathed out. "We need to get moving. If he was willing to grab me here, it means that whatever he intends is escalating. I don't know how much time we have left."

Alec guided her back out, and they reached the area outside the ward. The doors were still closed, but Beckah was missing. Alec frowned. He cracked the door, peeking inside, and saw the master physickers all still there, speaking animatedly. Master Helen seemed to be pointing at Master Carl, and Alec wondered what they were saying to each other, and whether there was anything he could do, but he needed to find Beckah. He searched for signs of Master Jessup, but he wasn't there.

When he closed the door, Alec turned back to Sam. "Beckah is missing, and Master Jessup hasn't returned," he said.

"He's taken her."

"Why would he have taken her?"

But Alec thought he knew. Master Jessup must've discovered that Beckah was Tray's Scribe. And if he had discovered that, then they needed to find her before something else happened.

31

THE PRINCESS ANSWERS

Sam scanned the grounds of the university, looking for signs of movement. Years spent as a thief had trained her to identify movement, but it might be her Kaver training that was the most valuable now. She saw nothing.

She glanced over at Alec. "I don't know where he would have taken her."

She felt helpless. With all of the power they possessed, and all of the abilities they had, an old man had managed to capture her—*twice*—and now had taken Beckah away.

She didn't want to worry about Beckah, and probably wouldn't were it not for the fact that Beckah was tied to Tray. If Ralun discovered that, and if he managed to use Tray, then both of them might be in danger.

There weren't many places she could go for help, but it seemed like now was the time to ask.

"Come on," she said.

"Where are we going?"

"To talk with my mother."

She stormed off toward the bridge and thrust Alec's hand forward before realizing that he didn't have the ring.

Kyza!

The guards watched her, glaring at her with their arms crossed over their chests. It was unlikely that they would allow her to pass, but somehow, she had to get across the bridge and over to Elaine. She still had her canal staff—for some reason, Jessup hadn't taken it from her, likely because she was not much of a threat when he had her confined—but she wouldn't be able to jump the canal with Alec.

She briefly entertained the idea of placing an augmentation that would grant her strength and allow her to jump over the canal while holding him, but they needed to conserve their strength, and might need to rely upon an augmentation later. If they wasted it now, they might not have time when they actually needed it.

"I need to get past," Sam said.

"You don't bear the mark, and—"

Sam pulled out one end of her canal staff and swung around, smacking the two men quickly with it, knocking them down. She would have to apologize later, but she wasn't about to be slowed by the guard when she needed to reach Elaine.

She grabbed Alec's arm and pulled him forward. They hurried across the bridge, and when they reached the palace grounds, she heard a shout behind her. One of the guards was already up and chasing her.

"Kyza!" She dragged Alec after her, hurrying toward the palace entrance. Once inside, she raced along the hallways, and found Elaine's quarters.

"What if she's not here?"

"Then we go after him on our own."

"We don't even know where to look."

"We don't, but there might be someone who can help," she said.

"Who?"

"I've asked Bastan for help a few times recently. If Elaine isn't here, I will have to see if Bastan might be able to help us." She remembered her mother's warning not to involve Bastan in this any further.

She didn't like the idea of needing to run through the Caster section to get to Bastan, but she also didn't like the idea of waiting too long, and allowing Ralun to have access not only to Tray, but to his Scribe. If he had them both, there might be no reason for Tray to remain, and no reason for him not to go with Ralun. She would lose Tray entirely.

Sam wasn't about to lose her brother, not like that, not for good. She would find a way to keep him safe, regardless of what it took.

She knocked before quickly pushing the door open.

The room was empty.

Sam stormed back out into the hallway, closing the door behind her. She hurried toward the princess's quarters. If Elaine wasn't in her rooms, the other place she might be would be with the princess, though since it was the middle of the day, it was possible she wouldn't be there, either.

At the princess's quarters, Sam knocked, waiting.

"Whose room is this?"

"This is Princess Lyasanna's room."

Alec paled.

Sam knocked again. When the door opened, the princess looked out and glanced from Sam to Alec.

"Can I help you?"

"I'm looking for Elaine."

"I'm afraid your mother is not here. She is off on an assignment for me."

Sam breathed out heavily. If Elaine was gone, and on an assignment, it could mean that she was outside the city. There were times when she would be gone for days at a stretch before returning.

They didn't have that kind of time.

"I need your help. We figured out who Marin's Scribe is, and he has gotten away."

Princess Lyasanna pinched her mouth together. "What do you mean you figured it out? Did your mother ask you to do this?"

"No, but—"

"Then why would you have gone searching? You are still in training, are you not?"

"I'm still in training," Sam said. "But I also was the only one who had encountered him. We figured out a way to determine who he is."

"He would be a master physicker. We are well aware of that."

If they were aware, and if they were doing nothing, then Sam coming here would not change anything. Could they have hoped to use the Scribe to try to draw Marin out? It wouldn't work, especially not since Tray had her—at least, he once had her. Sam no longer knew whether he did.

It was time for a different type of question.

"He told me that Tray is descended from the Anders."

Princess Lyasanna looked both directions down the hallway then grabbed Sam and dragged her into a room, motioning for Alec to follow.

"He told you this?" she asked Sam after shutting the door.

"Is it true?"

The princess glared at Sam for a moment before her expression softened. She motioned to a pair of chairs and took a seat, waiting for Sam to sit before she answered. "That fact should not be known to anyone other than Elaine."

"Why?"

"Because she's the only one who has always known the truth. Tray—the young man you know as your brother—is my son."

Sam blinked. "Your son?"

"It happened when we were on a mission, serving as emissaries, trying to end this conflict with the Thelns. There was a celebration one night, and I was given too much to drink, and..." She shook her head. "It doesn't matter. Mistakes were made. And I had him. Up until you reappeared, I thought him dead."

"Who's the father?"

Sam had to know, though she had her suspicions, even without Lyasanna telling her.

"It was a long time ago," Lyasanna said.

"That's not an answer."

"He was powerful. I could feel it. He exuded it and told me that he had a claim to rule. With the wine, and with the celebration, there was..."

Lyasanna squeezed her eyes shut.

"It was Ralun, wasn't it?"

She took a deep breath and looked over at Sam. "He was angry when I left, and angrier when he learned that I was pregnant. There have been attempts at unions between our people before, but none have succeeded."

"But you are a Scribe. How is it that Tray has Kaver abilities?"

Lyasanna has breath caught. "Kaver?"

Sam cocked her head to the side. Had Elaine not shared that with her?

"He has Kaver abilities. We discovered it when Marin attacked and left him injured," Sam said.

"If you discovered that, that means you discovered…"

Sam nodded. "His Scribe. Yes."

"Ralun can't know this. He would use him, and he would attack."

"I'm well aware that Ralun would use Tray. He has made that clear to me." Sam frowned, a question coming to her. "Tray obviously doesn't know, much like I didn't know. Why is that?"

"It doesn't matter."

"I would disagree. I think it matters quite a bit," Sam said.

"We need to stop Ralun. He shouldn't be in the city. He remains angry with me."

"Is that why he poisoned you?"

"At that time, neither of us knew of Tray's existence. His attack on me was simple vengeance for leaving him. He feels I wronged him," Lyasanna said.

Sam couldn't believe that all of this was tied to Tray and his birth history. Probably to hers, too. She had many more questions, and she doubted that Lyasanna would answer them easily. Most of them were questions about how all of this came to be? How did they arrange for Tray to be raised as her brother? How did a royal princess hide a pregnancy and birth of a son? What role did her mother play? Is that why she disappeared? There were questions about Marin, and the role that she had, too. Why would Marin have claimed to be Tray's mother? Did she know that the princess was Tray's real mother?

If she could only get her hands on the Book, might her memories answer some of these questions?

"I need to find him," Sam said.

"You don't need to find him. Others have gone after him."

Sam frowned. "Others? Is that where Elaine has gone?"

"You aren't fully trained."

"I'm trained well enough to know that I can help."

"If you were able to help, she would have asked you to go with her. That she didn't tells me that she doesn't think that you can be of assistance."

The comment stung, more so because it meant that Elaine doubted her ability.

"How long has she been gone?"

"Long enough that she should have taken care of Ralun by now."

"Should have, but if she hasn't?"

Could that be where bushy brow had gone? She looked over to Alec, and he remained silent. He hadn't said a word since they had gone into Lyasanna's rooms.

"Listen. If she's gone after Ralun, then she's in more danger than she realizes. I can help."

"She wouldn't want you to help."

"It doesn't matter what she wants. What matters is that I can offer a way to help her."

Lyasanna looked like she was going to say something, but then shook her head.

"Kyza! You're the princess. Make a decision that can help. You don't need to wait for Elaine's permission."

Lyasanna stood. For a moment, Sam thought that she might have gone overboard. Pushing the princess was a risky maneuver. Especially as she didn't know how she might respond. She barely knew anything about the princess.

"You may find her in the swamp."

"The swamp?"

"There's a place the Kavers keep there, though few know of it. If I wasn't worried about what Ralun might do, I wouldn't even tell you this."

As Lyasanna explained how they might find Ralun, Sam glanced over at Alec. It wouldn't be easy, and she wasn't certain that finding Ralun would lead them to bushy brow and Beckah, but what other option did they have?

32

RETURN TO THE SWAMP

The air stank. Alec pinched his nose, trying to ignore the smells all around him. Even though he'd experienced his share of odors, treating patients with all manner of infections, his time at the university, surrounded by the fragrances of hundreds of flowers and the underlying aromas that came from the various medicines stored within the university, had lowered his tolerance for such foulness.

"Are you sure this is where we need to go?" Alec asked.

"This is where Lyasanna claimed we could find him," Sam said.

They stood at the edge of the city. From here, there was nothing but swamp stretching out into the darkness. Alec didn't like it, and Sam leaned on her canal staff, almost comfortable. It would've been better had there been other Kavers with them, but the princess hadn't been willing to send any. Alec had a sense that she wanted to keep her connection to Tray a secret, and anything that risked exposing that was to be avoided.

"How are we supposed to head out into the swamp?"

"Not we. Me."

Alec looked over at Sam. "I'm not letting you go in there by yourself."

"You're not letting me? I've gone out into the swamp more than once."

"More than once?"

"Well, the first time was a training exercise, and Elaine basically abandoned me out there, forcing me to figure out how to get back on my own. The other time was not quite as extensive."

Alec waited for her to share more, but she didn't.

"If Ralun is out in the swamp as you suspect, you can't do it by yourself."

"I can if you place augmentations."

"Any augmentation would be better if I knew what you were facing. I can help keep you safe, Sam."

"I know that you can, but I don't think you can travel the swamp."

There was movement along the canal, and Sam grabbed him, pushing him back.

Alec pressed his back up against the wall, modeling Sam's posture, trying to remain hidden. It was late at night, late enough that the shadows over the city should conceal them, but he didn't feel concealed. He didn't feel as if there was enough protection here.

"And who would be out at this time of night?" a voice boomed.

"Kyza, take him," Sam whispered and then stormed forward.

Alec tried grabbing her sleeve, but she pulled away and reached the edge of the canal.

"Bastan. What are you doing here?"

A narrow barge pulled up along the edge of the canal, and a rope was tossed over. Sam ignored it. Bastan appeared at the edge of the boat, smiling widely. "Are you going to help secure the barge, Samara?"

"What are you doing here?"

"I've been observing you."

"Observing me?" Sam asked.

Alec approached and nodded to Bastan. The man might be a thief and a smuggler, but he also seemed to look out for Sam, and because of that, Alec didn't mind him. Someone had to look out for Sam, especially when Alec couldn't be there.

"Yes, observing you. I knew that eventually you would find a way to reach this Theln again. He has taken something from me."

"Are you still mad about the fact that he beat on you the last time?"

"I am still mad about the fact that he shut down an entire section of the city to me," Bastan said.

"You don't know what you're getting in to," Sam said. "He's dangerous. I know that you hired the djohn, and I know they have some way of combating the Thelns, but this one is dangerous."

"Indeed, he is." Bastan patted his crossbow. "And I have found a way to slow him that I did not have the last time." His gaze flicked to Alec, and something of a knowing smile crossed his face.

Why would Bastan look at him like that?

"I'm not letting you come with us," Sam said.

"Not letting me? Oh, Samara, I think you misunderstand. I'm taking you with us."

"You're not taking me anywhere. I don't need your help to cross the swamp."

"No. I doubt that you do. But he does," Bastan said, nodding to Alec.

Alec glanced over at Sam, and then he jumped onto the barge. "Come on, Sam."

"Alec—"

"I'm not letting you leave me behind. I can help, but I can only help if I know what you're facing."

"You know what I'll be facing. And if they attack you—"

"You just have to make sure they don't. You need to make sure that you're fast enough to prevent them from getting to me."

"I can't guarantee that I will be," Sam said.

"I have faith in you."

Sam swore to herself and pushed off with her staff, flipping out onto the barge. She glared at Bastan. "Sometimes, you're a bastard."

Bastan nodded to the ship's captain, and they pushed off, the captain using a long pole to send them out through the canal and into the swamp. Alec hadn't taken a barge before and found it surprisingly stable. Were they not heading into the strange filth of the swamp, he might've found it enjoyable. As it was, he felt uncomfortable with where they were going and what would happen to them.

"Why out into the swamp?" Bastan asked.

"Because I've heard that's where he's hiding," Sam whispered.

Alec could tell that she didn't want to answer, but it was Bastan, and he also knew that she had a grudging respect for him.

"There aren't places in the swamp where someone can hide."

"There are. There are small islands scattered throughout."

"And how do you know which island we need to go to?"

Sam looked over to him. "Let's just agree that I know."

Bastan grinned. "I suppose we can."

They continued on in silence, and it seemed as if time stood still, but hours must've passed. Eventually, Sam motioned for them to turn. She leaned toward Alec and whispered, "We're almost there."

"What happens when we reach it? What if Ralun isn't there?"

"He'll be there."

Alec breathed out, nerves beginning to send his heart fluttering. He pulled a slip of easar paper out of his pocket and started thinking about what he might document, trying to think of what would provide the best protection for Sam. There had to be a particular combination of words, a way of limiting damage to her if she were to face the enormous Theln.

And Sam didn't want to kill him.

That was difficult for him, especially knowing that Ralun wouldn't hesitate to do the same to them.

But Sam wanted answers, and she thought she could only get them by having Ralun alive so that she could discover what he knew of the Book.

In the distance, a dark stretch of land was visible in the moonlight. The captain slowed, and Sam motioned for Alec. He leaned down and unstoppered the vial, quickly scrawling out a few words on the easar paper. A wave of cold swept through him as it often did when they placed augmentations. Weakness would follow, but hopefully not so much that he would be unable to focus. If he had been careful enough, he would have given them time with the augmentation. He prayed that he had placed it correctly.

"It's ready," Alec said.

Sam hurried forward and leaned into Bastan. "If you're going to do this, we need to move quickly."

"I will let you lead, Samara."

Sam glanced back at Alec, and he frowned. She placed her staff on the deck of the barge, and then she flipped into the air, leaving him to watch from a distance, leaving him feeling helpless. He was her Scribe. What other choice did he have but to observe?

33

REACHING THE ISLAND

"Stay on the barge," Bastan told Alec.

Alec looked past him. "If I stay on the barge, I can't see anything. If her"—he lowered his voice, shifting his gaze from Bastan to the two plain-looking men with him—"augmentations fail, I need to be able to see her so that I can help her."

"If they fail, then she is in much greater danger than we know."

"Keep me safe. I can help."

Bastan glanced from Alec to the two men. What had Sam called them? Djohn?

Whatever they were, she believed they were able to combat the Thelns.

"I don't like this," Bastan said.

"I don't like it, either. If it were up to me, Sam wouldn't face him."

"And who would? Do you think there's someone else who is more capable than Samara?"

Alec shook his head. "I thought you wanted to keep her safe."

"I do. I've done everything in my power to keep Samara safe over the years. And I will continue to do so." He pulled the crossbow from his shoulder and reached into a quiver that Alec hadn't seen before, pulling out a pair of arrows.

Not arrows. Sam would kill him for calling them that. They were crossbow bolts. They were the same thing that had nearly killed Sam the night they had met.

"I don't think those will work against the Thelns," Alec said, stepping off the barge and following Bastan.

Bastan glanced over at him, a grim expression on his face. "No? If they don't, then your father has something to answer to."

Alec blinked a moment. "My father?" As he asked, he thought he understood. "Eel venom?"

"He told you? That was supposed to be a confidential discussion."

"No. He didn't tell me. He only told me that he had collected eel venom."

"Ah. Then I guess he gets to live."

Alec didn't know whether Bastan was making a joke or not, but he didn't like the idea of Bastan threatening his father. "If anything happens to him—"

"You will what?"

"It's not what I will do, but I will make sure that Sam does something."

Bastan chuckled softly. "That's a threat I can actually worry about."

Once on the island, Alec tried to ignore the way his feet

342 | D.K. HOLMBERG

squelched. Each step was soggy, and he sank in. Had Sam experienced the same difficulty? Probably not. Not only was she lighter than he was, she likely used her staff the entire way, flipping across the bog as she had out in the swamp.

They were only twenty or so feet in when they came across the first fallen Theln.

"It looks as if Sam came through here," Bastan said.

He motioned to the djohn, and they took off, disappearing into the darkness.

Bastan held the crossbow out in front of him as he stalked forward. "You might want to stay behind me."

"Why does eel venom work against the Thelns?"

"Why do the eels prevent the Thelns from reaching the city?"

"You knew?"

"I didn't, not at first, but rumors have a way of spreading, especially after what Marin attempted recently." Bastan glanced over at him, and he quickly swung the crossbow over and fired.

Alec jumped back. Bastan grabbed him, pulling him toward him, and he looked over to see another Theln lying sprawled on the ground, the crossbow bolt sticking out of his chest. He convulsed before his body finally lay still.

Bastan grunted. "That answers that," he said.

"Answers what?"

"Answers the question about whether the eel venom would be effective."

"You didn't know?"

Bastan shrugged. "Not with any certainty."

"You were willing to risk yourself here even though you didn't know?"

"I've learned that you need to take risks if you want to be rewarded. Everything in my life is about that. Now. Let's see how many others we can find."

They continued forward, and Alec stayed behind Bastan as he suggested, not wanting to have to confront one of the Thelns himself. He wasn't sure if he would even be able to. All it would take would be one massive strike, and he would be knocked out—or killed.

"Where—"

Bastan turned and fired again, sending a crossbow bolt streaking across the distance.

It struck a Theln, and he fell, twitching. There was another Theln next to him, and beyond that, Alec saw Sam frozen in place.

It took a moment for him to realize why.

Ralun held Elaine.

Alec stopped, quickly pulled out a sheet of easar paper, and began writing.

34

ATTACK ON THE THELNS

The night air whistled past her as she flipped, and Sam held her breath, trying not to focus on the foulness that was the stench coming off the swamp. It was a horrible odor, and she found it worse now than she had before. Was that because the Thelns were here?

She landed in a roll and swung her staff up, preparing for whatever might be on this strip of land. Lyasanna had finally revealed where to find Ralun. She worried that it was already too late.

The island appeared empty, but there was a stink to it that wasn't accounted for by the swamp. The swamp carried a distinctive odor, and what she detected here wasn't quite that. It was what she attributed to the Thelns.

She hurried forward, wanting to finish this before her augmentations failed. Alec was watching, but there were limits to what he might be able to see and how he might be able to help, and she didn't want to put him in a position where he needed to try and do something. Besides, she had Bastan, and the djohn he'd hired. Maybe that would be enough to balance things out.

The swamp consisted of mostly reeds surrounded by water, though there were strange trees that grew up in the midst of the swamp as well. More of those trees grew in dense clusters on the island, and she moved through them, realizing that the full length of her canal staff would be ineffective. There was not an easy way for her to navigate here, and if she did get into a fight, the staff would be more of a hindrance than anything, at least in its current form. Sam disassembled the staff, and held the two ends.

She approached slowly. If this was the place that Lyasanna believed, then it would be here. They would be here.

Movement caught her eye, and she dropped. It was just in time.

A Theln darted forward. It wasn't Ralun, and the person wasn't nearly as massive as some of the Thelns she had faced, but he was quick. Almost too quick. She spun around, using the end of her staff to strike at him, going high and low at the same time. With her augmentations, she was better able to fight.

He fell, and she clubbed him brutally on the head with the ends of her staff.

Sam gathered herself and remained crouching as she looked around. At least now she knew this was the right place.

She started forward, this time staying closer to the trees, darting from one tree to the next, looking for movement.

Only the thin moon overhead provided light. It would've been helpful had Alec given her some way to see more easily. Maybe she should have suggested that to him, rather than letting him decide on the augmentation. He was better at writing them, but she knew what was effective for her.

There was a shadow that shifted near the space between a pair of trees, and Sam slithered forward, wanting to determine whether it was a Theln or someone else.

It was another Theln.

Much like the one before, this Theln wasn't nearly as sizable as Ralun.

Was there some reason for that?

She hurried forward, catching him with her staff.

Not a him. As the Theln fell, she realized it was a woman.

She struggled to find remorse. The Thelns would harm her without any question. She needed to be brutal with them, the same way they would be brutal with her.

How many more were here?

Sam continued to sneak forward.

With each step, she expected to find more Thelns, someone else who might attack, but there wasn't anyone. Where were they? What were they after?

And where was Elaine?

Better yet, where was bushy brow? He was here; he had to be.

She needed to draw them out, which meant she would have to risk herself.

Sam darted forward, keeping herself visible, readying for attack. She watched for movement, and it came suddenly—almost too suddenly.

Another Theln, and this one was more typical of the Thelns she'd faced in the past. Worse, he wasn't alone.

They stepped off to either side of her came at her simultaneously. Her augmentations began to fade, and Sam wondered how much longer she had. She hurried forward on the offensive, needing to finish them off before anything happened to her.

As she advanced, she screwed the ends of her canal staff together.

With the staff in one piece, she pushed off, spinning into the air and swiping at the Thelns with her staff. She flipped, the same technique as when she flipped out over the swamp used now so that she could best defend herself. She brought the staff down, crashing it into one of the Thelns heads, and he crumpled. Sam spun, sweeping the staff along the ground, quicker than the other one could react, and he went down. She brought the staff around, connecting with his skull, and he went out.

"You have gotten skilled," she heard.

Sam spun around. Ralun stood before her. He held Elaine, one hand around her throat.

"But you Kavers are all the same," he said.

"How are we the same?" Sam asked.

"You all believe that the key to your power is through augmentations. I have seen it so often over the years. This one especially," he said, shaking Elaine. She tried to fight, but Ralun was simply too strong. He didn't rely upon augmentations for his strength. It was a part of his Theln makeup. It was simply who he was.

"How did you know she would be here?"

"How did I know? I've been watching this one."

Sam glanced over at Elaine. She had worried that she was the reason the Thelns had attacked, but it had been Elaine. She would give her a hard time about it—if they survived.

"Let her go."

"I don't think so," Ralun said.

"Let her go, and you can take me."

Ralun snorted. "I'm not sure that is an equal trade. You see, I know exactly who she is and who she serves."

"And I know exactly what you want as well as why you want it. Let her go, and I will help you find Tray."

Sam hated the idea of going with Ralun, but what choice did she have? She wanted to free Elaine so they could work together to trap Ralun, but first, she needed to help Tray. If that meant agreeing to go with Ralun, then she would do it.

"I think not. Why should I make such a bargain when you stand here before me without any augmentations? Especially given that I already have Tray."

Sam realized that her augmentations had indeed worn off. Would Alec have realized that? If he did, she would need him to place another so she could escape, but with the swamp and the trees and everything that could be blocking his view, it might be that Alec didn't know.

Two Thelns approached. One of them was smaller and reminded her of the female Theln that she had just faced.

The other was Tray.

"Sam. You shouldn't be here."

"I was thinking the same thing about you. I don't know how safe it is for you to be here with these people."

"These people are going to help me understand who I am and what I can be," he said.

"No. They want to use you."

"What about you?"

Sam looked over to Ralun. He watched her, amusement burning in his dark eyes. Elaine struggled, and if nothing changed, he might choke her before Sam could do anything.

But all Sam really needed to do was buy some time. If she could, she might be able to hold off until Bastan arrived. And he had to be arriving soon, didn't he? He was out there, and with his djohn, they could confront the Thelns.

Except... if they did, she ran the risk of Bastan harming Tray. She ran the risk of the djohn harming Tray.

Kyza!

It needed to be easier. Somehow, she needed to get through to him. Somehow, she needed to keep Tray from attacking, but she wasn't sure that she could.

"Tray, don't do this," she said.

"I haven't done anything."

"Keep it that way. Help me get Elaine free, and—"

"Why should I help you free Elaine?"

"Because she's my mother."

Tray looked at her, fixing her with a long expression. "And Ralun is my father."

Sam breathed out heavily. He knew.

35

FINDING MARIN

A wave of cold washed over Sam as the augmentation took place. It happened almost at the same time as she saw Tray fall, kicking briefly.

"No!" she screamed.

She spun around and saw Bastan holding a crossbow. She wasn't sure that a crossbow would make a difference —not to a Theln—but Tray twitched.

"Alec! You need to help Tray."

He looked up from where he crouched behind Bastan.

"And give me better sight."

She met his gaze and he nodded.

She didn't wait, jumping forward. Ralun tried to squeeze Elaine by the neck, attempting to shake her, but Sam reached him before he could snap her neck. At least, she hoped that she did. She slammed her staff into his side and spun around, already jumping, bringing her staff around.

She clubbed him on the arm, and he released Elaine.

Elaine staggered forward.

"Bastan! Watch Elaine!"

She wasn't sure whether Bastan heard her, but hoped that he did. How badly was Elaine injured? And how had Ralun managed to capture her?

There would have been other Kavers with her.

Her next attack sent Ralun staggering forward. She didn't let up, bringing her staff around again and again, striking him with as much force as she could. Each time she hit him, he grunted. She struck until he stopped moving.

Sam hesitated, her breathing ragged.

Was that it?

No. It couldn't be it. They still didn't know where Marin and her Scribe had gone.

Sam surveyed the area. The djohn seemed to have taken down the other Thelns. Alec crouched in front of Tray, and Sam went running over to him.

"Will he—"

Alec looked up at her. "I don't know. Bastan was using eel venom on these bolts. He was able to kill at least one of the Thelns with them." He looked back down at Tray. "I might have gotten to him in time, but I just don't know."

Sam looked at her brother. "Tray. I need you to wake up."

Tray rolled his head toward her weakly. "Sam? Did you kill him?"

"I didn't." She had thought about it, and considering that Ralun wanted to kill her, she probably should have, but Tray was right. He deserved the chance to know his father. He deserved to have questions answered. Wasn't that the same thing that she wanted? "Where is Marin? Where is her Scribe?"

"It doesn't matter. I've taken care of Marin. She won't cause any more trouble for you."

"It does matter. She has your Scribe."

Tray blinked. "Then she's already dead."

"Don't say that. I don't believe that you would have allowed Marin to harm her."

"You think that I'm in control of the things that Marin does?" Tray sat up and grabbed his stomach where the crossbow had struck, peeling away the fabric. His skin looked uninjured despite the bloody mess of clothing overtop of it. He glanced at Alec and nodded. "Thanks."

"Tray?"

He turned and looked at her. "Don't try to stop me, Sam."

"I don't want to stop you. I only want to help you."

Tray took a lumbering step forward, his strength slowly seeming to return. He went over to Ralun and scooped him up. Ralun was an enormous man, and Tray handled him easily.

Bastan aimed the crossbow at him.

"Don't," Sam said.

"Samara, you know who this is, I presume."

"I know who it is, and I know what he's done, and I know what he might continue to do." She put herself in between Bastan and Tray. "You can't hurt him."

"If you let Ralun leave, you set the city up for ongoing attacks," Elaine said. She stood near Bastan, almost too comfortably.

"Tray. Stay here with him. Let's keep them confined—"

"No. I'm done doing what others want of me. I'm going to understand who I am and what it means." He looked at Sam and then Alec. "I wish it could be some other way, Sam, I really do, but I need to do this."

He bounded off into the darkness, but Sam watched him until he reached the edge of the island and jumped off onto the barge. He smacked the captain, sending him into the swamp. The man frantically swam toward the shore. Tray set Ralun down and picked up the barge pole and began pushing off. "Don't follow me, Samara," he called out.

"Where is Marin? At least tell me that," she shouted as the barge got further away.

She could follow him, but at what cost? Doing so would drive a wedge between her and her brother, and it was a wedge that she didn't want. Tray had been all she had for so long. She couldn't fathom the idea of losing him.

Tray said nothing until the barge was in the middle of the swamp. When it was, he called back. "She intends to head north. There will be a ship, and that's where you'll find her."

"Why did you let her go?"

"She's my mother," Tray said.

"She's not. I don't know why she deceived you and me, but she's not. Your mother is—"

Elaine grabbed Sam's arm and turned her to her. "Now is not the time, Samara. If Ralun shares that information with him, then he can know."

"Why isn't now the time?"

"Because it will raise complications."

Sam glared at her. She bit back the first few responses that she wanted to say before shaking her head. "Now we need to go get Marin."

"That I think you should leave to me and the other Kavers."

"If you think to exclude me from this—"

Elaine patted Sam on the arm. "There will be no excluding you, not any longer, Samara. You've proven that you need to be included. But, I think your Scribe needs to return, and you may need to help with the explanation."

"I'm going to go with you for Marin."

Elaine looked as if she might argue, but stopped herself and nodded.

Sam looked over to Alec. He had folded up the sheet of paper and tucked it into his pocket. Bastan was watching them, and when he realized that she was looking his way, he turned and spoke quietly to the djohn.

"Who is Bastan to me?" she asked Elaine.

"He's someone who has watched over you."

"I'm aware of that. But why do I get the sense that you and Bastan know each other?"

"I'm not sure why you would get that sense."

Sam sighed. Alec approached, keeping her from asking any more questions. Instead, she turned her attention to him. "I think it's time you get back to the university to see how the testing turned out."

"I don't think it matters. Since I disappeared, I doubt there will be much support for my request for promotion. Maybe you better just take me back to my father."

"I think you need to return," Sam said. "If nothing else, you need to confront them."

"How do you think we're going to do that? Without the barge, we're trapped here."

"Not entirely," Bastan said, striding forward. He studied Sam, his face unreadable. "It seems the barge the

Thelns used to get to this island is still here. I will take your physicker friend back to the city. Go find Marin."

"Thanks, Bastan, for... well, for all of this."

"You will come by the tavern later. I have questions that will need answering."

Sam couldn't refuse, not with as much help as Bastan had been. She wouldn't have been able to do this without his—and the djohn's—help. "After I deal with Marin."

"Are you sure you want to come with me?" Elaine asked.

Sam stared at her. "After all of this, after everything that has happened between Marin and me, do you really need to ask that?"

"There are other Kavers who can help with this."

"Other Kavers don't know Marin as well as I do."

Elaine glanced over at Bastan, and he continued to watch them, though he remained near the djohn he'd hired. Sam had more questions about them, including how exactly they had the ability to face the Thelns, but those would be questions she could get answered later.

"Then it's time to go."

Sam followed Elaine, flipping across the swamp, and Elaine took her a circuitous route, navigating through the dark waters with ease, clearly having been here many times before.

"Lyasanna told me the truth about Tray," Sam said as they made their way through the swamp.

Elaine glanced over. "Did she, now?"

"She told me that she is Tray's mother."

Elaine paused, resting on her staff and looking over at Sam. "There are very few who know that information."

"Why keep it quiet?"

"It's dangerous. Knowing that Tray is descended from the Anders is dangerous."

"For who? It seems Tray is already in danger, especially considering who his father is."

"That's exactly why it is dangerous. Lyasanna's parents don't even know that she had Tray."

"Why would that matter? Wouldn't they want to know that Tray is theirs? He would be an heir to the Anders."

"Not only an heir to the Anders, but also for the Thelns. And we've managed to keep the relative peace—"

"Peace? Is that what you call this? Ralun and the Thelns have attacked several times over the last year. It seems that we have no peace."

"And why is that?" Elaine started off again, and the outer edge of the city became visible, though not the same section they had departed from. Elaine must have some idea about where to find this ship Tray had mentioned. He had said that Marin would travel north, but none of the northern sections would have ships. Most of them would avoid the swamp.

"Marin abducted him."

Sam frowned. If Marin had abducted Tray, and she believed that she had, she still didn't know why. What did Marin hope to gain in abducting Tray? Not only abducting him, but essentially forcing Sam to have a relationship with him.

"It doesn't make sense," Sam said.

Elaine paused as they reached the outer section. "Nothing that Marin did make sense."

""That's why we've remained vigilant. Those of us who've known about Tray have searched for answers while the rest have watched for movement, knowing that Ralun would plan something else."

"So, you thought Ralun had Tray?"

"We believed Ralun was responsible for what happened to him. That he'd somehow gotten to Marin. Lyasanna thought the child dead, killed by Marin, but there were rumors—enough that were believable—that made us question whether that was true or not."

"Ralun hadn't known about Tray before, had he?" Sam asked.

Elaine sighed. "It seems that when Ralun used the Book on Lyasanna, he discovered more than your presence. He discovered Tray's existence."

They reached the shore, and Sam shook water from her staff. "Why do the Thelns hate Kavers and Scribes? It's about more than what happened between Ralun and Lyasanna."

Elaine paused. "The city has been home to many people seeking safety over the years. Not all people living within the city originated here. There are many immigrants, though less now than there used to be. The first Kavers and Scribes came to the city to escape violence from the Thelns in their own land."

"Why was there violence?"

"The reason why has been lost over the years, but the violence between us has persisted."

"You've been to the Theln lands. You've seen them."

"I've seen only the edge. No Kavers or Scribes have been allowed access to anything more than the outer edge of their lands."

"What are their lands like?"

"Dangerous. Bleak. Deadly. Much like the Thelns."

Elaine glanced over, and she tapped her staff on the ground. "Now. Have you had all of your questions answered well enough for you to come with me or do we need to keep talking?"

There were still questions Sam had, but they were questions that Elaine might not have the answers to. Most of those questions were for Marin, and until she had a chance to sit and talk with her, she wouldn't know why Marin had allowed Tray to live, especially as she obviously hated Lyasanna. There was more to this.

They reached the port, and as they did, Sam frowned. This was a section Sam had rarely visited, not needing to come through here too often. Most of the things Bastan had her take were from merchants, and it was easier to steal from the warehouses rather than off the ships or the docks. Safer, too. There was a certain bustle to the docks, activity that reminded her of Caster in a way. Everyone seemed to be hurrying, some carrying baskets while others pushed carts, and some were dirty, stinking of fish and the sea.

None of that really caught her attention.

What did catch her attention were the dozens of soldiers dressed in the colors of the Anders marching along the streets.

"What is this?" Sam asked Elaine.

Elaine frowned and hurried forward, thrusting herself into the line of soldiers. Sam followed carefully, and her eyes widened when she saw Master Jessup. Bound in chains around his wrists, he looked around, a defiant glare on his face. Next to him, head slumped forward and obviously unconscious, was Marin. Two men carried her, and her wrists were bound, as were her ankles. Sam didn't know whether Marin could escape from them easily, not without an augmentation, and seeing as how her Scribe had been captured along with her, Marin was unlikely to receive such augmentation.

"Sam?"

Sam turned to see Beckah looking at her. Her eyes were red, as if she'd been crying or drugged. Either was possible, especially considering who she'd been captured by. Other than that, she didn't look unwell.

"What happened to you?" she asked, then glanced at the soldiers. Elaine was talking to one of them, a dark-haired man who seemed to be in charge.

"They found us," Beckah said, nodding toward the soldiers. "I've never been happier to see soldiers."

One of the soldiers turned, and Sam noticed the crest emblazoned on his cloak. One of the Anders' personal soldiers. "Why would they have come and not the city guard?"

Elaine joined them, and the soldiers continued to head off through the streets, making their way in the direction of the palace. "It seems that after your conversation with Lyasanna, she sent her men in search of Marin and Master Jessup."

Sam frowned. "She was the one who told me about the island in the swamp, suggesting that might be where I'd find Marin."

"That might be, but Lyasanna also planned for the possibility that they would have gone elsewhere. It seems that they found her attempting to board a ship."

It made sense, but as Marin was carried away, Sam couldn't help but feel disappointed that she wouldn't get a chance to question her. Once they reached the palace, Lyasanna would surely have her own plans for Marin.

"Don't look disappointed, Samara. We've won. Not only is the master physicker who has betrayed the university been captured, but so is Marin."

While that might be true, Sam couldn't help but feel like there was something more. Tray had left the city, taking Ralun with him, along with answers to questions that still troubled her.

She looked up to see Elaine watching her, and she forced a smile. Marin might have been captured, but Sam's task was not complete. Tray might not be her real brother, but that didn't change that there was a connection between them, and it was one that she didn't fully understand. Now that he had left Verdholm, she had to go after him and ensure his safety. It was her turn to help him get answers to his questions.

It would mean leaving the city and her training, and it might mean Alec leaving the university since she couldn't imagine doing what she intended without him—though if his testing had gone poorly, that might not matter—but didn't she have to? Didn't she owe it to Tray?

And didn't she want to understand why Marin had paired Sam up with Tray to begin with?

That was an answer she might be able to get without leaving the city, but Elaine would have to be willing to let her get close enough for those answers. And then she would go after Tray.

36

TEST RESULTS

Alec approached the university wearily. It was early morning, and sunlight had just begun to stream through the city. The barge ride back to the city had gone quickly, but he had traveled between sections slowly, dreading what he would learn when he returned. Had he been expelled?

He heard a splash and looked over to see Sam approach. "What are you doing back here already?"

She waved her hand. "It's a long story, but Marin and Jessup were captured and are being brought back to the palace by Princess Lyasanna's personal guards." She glanced toward the palace frowning. "I need to find out what Marin might know, but first, I thought I'd offer my support to you."

"As much as I'd love you to, I think this is something I need to do on my own."

"You don't want me to be here?"

Alec looked over at her and smiled. He felt closer to her than he had in a long time. "That's not true at all. It's just that I need to face whatever the master physickers have for me on my own. If they choose to expel me, then I'll come find you."

"You don't have the ring anymore, remember? I'm sure I can get you another one, but it might take some time."

"Fine. Then I'll go to my father's apothecary. If you don't hear from me, that's where you can find me."

Sam glanced over at the palace. "I don't know how much longer I will be there."

"What do you mean?"

"Tray has gone to the Thelns. I can't leave him to them. I need to know what might happen to him. I need to know why his history has been suppressed."

"You're more concerned about *his* now?"

"I still want to know why Marin took my memories, but right now, I think Tray needs my help more than he realizes."

"I will go with you. Whenever you choose to leave, I will go."

Relief washed over her face. "Send word to me either way."

They embraced, and Alec held on to her for a long moment before stepping away. He watched as Sam reached the edge of the canal and flipped over it. After a while, he made his way into the university. He entered the hospital ward and found it empty except for a few junior physickers. He turned away and made his way up to his room. He stood for a long moment staring at his stack of journals on the desk before taking a deep breath and heading back out and up to the masters' quarters. At the top of the stairs, he nearly collided with Master Carl.

"Mr. Stross," he sneered. "Now you finally decide to return?"

"There was something that I needed to address. There was someone who needed my help."

"I'm sure there was. You always seem to believe that everyone needs your help."

"Not everyone." He hesitated but decided to press forward. "What happened with the testing?"

Master Carl grabbed his arm and guided him along the hallway. At the end of the hall, he raised his hand. "Wait here."

Alec stood, fearing the worst.

He didn't have to wait long. Master Carl returned with Master Helen and surprisingly, Master Eckerd. Where had he been? How could he have been gone all this time when they needed him?

"Mr. Stross," Master Helen said, stepping forward. "You demanded testing, something that has not been done in many years. The last time it was done was…"

"You," Master Eckerd said.

A hint of a smile played upon Master Helen's face. "That is correct. The last time was me. I grew tired of the steps involved in the training. As it seems you did."

Alec swallowed. "You demanded testing?"

"I did. It is something that had never been successfully completed before me."

The bit of hope that had surged in his mind at the idea that he might have succeeded faded. If Master Helen had been the only one who had ever succeeded, what hope did he have? Master Helen was the brightest physicker he knew.

"Mr. Stross. I will tell you that the vote was not unanimous," Master Helen said.

She looked over at Master Carl.

Alec's stomach sank. For him to pass from student to junior physicker required a nearly unanimous vote. It didn't require all the master physickers, but he suspected from the way Master Helen was telling him that he had failed. "So that's it? I'm expelled?"

Master Helen held her gaze on Master Carl for a long moment. "There were a few objections to you being raised to junior physicker. Master Carl was among them." She turned and looked earnestly at Alec. "So unfortunately, that means that you will not be promoted to junior physicker."

Alec felt nauseated. Had he wanted this promotion that badly? That he'd been willing to face expulsion if he failed?

It had been worth it. They had discovered Master Jessup. But... he wouldn't be able to continue his studies.

Master Helen regarded him a moment. "You did manage to demonstrate a depth and breadth of knowledge that convinced many of us that you are deserving of something else."

Alec's breath caught. "What something else?"

"There is another route to promotion, and one that is more difficult. With it, you need the support of each of the most senior physickers. There are five of us, and you had the support of four for this promotion."

"Five. I came around," Master Carl said.

"What promotion is that?" Alec asked.

Master Carl looked at Alec, and he couldn't tell if there was irritation or something else on his face. "Mr.

Stross," he began, "you have been promoted to full physicker."

Alec blinked. What did that even mean? "Full physicker? You mean I—"

"You have bypassed junior physicker. It was clear during your testing on the wards that you have a grasp of physiology that exceeds what most junior physickers possess. Because of that, you have been promoted to full physicker."

Alec didn't hear much else. They congratulated him, Master Eckerd the last of all. As he made his way down the stairs, back to his room, he was numb and unable to fully comprehend what had just happened.

When he reached it, he found Beckah inside.

"Beckah?"

"Alec. You're here."

"How are *you* here?"

"Soldiers came for Marin and Jessup. When they captured them, I was free to go. I saw Sam and her mother…"

Alec sighed. Why hadn't Sam mentioned that? Then again, she was distracted by what had happened to Tray, so maybe she hadn't thought to say anything. "I'm so glad that you're okay."

"What happened with Tray?"

He told her about the attack and about Tray taking Ralun away.

"So that's it? He's gone back to the Thelns?" she asked.

"Sam intends to go after him. She feels that she owes it to him."

"Which means that you are going to go with him."

"That's what it means," Alec said.

"What happened with your testing?"

He smiled. He still couldn't believe what had happened.

"You weren't expelled?"

He shook his head. "I wasn't expelled."

"Are you going to tell me what happened? Or are you going to keep me wondering?"

"Well, now you get to study under a skilled physicker."

"Who?"

"Me."

"Physicker, and not junior physicker?"

Alec nodded. "Not junior. Full physicker."

"That's one step below master physicker. Alec—that's never happened before."

"That's what Master Helen said."

Beckah looked around his room. Alec expected her to comment on something about the changing dynamics, or the fact that they wouldn't have the time to study together anymore, or any number of other things, but what she said instead made him laugh.

"Gods. Now you will be absolutely impossible."

Grab the next volume in the Book of Maladies: Comatose

Finding the truth in the present means understanding their past.

Newly promoted to full physicker, Alec still struggles with his place in the University. Friends treat him differently and the master physickers no longer allow him to study with them. After everything that has happened, he's still an outsider. When his father arrives at the university for healing, Alec must use everything he learned from him in order to save him, but even that might not be enough. He must discover the secret of his illness by finding a way to work with the master physickers, but what he finds is unexpected and hints at a greater plot taking hold.

Sam wants nothing more than to head toward the Theln lands after her brother, but with Alec needing her help, she postpones the journey. Rather than having the opportunity to help Alec, she finds herself chasing details of the past Marin has hidden, only to realize the deception to the city runs much deeper than she could ever had imagined. Could it be that Marin had actually saved Tray as she claimed?

Though they have both progressed in knowledge and

ability, it still might not be enough to stop a plot against the city that has gestated for years and finally threatens to come to fruition. The truth behind the plot has the potential to destroy the city, if it doesn't destroy Sam and Alec first.

NAMES AND TERMS

People:

- Aelus Stross: An apothecary and skilled healer. Alec's father
- Alec Stross: an apprentice apothecary
- Bastan: a thief who essentially runs Caster
- Hyp: a moneylender in the Arrend section who frequents Aelus's shop
- Mags: a painter with a unique talent
- Marcella Rubbles: owner of a stationary store in Arrend
- Marin: a thief who knew Sam's mother
- Samara (Sam) Elseth: a thief
- Trayson (Tray) Elseth: Sam's brother

Places and Terms:

- Arrend section: a merchant section

- Balan Day: a day to celebrate the festival god
- canal eels: possibly mythical creatures living in the canals
- Callesh section: a merchant section
- Caster section: a lowborn outer section of the city
- Central Canal: the canal that separates the lowborn sections from the merchants and highborns
- Drash section: a merchant section
- easar paper: magical paper
- Farnum section: a merchant section
- Highborn: a term for the wealthier living in the center of the city
- Jaku section: a highborn section where easar paper was found.
- Kyza: one of the many gods worshipped in Verdholm
- Lostin section: a merchant section
- Lowborn: a term for people living in the outer sections of the city
- Lycithan: a southern nation. Known for their skilled artisans.
- Narvin Plains: east of the city, thin stretch of land
- Physicker: healers with specialized training at the university
- Piare River: connects to Ralan Bay and the canals
- Ralan Bay: a trading hub along the coast of Verdholm
- Sacred Alms: the healing religion Alec follows

- Sornum: Bastan's tavern
- Thelns: dangerous brutes
- Valun: a country known for various artifacts, including the stout rope Sam uses
- Verdholm: an isolated city situated near the coast with canals running through it separating it into different sections
- Yisl: one of the many gods worshipped in Verdholm

Printed in Great Britain
by Amazon

12695902R00217